The River of Souls

The River of Souls

Robert McCammon

Subterranean Press 2014

Second Printing

Limited Edition ISBN
978-1-59606-629-8

Trade Edition ISBN
978-1-59606-630-4

Subterranean Press
PO Box 190106
Burton, MI 48519

subterraneanpress.com

One

A Constant Player

The bootpound drumbeats continued across the floor, step by ominous step, until the new arrival at the party stood looming over Matthew Corbett.

"Not again!" said Pandora Prisskitt, her red-lipped mouth twisting. The violet eyes in her heart-shaped face flashed with both anger and supplication. "Please! I'm *begging* you!"

The man shook his head as absolutely as a demon on doomsday. "No use beggin'," he answered, in a voice as deep as the Pit and as rough as a rocky road. "What's got to be done."

Matthew did not like the sound of that. "What's got to be done?" he asked Pandora, and to his chagrin he heard his voice tremble just the bit.

"*You*," said the huge black-garbed man, who put a thick sausage of a grimy dirt-nailed finger upon Matthew's chest, "have got to *die*."

"It's a necessity?"

"A certainty," said the beast. "Now. Let's get us to the fine points of the thing." Reaching into a pocket of his long coat—which seemed to Matthew to be very much out of season on this sultry Friday night in late June—the man brought out a black leather glove which for all the world must've seen both the bottom of a pigsty and the floor of a horse-figged stable. He wasted no time in slapping Matthew across first the left cheek and then the right. Around the room there were gasps and shudders and a few licked chops of delight, for even the finest lads and ladies loved a spirited duel.

"I challenge you!" the man growled, in a tone that made the fresh glasses on the table clink together and the harpsichord's strings hum.

"Magnus Muldoon!" said Pandora Prisskitt, her cheeks reddened. Her long hair was the color of the richest sable, clasped with a golden pin in the shape of a P. She wore a French gown the hue of the reddest rose in Colleton Park, enhanced by light pink ruffles at the throat and along the arms. "I won't have it! Not another one!"

"Another one *what*?" Matthew asked, thoroughly poleaxed.

"Another dead man on my conscience," she told him, without taking her gaze from the monster of the moment. "Listen to me, Magnus! This has got *to stop*!"

"Will stop. When all of 'em are dead."

"You can't kill every one of them!"

"Yes," said Magnus Muldoon, the iron-gray eyes above the sharp nose and the beastly beard staring daggers through Matthew, "I *can*."

"I think," said the young problem-solver from New York, "that I have come into this play in the second act." He then happened to look up, and noted with some distress that hanging on leather cords right above his head was the symbol of the night's festivity, a large painted wooden sword. It was, after all, Charles Town's famous annual Sword of Damocles Ball.

"All right, then!" growled Magnus Muldoon, oblivious to Pandora's expression of pleading and her hand across Matthew's chest as if to protect his heart from being ripped clean out. "How do you want to—"

"I have had quite enough of this," said the older gentleman who had just come to the side of the mountain, drawn a pistol from under the waistcoat of his dark blue suit, cocked the mean-looking weapon—as it did have a small bayonet beneath the barrel—and placed it alongside Muldoon's fly-swarmed cranium. "You will withdraw from the sight of my daughter, sir, or blood shall be spilled!"

Matthew felt like a loose button on a tight coat. Indeed, this second act was proceeding apace with him being a central character yet not having a dap of knowledge concerning the script. He felt he must have unwittingly stepped into a role as a Charles Town Player, but whether this was yet to be a comedy or tragedy the problem-solver had no clue.

In this early summer of 1703, as his world seemed poised between gun barrel and grim brawler, Matthew Corbett was all of twenty-four years old, having turned that age in the merry month of May. He sometimes wondered, usually late at night in the silence of preparing for bed in his small residence in New York, how one could be young and old at the same time, for surely some of the things that had both perplexed him, challenged him and attached themselves to his life had the power to dim the candlelight of youthful exuberance and for certainty one's outlook upon the world. He was older than his years, and more seasoned in his experiences. In the course of his investigations for his employer, the London-based Herrald Agency, he had been by turns fascinated, wary, burdened with despair, jubilant beyond measure and just plain scared nearly to death. And, it must be said, very nearly *put* to death on more occasions than he might like to recall. Yet recall he must, for such was his mind. He was a constant player at chess, though he might be sitting at no board and facing no physical pieces. It seemed also to him that he had become a constant player at the game of survival, and that this chess match he had unwittingly entered into with the eerie and powerful individual known as Professor Fell went on day and night whether he was present at the game table or not.

Matthew was yet troubled from his encounter with Professor Fell, the emperor of crime whose eyes and appetite had now fallen upon the New World as well as the Old. Back in March on Pendulum Island, in the Bermudas, Matthew's clock had nearly been wound down. He still carried many unpleasant memories of that excursion into the criminal realm, during which he himself had played the part of a rather wicked individual to mask his role as a Providence Rider. He had wished to withdraw from New York—that seemingly sleepless and perpetually active burg—for a time, to rest and recuperate, and to bask leisurely in the Atlantic breezes that rustled the palm trees of Charles Town and spread the scents of lemon and cinnamon at night through the lamplit streets.

Alas, here stood Magnus Muldoon, smelling neither of lemon nor cinnamon, and though the pistol was aimed at the mountain monster's brainpan Matthew suspected this was not the end of a story, but the beginning of one.

"Father Prisskitt," growled Muldoon, with a wry smile pulling at his whiskers, "you won't kill me. Not the man who's gonna marry your daughter."

"Silence, you filthy beast!" came the retort from Sedgeworth Prisskitt, who was slim and tall, gray-haired and handsome in his fifty-third year, his nose and chin carved from the stone of nobility, his forehead graced with the lines of intense thought, his eyes more blue than the compelling violet of his daughter's. Now, however, they were equally as angry. "I'd have a jackass as a son-in-law before the likes of you!"

"Many jackasses have been standin' where this one stands," said Muldoon, with a glance at Matthew. "Look at all the stable cleanin' I've saved you."

Matthew held stock in the pistol, but not in its holder. A bad sign: the barrel wavered.

"Why do you torment us so? What have we done to you?"

Muldoon's narrow eyes narrowed still. He pondered this question as if it carried the weight of God's Kingdom. "You," he rumbled like an avalanche, "and your dear departed missus have made betwixt you this angel who stands next to a dandified jackass. You have put upon this earth the one female I should have...must have...and *will* have. The one female who walks through my dreams at night and shatters my sleepin'. But will she have anythin' to do with me in the light of day? Nossir! I am the dirt beneath her lovely heels...as I am the dirt beneath *all* your shoes!" This he announced loudly to the assembled and transfixed listeners. "Well...Magnus Muldoon ain't nobody's dirt! And when Magnus Muldoon falls in love, as he has fallen such a height for the vision of beauty, this angel Heaven wishes other angels might be, he will not stop 'til he has her in his arms and in his weddin' bed...no matter how many men he has to kill to win her heart."

"You're insane!" sputtered Sedgeworth. "I ought to put a ball between yours ears this instant!"

"*Ought to*," replied the mountain monster, "is a far holler from *will do*. I have challenged this...this whatever it is to a duel. A fair and square fight to the death. Which I'm plannin' on winnin', naturally. Duels are legal fightin', as you know. Now...you kill me and that's cold-blooded murder. Seems I see a few constables in here amid the highwigs. They'd have to throw you in irons and be knottin' a noose for your neck, Father Prisskitt. So...I think what you *ought* to do... is put down that little popper 'fore it goes off and sets you swingin'."

To Matthew's heart-stopping horror, the little popper was lowered and Sedgeworth Prisskitt gave him a sad-eyed look that said *I am sorry you have to die.*

And no one was more sorry than Matthew, that he had come to this place and moment in time. How he wished to be walking on The Broad Way, even though it be dappled with horse apples! How he wished to be drinking a glass of wine at the Trot Then Gallop, and playing chess with his friend Effrem Owles. He even wished to be back in the office at Number Seven Stone Street, listening to Hudson Greathouse go on and on about the charms of his own lady love, the lusty widow Abby Donovan. Or...the worst of his wishes yet one he wished he might correct...suffering the cold winds of silence that eminated from Berry Grigsby, the print-master's granddaughter and—truth be told—a red-haired adventuress who had more than once caused trouble for Matthew. Yet Matthew knew he had more than once caused trouble for her, and at present wished to keep her *out* of trouble. And yet she bridled at his efforts, misunderstood his meanings and had the ability to pierce his tongue upon the thorns of language, and now they were two icebergs that passed in the night.

So be it.

Matthew faced his mountainous foe with an expression of impassive dignity, his chin uplifted not in defiance but because the fellow was so lofty. He was tall and slim, with a lean, long-jawed face and cool gray eyes that held hints of twilight blue. His thatch of fine black hair was neatly combed, as suited this evening of fine graces. As suited also the fine company, his pale candlelit countenance bespoke his intellectual qualities of reading and chess-playing, both interests that claimed many hours. He had been well-educated in a New York orphanage, and better educated by his experiences so far in the rough and rugged world. He was by profession a problem-solver, and well-tempered by such rigors as an ex-magistrate's clerk would have never dreamt—or feared—to know. One lasting mark of his journey through an uncertain and certainly demanding life was a crescent scar that curved from just above the right eyebrow into his hairline, a gift that Magnus Muldoon was now regarding with obvious interest.

"Bear got you?" the mountain asked.

"Not all of me," was Matthew's calm reply. The claw slash from Jack One Eye when he was trying to save Rachel Howarth—his "nightbird," so to speak—from being burned as a witch not far from this very town was yet a painful memory, but still...only a memory.

"Hm," said Muldoon. "Mebbe you ain't a *pure* dandy after all, to be carryin' such a token. But no matter. You have got to die for darin' to bring my angel to this gatherin'."

"I won't allow it!" spoke the violet-eyed angel, with some devilish heat. "Magnus Muldoon, you don't own me! You can't be trying to win a woman's heart with bloodshed! It's not…not…" She hesitated, struggling for words.

"Natural. Nor is it Christian," Matthew supplied.

"Oh, you're wrong there!" came the answer from the growly-throated voice within the busky beard. The eyes above that black forest glittered with feverish intent. "It *is* natural for a man to use bloodshed when he has seen the woman he loves more than the stars love the night. More than the river loves the sea. More than a bird loves the free wind. It *is* natural, if that's the only way to win her… by killin' every damn pretender to her heart who dares to take her arm and sport her about like a silver button on his cuff. And it *is* Christian, you low-assed heathen, for even Jesus shed blood in the name of love…"

"His *own* blood," Matthew said, to no avail.

"…and I'm riddin' this world of those men who can't carry a candle to the torch of her beauty, and they dress 'emselves up like jouncy crows and hop hither and yonder tryin' to prove they're made of some mettle, when right before her stands a man of pure iron!"

"A little rusty, I think," said Matthew. He regarded the circling flies and wrinkled his nose at what they swooned upon. "And *musty*, also."

"He won't be the last," Pandora said to her hulking suitor. This did not go over very well with Matthew, who nevertheless remained silent. "I would never marry a beast like you! I want a civilized man of refinement…a man to be proud of, not a…not a…"

"Man not to be proud of," Matthew supplied.

"That," said the most beautiful woman in the world.

The grim-faced head nodded. "I'll kill every man livin' who stands in my way, Pandora Prisskitt! Sooner or later…I'll be the last man standin'."

"You can stand on your head or stand on a pile of gold! I can't bear to look at you, much less *smell* you!" She put a hand to her throat and reached out for a handkerchief. "Father!" she cried, and staggered toward him. "I'm going to be ill!"

"Your time has come," said the bearded beast to Matthew Corbett. "I challenged you to a duel, and if you're any kind of man you'll accept that challenge. If not, turn tail like the yellow-belly I figure you to be and light out of here this minute. Many others have, and everybody at this social loves a good laugh. So I'm askin' you… what weapon do you choose? Sword? Pistol? Axe? What are you wantin' to fight me with, you little pale piece 'a parchment?"

The pallid problem-solver pondered this. He looked up once more at the Sword of Damocles that dangled above his skull. Then he stared into the eyes of Magnus Muldoon and saw there something he had not seen before. Something, perhaps, he had not expected to see. He decided, then, what was his choice. But before he spoke it, Matthew thought of how he had come to this place and this moment, and how when he got home he was going to give Hudson Greathouse such a kick in the pants that the squabbling ghosts of Number Seven Stone Street would stop their eternal fight to applaud his determined application of the boot.

Two

"I SAY, *go!*"

"And I say, *no.*"

"Well my God, Matthew! It's an easy fifty pounds! And I think, according to this gent's taste in stationery and his oh-so-precious seal, I can ask another twenty pounds and get it. Easy money for an easy task."

"Too easy," said Matthew, as he turned from the pair of windows that—now opened to the warm air of early June—afforded a view to the northwest of New York, to the wide sun-sparkled river and the mossy cliffs and vivid green hills of New Jersey. Fishermen in their small skiffs were at work upon the river, and a sailing boat carrying crated cargo of some sort on deck had come drifting down toward the docks of town, its sails bloomed before the breeze. The ferry was making its long, slow but usually reliable crossing from Manhattan to New Jersey, with a coach and four horses aboard. Matthew had noted with interest that the frameworks of two houses were being built up on the Jersey cliffs where no dwelling had stood before he'd been kidnapped by Professor Fell's cohorts and taken to Pendulum Island.

The pristine nature of the cliffs was no more; such was progress, and ever would be. Directly below the windows were the streets, houses and businesses of New York, a jumble of nautical warehouses, stables, blacksmith shops, rope makers, timberyards, tallow chandlers, carpentry shops, soap makers, poulterers, coopers, peltry sellers, bakeries, japanners, horners, creditors and a dozen and one other areas of occupation. It seemed to Matthew that more people had come since he'd been gone, and on some mornings the bustling traffic of horses, wagons, carts and carriages along the Broad Way reminded him of an anthill scraped open by an errant boot.

"Too *easy*," he repeated to Hudson Greathouse's bearded face. "And it's not a suitable task for me. Or for any problem-solver worth a pinch of salt, for that matter."

"I saved this letter," said the Great One, holding it aloft at his desk, "because I thought you might detect a little *pepper* in it. And I assumed it would stir your juices and make you wish to get to the meat of it."

"Is it a letter or a beef stew? Keep on like this and I'll ask you to pledge yourself to buying my noonday meal at Sally Almond's."

"Pah!" said Hudson, and let the missive drop like a dead leaf upon his desk. He had grown his silver-touched beard out ever since Matthew had arrived bearded from his time at sea upon Captain Jerrell Falco's *Nightflyer*, and the widow Donovan had remarked upon her attraction to a hairy face. Which presently had set Hudson to lay aside his razor and reap the rewards, of which Matthew wished to know nothing. Of Captain Falco and the *Nightflyer*, the good captain's ship was now many hundreds of miles out in the Atlantic on the mission of returning the ex-slave Zed to his tribal homeland. Matthew had seen the ship off on that morning, as had Zed's ex-owner, the town's eccentric coroner Ashton McCaggers. And...on that morning also, stood with McCaggers Berry Grigsby in a dress the color of the April meadows and wearing a floppy-brimmed straw hat banded with wildflowers. Matthew had sneaked several glances at Berry but had received nary a one in return. But what had he expected? He recalled his speech to her not so long ago...recalled it, in fact, as one might recall a stab to the gut.

I was wrong to have confided in you on the ship that night. It was weak, and I regret it. Because the fact is, I have never needed you. I didn't yesterday, I don't today and I will not tomorrow. He had seen the little death in her eyes. And it had killed him, most of all. *Fine*, she had answered. *Good day to you, then.* She'd begun walking quickly away, and six strides in her departure she had turned again toward him and there were tears on her face and she'd said in a voice near collapse, *We are done.*

Three words. All of them small. All of them terrible.

So...what had he expected?

He had played and replayed this scene, in the silence of his diminutive abode behind the Grigsby house. In the shaving of his face before his mirror he had replayed it, and in his reading by candlelight it interrupted the pages. In his walks to and from this very office it followed him like a silent shade, and as he sat alone at Sally Almond's or in some other establishment it mocked him like a cuff upon the ear.

Gone too far, he thought. Too far by many steps.

But he had no choice now, only to keep walking the path. What he would have liked to say to Berry was lost to him. He would have liked to tell her that as long as Professor Fell was alive or at the least uncaged, he must fear the unsleeping eye and the stealthy hand that held a dagger aimed for the heart. And not only fear a sudden death for himself, but for others who dared to befriend him. He didn't worry much about Hudson Greathouse, who knew what he was getting into when he signed on with the Herrald Agency. No, it was those like Berry—and especially Berry—whom Matthew thought the professor would target, as a method of revenge. Matthew had already led her along dark passages and into dangerous situations that he regretted; to lead her into more intrigues and dangers would mean he did not care for her nearly as much as he really did. Therefore...the silence.

Silence, however, was not Hudson's *forte*.

"Here you are," said the Great One, "with an opportunity to refresh yourself with a *minor* task to carry out—something I'd surely do if I was up to the dance, my lady was more understanding and I was as *young* as you—and you spurn it as if you were given a horse-shit pudding. There's nothing so vital on your schedule! Go to Charles Town and relax! Get that episode of Pendulum Island out of your sails! And bring us back a nice chunk of money, for nothing more dangerous than escorting a rich man's daughter to—" He checked the letter again. "The Sword of Damocles Ball." A little chuckle rolled from the corner of his mouth. "Some imaginations, these Carolinians have. And, it appears, a little too much money. Why Mister Sedgeworth Prisskitt can't find a local escort for his daughter is a mystery." He stared at Matthew with a more serious intent. "Don't you wish to find the answer?"

"I wish to enjoy the summer in my own way. I have several books to read." The truth was, Matthew might be interested in the *why* of this situation, but his inclination for travel had been dulled by that sea voyage to the Bermudas imposed upon him. At this late date, he would have to take the packet boat from here to Charles Town. He and Berry had worked as crew on the *Nightflyer* during the passage home, and during his own night flying Matthew was still awakened by the ringing of phantom ship's bells, the hum and thrum of wind through rigging and the creaking of sea-strained timbers. It seemed at times his little residence was pitching back and forth as if in a white-capped sea.

"I think the answer," Matthew ventured, "is that Pandora Prisskitt is so homely no man will be seen in public with her. Far be it from me to upset that equilibrium." He returned to his own desk and sat down, ignoring his friend's snort of derision. He had nothing on the docket that shook his earth. Three letters...two requests for a rider to safeguard property papers between New York and smaller towns, and one missive from a farmer in Albany asking for help in unmasking the fiend who had stolen his scarecrow. None of those inflamed Matthew's imagination, enticed him to act as a champion for justice or caused him to want to travel any of the hard roads out of town. Still...he did wish to be active in some way, to get his mind back onto the business of problem-solving. And of course because his abode—which used to be a dairy-house belonging to New York's prickly printmaster Marmaduke Grigsby—was just steps away from Berry's door, the house she shared with her grandfather, Matthew was painfully aware of how long a short distance could be. On the matter of distance, the best news of the season was that the spindly-framed High Constable Gardner Lillehorne had announced he was leaving for London with his shrewish wife 'the Princess' at the end of the month to accept a position as Assistant to the High Constable in that teeming city. The surprise to this was that the little red-faced bully Dippen Nack was going with Lillehorne to become *his* assistant. Matthew thought London must certainly be desperate for assistants these days.

He shuffled some papers while Hudson busied himself answering a letter from a woman in the town of Huntington inquiring as to help in finding a missing horse, the animal having been taken from her barn in the middle of the night. Perhaps, Matthew thought as his mind wandered, its current rider was a scarecrow.

He recalled quite vividly the day that Zed departed New York aboard Captain Falco's ship. His recollection was keened by the fact that after the ship had parted ways with the harbor, Berry had left the scene arm-in-arm with Ashton McCaggers. This time, though Matthew might have fervently wished it, neither of McCaggers' shoe heels snapped, and neither did the coroner step into a hole or a mud puddle or suffer any disaster of Berry's supposed "bad luck". Which perplexed and bothered Matthew no end, though he wasn't sure exactly why.

"You are not here," said Hudson, looking up from his letter and frowning. His frown made a thundercloud appear jolly. "You are not *there*, either. So the question is…*where* are you?"

Matthew replied after a moment of reflection, "Neither here nor there, it seems."

"Exactly. Which is why you should find a destination. I'd think you would want to—" He was interrupted by the sound of the door at the bottom of the narrow stairs opening and then closing. Came the noise of someone ascending, and in another moment the inner door opened and there stood the *grand dame* of the Herrald Agency, Katherine Herrald herself.

"Good morning, gentlemen," she said, with an uptilt of her solid chin. She was wearing a pale blue gown nearly the same shade as her eyes, which with a single sweep took survey of the office and her two associates. She wore white gloves. Her right hand held a red clay vase that brimmed with yellow flowers. Though she was about fifty years of age, Katherine Herrald was trim-figured, straight-backed and elegant. She wore tipped at a jaunty angle a pale blue hat with red piping, her dark gray hair streaked with pure white at the temples and at a pronounced widow's peak. She was, lamentably, a true widow; her husband Richard had originated the agency and been brutally murdered in his pursuit of the enigmatic and viperous Professor Fell.

"Good morning, madam," replied Hudson, who pushed back his chair and rose to his feet at the same time as did Matthew. Hudson, a broad-shouldered and some might say supremely overconfident bull of a man, stood three inches over six feet and wore a plain white shirt with rolled-up sleeves, tan-colored trousers and white stockings. His thick iron-gray hair was pulled back in a queue and tied with a black ribbon. He was forty-eight years old and had a ruggedly handsome, craggy face that had quickened the hearts of many women before the widow Donovan. The scars he wore attested to his dealings in the world of men armed with swords, daggers and muskets, but actually the scar that cut across his left eyebrow had been caused by the treachery of a broken teacup thrown by his third wife. Hearing the tales of Greathouse's exploits, Matthew had often wondered how the man had stayed alive so long. Indeed, in one case involving the killer Tyranthus Slaughter, Matthew had almost been the cause of the Great One's demise. For a time Hudson had counted on the support of a cane to get around; a knife plunged repeatedly into the back followed by near-drowning at the bottom of a well did tend to make the legs unsteady. Happily now in these warmer days, however, Hudson showed his mettle by no longer depending on the cane as much, and he was getting more nimble at taking the stairs up from Stone Street.

"I have seen Lady Cutter off," said Madam Herrald, with a quick glance at Matthew. "And I've brought something to brighten your day." She walked to the small hearth of rough gray and tan stones, unused now these last two weeks. She leaned down to place within it the red vase of flowers. "There!" she announced. "An improvement over cold ashes, wouldn't you say?"

"I would," Hudson agreed. "As a matter of fact, I was about to suggest that Matthew clean the fireplace out today. It seems he's so free with his time at the present." He followed this with so slick a smile Matthew wanted to rip his beard off and throw it out the window so someone might use it as a horse-brush.

"Indeed?" The woman's penetrating blue eyes fixed upon the younger problem-solver. It was apparent she was not simply appraising

Matthew's light gray suit and spotless white shirt. "Time on your hands, you say?"

"A bit sullen this morning," Hudson spoke up, rather too cheerfully for Matthew's liking. The letter from Charles Town rose again from the dead in the Great One's grasp. "We have here a request from a Mister Sedgeworth Prisskitt concerning the employ of an escort for his daughter Pandora to an occasion called the Sword of Damocles Ball, held the last week of June."

"I've heard of that," said Mrs. Herrald. "An annual occasion for the elite of the town, to see and be seen. Sounds more than a little pretentious to me."

"My thoughts exactly," Matthew supplied, bellowing the sail while this tide was turning to his favor.

"Pretentious or not, we're being offered fifty pounds for what appears to be *one night* of work. If you want to *call* this work." Hudson waved the letter like a battleflag. "A few days aboard a packet boat for Matthew, he attends the ball and escorts the dear daughter, he gets back aboard another packet boat the next day or so...and there you have it. Anyway, I'm of the opinion that Matthew could use a trip to refresh himself. His last trip was...how shall I say this...? Eventful, for all the wrong reasons. Matthew's been dragging himself around these past couple of weeks. Look at him, he's a ghost in his own skin."

Matthew thought he could well be a ghost by now, and stumbling through the invisible world inhabited by the spirits of Number Seven Stone Street's fighting coffee-bean dealers if not for the courage and faith of three women: the princess of blades Minx Cutter, the lonely Iroquois wanderer Pretty Girl Who Sits Alone, and the indefatigable but unreasonable Berry Grigsby.

He did have another bitter seed from his apple of fortune to chew upon. The fact that Minx Cutter's first assignment since agreeing to become an associate with the Herrald Agency was taking her to Boston. She was on the case of a stolen piece of jewelry said to be in the shape of a scorpion, and supposedly endowing mystical "gifts" of some kind upon its wearer. Matthew would have wished for such a problem to solve, but that honor and opportunity went to Minx. He thought this totally unfair, since Minx had not yet proven her worth. Or...for that matter...proven she wouldn't abscond with the scorpion herself at the first chance she got. He could only surmise that Mrs. Herrald had given Minx the enviable job because of information Lady Cutter had offered concerning Professor Fell's organization. After all, Minx had been involved in the forgeries realm of that operation and also knew more than a passing bit about other areas of the professor's criminal world. Which made Minx a source of valuable wealth, if she could be trusted. Perhaps giving Minx the task of finding the jewelled scorpion was Mrs. Herrald's way of verifying if indeed Lady Cutter *was* trustworthy. Minx had just left for Boston aboard a north-bound packet boat this morning, so the issue of trustworthiness—and the recovery of the mystical scorpion—was yet to be asserted.

Matthew had bitten his tongue when he'd learned Minx was given the assignment. But it was he who had talked Minx into meeting Mrs. Herrald barely two weeks ago and considering a position in the agency of problem-solvers. Still, it was a damnable affront to his own abilities. And here he sat, with Hudson Greathouse waving that blasted letter around! He had to voice his opinion to Mrs. Herrald, now or never.

"I believe," he said calmly, his attention focused on Katherine Herrald, "that this Pandora Prisskitt must be one of the most... shall we say...unlovely creatures upon the face of the earth. I recall that we received a letter sometime back from this same gentleman requesting an escort for his daughter to the...if my memory is not faulty...Cicero Society Ball at the end of March. Why else would her father want to *hire* someone? *And* pay what is really a ridiculous amount? I mean...think of it! Hiring an escort to come to Charles Town *all* the way from New York? Why doesn't Mr. Prisskitt just find a *local* escort and pay him the same? Surely there are young men in Charles Town who can be paid to squint through their spectacles at a female of an unfortunate proportion, a wayward eye or a dark-haired lip. So...how does it make sense that this gentleman proposes to secure an escort from a place some seven hundred miles away?"

"Oh, you've tracked the distance, have you?" Hudson's scar-cut left eyebrow went up.

"I *know* the distance. I lived in Charles Town long ere I met you, and certainly had a trying experience in its vicinity."

"Yes, the Nightbird thing," Hudson recalled. "Well, you were but a lad then."

"Old enough," was Matthew's reply. *The Nightbird thing* was an improper way to put it, but understandable coming from the Great One's unruly tongue. It was a reference to his association in the spring of 1699 with Rachel Howarth in the fledgling town of Fount Royal. The magistrate Matthew had clerked for, the late and lamented Isaac Woodward, had called Rachel his "nightbird", due to the fact that she'd beguiled him just as the singing of a nightbird might beguile any ordinary man from his daytime duties. Matthew had told Greathouse the whole story of that, and now was rewarded with this jab to the groin biscuits.

"Interesting," said Mrs. Herrald, who motioned for both gentlemen to be seated again. She gave Matthew a bemused smile. "I mean to say your impressions on this are interesting. You have correctly identified the questions involved, but you jump to a strange conclusion. Even if the young lady is as...*hideous* as you suggest, surely a man might be found to escort her to a ball for somewhat less than fifty pounds."

"I'm thinking the local gents don't wish their reputations to be sullied. Even for such a sum," Matthew said as he sat down at his desk.

"Possibly not. But you surprise me, Matthew. You are presented with a..." She paused, obviously debating some nuance of language. Then, satisfied with her decision, she went on. "A Pandora's box of mysteries. It seems to me this is a simple matter, yet one I'd think you'd surely consider taking on if just to answer these questions for yourself. You have nothing pressing, it seems. I think you have a respite from the attentions of Professor Fell, who will certainly be busy cleaning up the mess you've delivered to him. Not to say he won't be attentive to you in the future, but for now...I believe he's busy in England, trying to repair the damage. I wouldn't have sent Lady Cutter to Boston, if I didn't think she would be secure in her travels. Again, I say...for *now*." A white-gloved hand motioned toward the windows that looked toward the green New Jersey hills and meadowlands. "But Matthew, you should take advantage of the season! You ought to enjoy this opportunity for some *safe* travel yourself. Consider granting the gentleman's request, won't you?"

Matthew shrugged. "I'll give it some thought," he decided, though he wished he were on his way north to Boston rather than planning a southern trip.

"You might take some extra time in Charles Town," Mrs. Herrald continued. "Rest and recover in the breezes. I know what you've been through." She offered him a saintly smile. "You should be kinder to yourself, Matthew."

"Just what I've been telling him," said the Great One, who made it sound as if he were the wisest physician of the age.

Matthew discounted Greathouse's bluster and turned his attention to a more important—and more personally disturbing—matter. "I would ask if you've had any news?"

"Nothing positive," came the woman's answer. "I've sent off a dozen letters. So far three have come back from my contacts in Philadelphia and Boston. None of them have ever heard of Brazio Valeriani. But I'm hoping my associates in London can shed some light on it."

"Hopefully," said Matthew. Now *this* was a problem worth the solving...and perhaps, Matthew thought, it *had* to be solved before Professor Fell lay hands upon this man, for whatever foul reason. Replies from London might take more than a year to arrive in New York, and Matthew had the feeling that time was of the essence. At a dinner one night during Matthew's enforced stay on Pendulum Island, the professor in the guise of a masked automaton had offered the statement and challenge: *I am searching for a man. His name is Brazio Valeriani. He was last seen one year ago in Florence, and has since vanished. I seek this man. That for the present is all you need to know. I shall pay five thousand pounds to the person who locates Brazio Valeriani. I shall pay ten thousand pounds to the person who brings him to me. Force may be necessary. You are my eyes and my hands.*

Seek, the professor had said, *and ye shall find.*

It sounded to Matthew as if Brazio Valeriani did not wish to be found. And mayhaps there was some desperation in Valeriani's disappearance from Florence. Fear of Professor Fell? Of course... but exactly why did the professor want him? Certainly not dead, but brought before him by force to the tune of ten thousand pounds?

And Professor Fell had even approached Matthew directly about finding his quarry with the declaration: *If you found him I would pay you enough to own that little town of yours.* So the question remained: who was Brazio Valeriani, and why did the emperor of crime want him so badly? *Badly* being the operative word here, Matthew mused.

"Beautiful flowers," said Mrs. Herrald as she surveyed the vase in the hearth. "Some of the most beautiful are often the most trouble to gather. Don't you agree, Matthew?"

The problem-solver had no clue. He wondered who might be filling the woman's ear about his difficult relationship with Berry Grigsby, if indeed this was her point. He decided at that clear and precise moment that he didn't wish to be around Berry and her new beau. He didn't wish to see them walking together and find them sitting at Sally Almond's or drinking coffee at Robert Deverick's establishment. No, Heaven forbid! It would be torture to have that sight thrust before him day after day!

Matthew sighed. It was the sound of a soul in pain, yet to Mrs. Herrald and the Great One it was simply a sigh of resignation.

"I believe I *will* go to Charles Town," said Matthew. He nodded, his face more grim than gracious for this sterling opportunity. "Yes. I will pack my bag and take the packet boat." He slapped his palms upon his desk for emphasis. "I *do* need a change of scenery. Do me some good, I think."

"There you are!" grinned Greathouse. "The young man at last has come to his senses! *And*," he continued with a slyer smile, "added at least fifty pounds to our coffers!"

"Far be it from me," Matthew relented, "to stand between a fool and his money." Which made Greathouse's smile slip a notch simply because Hudson wasn't sure if he was the fool in reference or if it was Sedgeworth Prisskitt, but the morning was bright and the hills were green and the birds were singing and soon it would be time for a bowl of hearty corn soup and a mug of apple beer at Sally Almond's, so all was right with the world.

That had been three weeks ago. Now, as Matthew stood beneath the Sword of Damocles and stared up into the black-bearded and ferocious visage of Magnus Muldoon, all was not so right with the world, even though the ballroom was ringed with silver candelabras that shed golden light and the air was perfumed with lemons and the faint tang of the Atlantic from Charles Town's harbor only a few blocks to the east.

The challenge had been made. The duel offered. Matthew stood alone, as both the most beautiful woman in the world and her father had withdrawn to a more comfortable distance.

"What weapon then, you little piece of puff?" growled the Magnus mountain. His eyes were as sharp as two bits of flint, and ready to strike fire. "What do you wish to die by?"

Matthew cleared his throat. It was a polite sound. The problem-solver was ready to speak.

Three

WOULD you agree, sir," said Matthew in a quiet voice, "that any implement causing injury can be considered a weapon?"

Muldoon scratched his beard. Possibly it was a trick of the light, but a few fleas appeared to jump out. "Reckon…I agree," he said, as cautiously as a human could speak it.

"And also that 'death' can have various meanings?"

"Hold up!" A huge palm was thrust toward Matthew's face. "This is smellin' of trickery!"

Matthew thought that at least the mountainous blackbeard was not a simpleton. "If I'm going to propose a weapon that might cause my death, sir, please allow me the ability to make the definitions clear."

A roar emerged from the cave of the man's mouth that might have sent a bear running. *"Are we gonna fight, or ain't we?"*

"We're going to *duel*, yes," said Matthew, with composure that even he felt was admirable. In truth, his stomach was churning and he was damp in his armpits. He glanced toward the tapestry of comedy and tragedy, not quite certain in which arena he was a player. Surely, both were rivers from the same fount, and both could easily capsize the most careful of boats. He returned his attention to Magnus Muldoon, who Matthew had realized in the last few soul-jarring minutes was the reason Sedgeworth Prisskitt had to pay an exorbitant fee for an escort for his daughter to the society balls *and* bring a young man from such a far distance.

He recalled his first visit to the fine Prisskitt estate and mansion three miles to the northwest, beyond the stone walls that made up the fortress of Charles Town. He had ridden up on a chestnut steed in the bright hot sunshine, fully expecting this day to turn dismal when he looked upon dear Pandora. And yet...when the servant had taken him to the red-carpeted parlor room, and the stately elder gentleman Sedgeworth had come to greet him and offer him a glass of spicy Sir Richard, and drinking this agreeable and quite head-spinning liquor Matthew had been guided out upon a glassed-in conservatory that overlooked meadows sloping down to the Ashley River...and yet Matthew was entranced by the hospitality and by such a beautiful vista, so much so that he forgot his trepidation and the sick little roll of his cabin in the packet boat and began to consider this task a pleasure.

He had not been half through his rum and only an eighth through Mr. Prisskitt's recitation of the family's huge fortune in timber and brickworks when spinet music began to issue from within the house. "Ah!" Prisskitt had said, with a proud and civilized smile. "That would be Pandora, playing her favorite hymn! Shall we make the introduction, Mr. Corbett?"

Matthew of course recognized the music as *A Mighty Fortress Is Our God*. He smiled also, his lips oiled by the rum, and pretended not to notice all the bad notes. It was indeed time for the introduction. No matter how homely Pandora was, Matthew was bound and determined to be the grandest escort the poor girl had ever had. Nay, he would be the King of all Escorts! He would kiss her hand and bow before her, and to blazes with Berry Grigsby and Ashton McCaggers, may they both be happy in his attic tomb of grisly curiosities. So there.

But yes, he would be the greatest escort ever to escort anyone. Ever. To the Sword of Damocles Ball. He wished he might have another jolt of Sir Richard, but now Prisskitt had him by the elbow and was pulling him to his doom. Or…meaning to say…*room.*

Matthew did not consider himself to be so superficial as he now found in the next moment that he was. For upon being pulled—escorted by the elbow, so to speak—into the music room and seeing the young woman who sat playing the intricately-etched Italian spinet he felt suddenly weak in the knees, not because of the assault of off-key notes but because…

…because if this vision was indeed Pandora Prisskitt, he was just about to be introduced to the most beautiful woman in the world.

It was amazing, how mangled notes could be healed by the smile of a violet-eyed goddess. Her lustrous sable-brown hair was done up in what Matthew presumed was the latest Charles Town fashion, its curly ringlets arranged about her shoulders and decorated with green ribbons. She wore a sea-green gown and a choker of perfect white pearls, probably worth the packet boat Matthew had rolled in on. Her face was fit to make any artist into a master of beauty, if such could be captured on canvas. Which Matthew doubted, for Pandora's serene loveliness would have unsettled the hand that held the brush and made the otherworldly into the commonplace, for her mouth, her cheekbones, the curve of her nose, the small dimples in her cheeks, the sleek arcs of her eyebrows and the violet coloring of the eyes…all would be too much for a brush to match. Matthew thought even Michelangelo might cry for his lack of talent in assigning the young woman's features to the body of an angel. Indeed, he thought as he staggered a bit beneath her steady gaze and the heavy presence of Sir Richard, she might be the most beautiful woman who had ever lived. Yes, she was that much. And another glass of this rum and he would be surely undone, and what might issue from his mouth would not be the refinements of an escort from New York but the gibbering of the orphan boy he used to be.

"Mr. Matthew Corbett," said Prisskitt, "meet my daughter Pandora."

And the vision had risen from her seat at the spinet and offered him her soft hand. Opening a Chinese fan before her face she had batted her eyes at him, lowered her head and said in a voice as sweet as the honey crust on a cinnamon cake, "I am so *enchanted*, Mr. Corbett."

In the two days to come before the ball, Matthew was the one who found himself enchanted by Pandora's manners and presence. He did find it odd, however, that such a creature should be lacking for a local escort, but an afternoon's ride along the river with Pandora's father had cleared up the mystery. It seemed that Pandora was so beautiful she had no suitors. "Too striking for the local men!" said Sedgeworth. "Can you fathom that! Yes, it's true! My daughter absolutely *loves* to attend the social events...and you do know it's important for a young woman of her status to be seen at these gatherings...but, Matthew—may I call you Matthew, as I feel I know you so well?—she is never *asked* by anyone! That's why I was forced to hire you. Yes, forced to hire a young gent all the way from New York, because no man in this town will ask my daughter to *anything*! And it's a shame on them, Matthew! Oh, I don't understand this younger generation! Well...I mean...*you* are of the younger generation, but...of course...you're a sophisticated sort, aren't you? Listen to me prattling on! Why don't we retire to the shaded porch, have us another glass—or two—of Sir Richard and relax as Pandora plays us a few hymns. Would that suit you, Matthew?"

"Oh, yes sir!" said the sophisticated sort, who didn't realize the power of the Southern sun upon his noggin. "I am well-suited for a stirring hymn!"

"Indeed you are, my boy," Prisskitt had replied, as he'd turned his horse back toward the stable. "Indeed you *are*."

One of the tapers in a silver candelabra to Matthew's left spat sparks, as above his head the breeze through the open garden door made the sword of Damocles sway back and forth...back and forth...

"Death," said Matthew, "can have many definitions as applied to the human condition, sir. For instance, there is the death of an idea. Or the death of hope. Do you agree that someone can be said to die of shame?"

"Of *shame*? What are you goin' on about? Either a man *dies* or he don't!"

"Precisely so, but there can be the death of the spirit as well as of the body...may I call you Mr. Muldoon?"

"Reckon. What's *your* name?"

"Matthew Corbett, at your service."

"Pleased to meet you."

"The same."

"*Now listen here!*" Muldoon roared again, the beast taking up its vengeful burden. "What are we gonna *fight* with?"

And here was the question that needed answering. Matthew had realized that Magnus Muldoon was the real reason no young man of Charles Town offered to squire the lady Prisskitt to any of these socials. No young man of Charles Town wished to wind up in the graveyard or laughed out of town for refusing this monster's challenge. A glance at the dandies and dames in this dignified dungeon told Matthew that there were a few too many grinning faces and glinting teeth for a civilized gathering. He had no doubt that several gents had been laid onto the banquet table for worms due to Muldoon and his fixation on the angel of the room, but probably many more had run for their lives. Matthew had seen in Muldoon's eyes that the man expected him to run...no...really, *wanted* him to. For the beast was not a born killer, it was just that he was somewhat bewitched by the awesome beauty of Pandora Prisskitt. And who was it who once said there was no such thing as witches?

Matthew had not desired to be the center of the evening's entertainment, but he stepped up to the task.

"My weapon of choice," he said firmly, "is a *comb*."

Muldoon cupped a hand behind one of his ears, which was hidden by his matted mane and might well be plugged by a thumb's-length of wax. "Must be goin' *deef*. Thought you said your weapon of choice is a comb."

"You heard correctly. A comb it is."

Magnus Muldoon shook his head as if he'd already been axed in the brainpan. "A comb. For the *hair*?"

"Exactly so. And I prefer to have satisfaction right *now*, at this moment." Matthew reached into a pocket of his waistcoat and withdrew his own simple wooden comb, and then he surveyed the onlookers. "Might one of you have a comb Mr. Muldoon and I can use in our—"

"You're *crazy*!" It was still a growl, but somewhat weakened. "How can a comb be a weapon in a duel?"

"I think you're about to find out, sir. Ah, thank you!" An older gentleman with a shock of white hair had brought a tortoise-shell comb also from his waistcoat and offered it to Matthew. "I will be glad to pay for the comb," said the problem-solver, realizing the fate of one of these implements.

"Are you suffering some insanity?" came the voice of Sedgeworth Prisskitt. The question was a polite repeat of Muldoon's. "What's a comb got to do with duelling?"

Matthew preferred not to answer the man nor give him and his daughter a glance. Suddenly Pandora was not so beautiful to him. After all, this entire scene had been set with him in mind as a sacrifice, just so dear Pandora could attend the ball. He could either wind up dead or running like a rabbit out of town, but it was all for the woman's vanity. He didn't think fifty pounds was enough for this job. Still...it was a challenge, and never more so than at this moment.

"Choose one, if you dare," Matthew told the mountain. There was hesitation in the black-bearded ogre. "Come on!" urged the piece of puff, in a voice that sounded like a man who had fought one or two uneven battles in his life and, in truth, didn't mind a little scuffle in the dirt. He held the combs forth. "If you have any courage, you'll take one of these. If not...*get out.*"

With that taunt, Magnus Muldoon bloomed red at his cheeks and came forward like a thunderstorm. He reached for the tortoise-shell comb first, but then his hand paused. He snatched up Matthew's wooden implement. "What am I supposed to do with this?" he asked, as if biting off a hunk of meat from a bone.

"My challenge to you," said Matthew, "is simply to comb your hair. Yes," he allowed to Muldoon's expression of bafflement, "that's all. I say that whoever can draw their comb completely through their hair is the winner of this duel. Oh...you're not *afraid*, are you?"

"Hell, no! Not feared of nothin' that walks on two legs or four, crawls on its belly or flies on the wing!"

"Good. Not fearful of a little *comb*, then are you?"

Muldoon regarded the teeth as if peering into the maw of an unknown animal. "No," he answered Matthew, his eyes aflame... yet his voice was more smoke than fire.

"Can someone count to three and start us off?" Matthew asked the assembly. No one came forth, and Matthew figured the throng was quite disappointed that they weren't going to either see a sword or pistol fight at dawn or a New York problem-solver's behind as he ran for the packet boat dock. "Mr. Prisskitt?" Matthew offered. "Count to three, please?"

"Well...I..."

"I'll do it!" said the young woman who was not quite now so beautiful. She actually wore the hint of a wicked smile, which proved that beauty was indeed skin-deep. "One...two...*three*!"

Matthew put comb to hair and began to smoothly glide it through. Magnus Muldoon put comb to hair and made another legion of fleas jump and a flight of flies grumble and buzz. In another moment, as Matthew continued to effortlessly guide the comb through his own hair, the Magnus Man found the going as tough as fighting upsteam through a barricade of beaver dams. His comb got hung up on one tangled and matted mess after another. When Matthew was finished, Muldoon was yet struggling and tearing out hair in the process. The bearded beast had to drop his tricorn and take hold of the comb with both hands, as if he were swinging the heaviest axe ever made. But he was no quitter, that was for sure, and though the bear-greased black sprigs clogged in the comb's teeth and the fleas jumped and the flies swirled and tears came to the eyes of Magnus Muldoon, still the hands wrenched and tore and the mouth grimaced with pain. He was hardly half-way to his crown, where the worst of his wilderness grew. The comb ripped, snagged and clogged with bear grease. Muldoon gritted his teeth and kept tearing. Suddenly rivulets of blood began to trickle through the man's hair down his forehead, along his cheeks and into his beard.

"Stop!" said Matthew, alarmed at this flowing of red rivers. "There's no need for this!"

But Muldoon wasn't listening. He continued ripping his scalp to pieces, tearing out hunks of hair with what had become a true instrument of pain.

"Muldoon! Stop it, you fool!" urged Sedgeworth Prisskitt, standing in front of his daughter. She had her hand up over her mouth, as if about to release all the stuffed victuals with which she was stuffed. Her eyes were no longer angry; now they just looked a little sick.

The madman would not stop. Matthew realized this was indeed a duel, and Magnus Muldoon was taking it as seriously as the New York dandy had not. Matthew was about to implore him to cease the struggle, as more blood ran over Muldoon's face, but then the comb clogged with its ugly mess of hair, grease and God-knew-what-all became well and truly stuck nearly to the man's crown, and try as he might with his beastly strength Muldoon could not move the comb a shilling's width through his unfortunate tangle. He staggered back and forth and struggled with it—God's breath, did he struggle! Matthew thought with equality of horror and awe—but as the blood trickled down Muldoon's forehead and cheeks and the comb refused to budge it was clear the duel had but one winner.

At last, with a *whuff!* of released breath that indicated even the Magnus Man had come to the end of his determination, the loser of this contest released his hold on the comb, which yet was held fast by the aptly-named locks. Someone in the watching throng—a woman, or perhaps a highly-excitable man—gave out a laugh in the upper register that cut across the room like a razor across a throat. Matthew saw Muldoon wince, saw his face tighten beneath the crimson streamers of blood that streaked his face as surely as if the sword of Damocles had fallen upon his head. Then Muldoon reached into his black coat, pulled a long knife from a leather sheath at his waist, and took two steps toward Matthew.

Matthew did not retreat. His legs wished to—and almost did—but it seemed to him the wrong thing to do, so he did not.

Muldoon stared into Matthew's eyes while he used the knife to cut the wooden comb free. Then he gave the quite unusable and disgusting instrument to Matthew's hand. He sheathed the knife, picked up his tricorn hat, and gazed around at the gathered throng who seemed to be waiting for the next act to what was yet this unknown tragedy or comedy.

"You lot," said the bloodied man, with a painful half-smile. "Thinkin' you're so high God has to reach up to you to wipe your tails with a pinecone, and you lookin' down haughty on me. Oh, you bagful of snakes and dirty sinners! Laughin' and laughin'...when there ain't nothin' funny at all."

Maybe someone further back in the room did give out an unfortunate and muffled chuckle, but mostly silence of the stony kind met this assertion.

"And *you*," Muldoon said to Pandora Prisskitt. "The loveliest vision I ever did see, or hope to see. You walk through my dreams. When everythin' seems dark out in the woods...you're the candle I hold tight to. I want for better things. Does that make me so bad?"

"You know what you've done!" Sedgeworth's voice was tight and strained. "You've killed three of my daughter's suitors, run a dozen more of them out of town and nearly ruined her life! Why don't you leave us both alone and keep to your own kind?"

"What kind would that be?" came the reply. "The animals of the field?" Again he directed his gaze toward the lovely one. "I thought... when I first seen you on the front street that summer morn...and I recall it, down to the minute...that if I could only walk at your side, and hold your hand, and have the favor of God's blessin' to look upon your face...that everythin' could change for me, and I would give you a life worth livin'. And a love you would never have known, straight from my heart. But...I kinda *see* you now. I kinda see...how you brung this fella all the way from New York, for me to kill...just 'cause you *have* to go to these fancy dances. That ain't right, Pandora." He let that hang in the air, as much as the sword hung in the air above the festivity. "Ain't right, to use a person that way." He faced Matthew. "My apologies to you, sir. I'll make apologies for *her*, too."

"You don't need to speak for my daughter!" said the father, getting more enraged by the minute. "How dare you! Speak for yourself! Or...let the world look at you and *smell* you, and that tells the story well enough!"

Magnus Muldoon opened his mouth perhaps to fire an angry volley at Father Prisskitt, but suddenly it appeared to Matthew that all the salt went out of him and all that was left was sad clay. "I reckon you're right," said the man. He nodded. "Reckon you are." His eyes found the loveliest vision, who stared at him with the warmth of a blizzard. "*Pandora*," he said, and the sound was like a heart breaking. "I know I done wrong...but I thought...maybe...with you at my side...I could be better than I was. *Am*," he corrected. "I would've given you love," he told her. "I would've held you like the finest cup in the world, and poured myself into you. Is wishin' that so wrong?"

"It is *hideous*," Father Prisskitt answered, and in it Matthew heard the hiss of the snake. "And if it did not make me so sick I would laugh myself to the floor."

"Get out of our sight!" the daughter nearly shouted, her face contorted and eyes glittering and not nearly so lovely as Matthew had thought at the evening's beginning. "Get out of this *world*, you black-bearded monster!"

With that, Muldoon straightened his boulder-like shoulders. He cast his gaze around the ballroom, at the grinning faces in the guttering light. He let his gaze fall upon Matthew Corbett, who felt the weight of the moment.

"You bested me," said Muldoon. "I ought to hate your guts…but I don't. I'm just gonna leave you here with 'em, all these fine ladies and gentlemen, and I'm gonna say…enjoy what you've earned." He gave Matthew a slight bow, and then turning around he walked across the boards and exited the event by the way he'd come, through the filmy curtain and into the garden where no weed dared grow.

In another few seconds Matthew found himself the hero of the moment. So many hands whacked him on the back—and some as hard as enmity—he feared he'd be bruised all the way to his lungs. Sedgeworth Prisskitt came up and clapped him on the back and said something unintelligible, because Matthew had ceased to listen to him. Fine ladies drifted up like pastel smoke to rub against his shadow. Highwigs puffing powder marched up and the chunky faces beneath them said how steadfast he was, and how cunning. And then Pandora Prisskitt came forward, radiant even in her darkness, and took his arm with the pride of ownership.

"You are *so* smart," she gushed, "and so brave too!"

The musicians were starting to take their places again, and allow a few notes to issue forth as invitations to more dancing. "Thank you for your compliments and your company," said Matthew, to Pandora's puzzled expression as he dislodged her hand from his arm. "I shall have to take my leave now, as I'm feeling a little ill."

"Oh?" Sedgeworth had heard this, and came forward. "What's the matter?"

"Nothing very much," Matthew replied. "Just a bit close in here for me. The air…seems oppressive."

"I'm sure a walk around the garden will help! Pandora, go with him!"

But Pandora was very intelligent, and she knew and pulled back. Matthew gave both father and daughter the smile of a gentleman who has done his duty. "I shall indeed walk around the garden on my way to the inn. It seems to me that there are several fellows here who might like a dance with your very gracious and understanding daughter. Oh...would you take this, please?" And so saying, he placed the comb matted with Muldoon's bloody hair into Sedgeworth's palm. Then he offered a bow to the lady and glanced up one more time at the sword of Damocles to count himself lucky. He left the room by the garden exit to walk beneath the star-strewn sky over Front Street, ruminate on how quickly life could turn comedy into tragedy and vice versa, and consider that he might appear to be one of the chosen elites who occupied the ballroom yet he in truth he had been there on a task and in depth he was more an outsider than ever before. And tonight, after having escaped either death or humiliation and seeing the reality of things, Matthew was very much more than content with his position.

Four

It was a fine morning to walk along Front Street in the warm sunshine, which if Matthew knew anything about Charles Town in the summer—and he certainly did from past experience as clerk to Magistrate Woodward here in his younger days—the warmth of the sun would turn to wretched heat as the day wore on and the shadows grew small. By noon the smell of the swamp would ooze over the town's stone walls and permeate the little shops selling coffees and teas and bon-bons for the genteel, and the odor of decaying fish afloat and abloat against the wharf would violate even the most sweetly-scented fragrance of a garden's roses or the perfumes sold to dab behind a lady's ear or upon a gentleman's cravat. In other words, at high noon it was time to get out the silk fans and employ the nosegays, so Matthew walked the street early and wisely before such aromas could embellish the air.

Besides, last night he'd gotten a strong enough whiff of this place. He had slept on a goosedown mattress in a comfortable bed in an inn owned by a Mr. and Mrs. Carrington, both agreeable people who were curious about New York and asked many questions concerning the life and manners there, and he had supped this morning on orange muffins with cinnamon butter followed by spiced ginger tea, and he appeared to be composed and content... and yet this was an illusion. For as he strolled along Front Street in his neat gray suit, his pale blue shirt and his gray tricorn with a dark blue band, even as he peaceably passed the shops and seemed to be at peace with all under God's eye, he was at war with himself.

He had come to this situation of internal combat sometime before dawn, just when the town's roosters began to crow. One part of himself wished to directly return to New York upon the next packet boat leaving port, and the other part...

...perhaps not so quickly.

He strolled on, from tree-shade to tree-shade. The scene—or rather, the *sense*—of last night's festivity would not leave him. Several well-dressed gentlemen and ladies who passed him nodded in greeting. He wondered if they had been present at the ball, and if they still thought him such the hero for besting Magnus Muldoon with a comb. But the part of it that particularly galled Matthew was the truth of something the bearded mountain had said: *I kinda see you now. I kinda see how you brung this fella all the way from New York, for me to kill just 'cause you have to go to these fancy dances. That ain't right, Pandora. Ain't right, to use a person that way.*

And Pandora's less-than-musical reply: *Get out of this world, you black-bearded monster!*

It was an ugly picture, Matthew thought as he walked. Made more ugly by the superficial beauty of the queenly Lady Prisskitt, which had beguiled him so completely and might nearly have crowned him as the king of his own coffin.

He walked a distance further, mindful of other people strolling on the street and the passage of carriages, the horses clip-clopping along. In a moment he stopped to gaze into the window of a tailor's shop that displayed some shirts and suits in light summer hues. He was thinking...thinking...thinking that thinking was often his undoing...but it seemed to him that Pandora Prisskitt should not get away completely free from causing the deaths of three men—however those deaths had been delivered by the hand of a man who loved her valiantly and in vain. Also, Matthew disliked the fact of being used, intended to be either the fourth corpse or another frightened fool running for his life. And there was also the issue of Magnus Muldoon, a sad and heavy-hearted soul who seemed to think himself more Lancelot than Luckless Lout.

So...the question being, in his state of internal war...should he board the next packet boat heading north...or should he stay for a few more days, and stir up the muddy waters of love?

A face appeared in the window.

Rather, it was the reflection of a face in the glass. A woman in a pale green hat and gown the same color had come to stand just behind his right shoulder, and when she spoke Matthew felt both a punch to his stomach and a thrill course up his spine.

"Matthew? Matthew *Corbett*? Is that *you*?"

He turned toward her, for he already knew. He brought up a smile, but his face felt too tight to hold it steady.

She was both the same and of course very different, as he also was. *Here is the witch*, he recalled her saying in the foul gaol of the fledgling town of Fount Royal, as she defiantly threw off her dirty cloak of sackcloth to reveal the woman beneath. He remembered the moment of her nudity quite clearly, and in truth he had carried that moment and opened it like a locket for a peek inside from time to time. His cheeks reddened a few degrees, which he hoped she attributed to the external temperature.

"Hello, Rachel," he answered, and he took Rachel Howarth's offered hand and almost kissed it, but decorum prevailed.

She had been weathered in her twenty-eight years, primarily by her ordeal of being accused of witchcraft in that nasty situation and her months facing the stake and the flames, but she was still very youthful and indeed as beautiful as Matthew remembered. Her heart-shaped face with a small cleft in the chin was framed by the fall of her long, thick midnight-black hair. Her eyes were pale amber-brown, verging on a fascinating golden hue, and her skin color was near mahogany as bespoke her Portuguese heritage. She was altogether twice as beautiful, Matthew thought, as Pandora Prisskitt considered herself thrice to be. And Matthew knew Rachel's soul as well, which was also a dwelling of beauty.

But also, he knew where the so-called "devil's marks" were on her naked body, and these little dark marks and flecks that appeared on everyone's flesh had almost sent her skin flaming. He had been her champion and had saved her from that imprisonment and from that fire, and the last he had seen of her was when he had left her to claim her own future in Fount Royal, and to find his own in the greater town of New York.

"I am *amazed*!" she said, with a smile that might have been described as giddy. She appeared to be about to throw herself into his arms, yet she was restraining her forward motion. "Matthew! What are you doing *here*?"

"On business from New York," he replied, in a steadfast tone. "I'm a problem-solver now."

"Oh? People pay you to solve their problems?"

"Yes, that's about it."

"If so, then," she said, "I owe you quite the chestful of gold coins. I cannot believe I am seeing you! Just out here, in the broad daylight!"

"I was in attendance last night at the Sword of Damocles Ball."

Rachel made a face as if the midday odors had come early. "Oh, with *those* people? Surely you haven't become—"

"One of them? If I gather your meaning correctly, I hope not. I was hired as an escort for one of the local ladies. The story is a bit complicated, but I survived the sword." And conquered with the comb, he thought. "But *you*...what are *you* doing here?" Did he feel his heart flutter just a bit, under her golden gaze? He had fought a bear to save her life, and bore the scar for that. Perhaps there was another scar that ran a bit deeper?

"Well, I..." She suddenly looked to her left. "David! You must meet this young man!"

Matthew followed her line of sight. A tall gent in a tan-colored suit and a darker brown tricorn was coming across the street. He paused to allow a carriage to pass by, and then he continued onward. He was smiling and healthy-looking and appeared to be in his early thirties. He walked with a purposeful stride, a man of energy and means.

"This is David, my husband," Rachel told the young problem-solver from New York. "I am Rachel Stevenson now." She smiled again, a little awkwardly, as if she could hardly believe this herself. "A doctor's wife!"

"Ah," said Matthew, whose hand extended almost of its own accord toward the approaching master of this beautiful woman's heart. He said, with his own smile fixed in place, "I am Matthew Corbett, sir, and I am very pleased to meet you."

They shook hands. The doctor had a grip that might put someone's hand in need of a doctor. "David Stevenson." He had a sharp-featured, handsome face and very blue eyes, which now blinked with sudden recognition. "Oh! *You* are the one!" And so saying, he rushed upon Matthew and hugged him and clapped Matthew upon the back with such fervor that a half-digested orange muffin nearly popped out. Then the good doctor Stevenson seized Matthew by both shoulders and grinned in his face with the power of the Carolina sun and said, "I thank God you were born, sir! I thank God that you did not give up on Rachel, when others might have. And I see the scar, and I know what you did for the woman I love. I should bow down on my knees before you!"

"Not necessary," said Matthew, fearing the doctor might actually do such a thing. "I was glad to do my part in that particular play, and I am surely glad that now her time of woe and worry has come to an end." And certainly it appeared so, for wife retreated toward husband and husband put arm around wife and wife who was once accused of witchcraft in a nasty little cell smiled very happily indeed, and the scarred champion nodded his approval for time had moved on and so must all men and women. She had made him what he was today, and because of her he had come very far from his first experience at "problem-solving"—though he hadn't known it at the time—in Fount Royal. Still, it was a bittersweet moment for Matthew, who had never felt so alone in a place in his life.

"We live on an estate just outside town," Rachel said. "You must come to dinner with us tonight!"

"We insist!" said Dr. Stevenson. "It's the least we can do!"

Matthew thought about it, but not too long. He had other business on his mind, and after this was done he planned on going home. There was no need to revisit his—or Rachel's—past any further, and besides he reasoned really that Rachel herself would begin to feel uncomfortable about this invitation as soon as he accepted it. Therefore he said, "Thank you, but I have to decline. My time here is very limited, but—again—thank you."

"Solving another problem?" Rachel asked. Was it Matthew's imagination, or did she look a mite relieved? After all, he recalled an event in an Indian village, when he was nearly insensible and recovering from the wounds inflicted upon him by Jack One Eye, in which he'd dreamed that this beautiful woman had crawled atop him to further the healing process by the heat of her body and passion of her kiss. But had it really been a dream? Only Rachel knew for sure, and though this was not a problem it was surely a mystery that Matthew knew he would never solve. Perhaps it was better that way, to keep some events in the realm of the mysterious.

"Well," Matthew answered, "as you mention it, *yes*. Or rather, a personal issue I'd like to address. May I ask if either of you know a man named Magnus—"

"Muldoon?" the doctor interrupted. "Of course! He's done work on the estate, clearing trees and such. A tireless worker, to be sure. And I tended to his father in the poor man's last days of swamp fever, just after I arrived last summer, Muldoon's mother having passed away several years ago. You have business with him?"

"I do. Might I ask how to find him?"

"I've never been to his house," was the reply. "He brought his father to me in their wagon to tend to. But I believe it's up the North Road past the town of Jubilee and the Green Sea Plantation, which is maybe eight miles from here." He gave an impish smile. "You might ask for further directions there, as the trails up along the River of Souls are...shall we say...for the adventurous."

"The River of Souls?" Matthew asked.

"Yes, the Solstice River, which branches off from the Cooper. The Green Sea Plantation grows rice along there."

"Ah." Matthew nodded. He'd heard of the Solstice River during his time spent here as a magistrate's clerk, but neither he nor Magistrate Woodward had ever had need to travel in that northward direction. For the most part they had remained within the town's walls, dedicated to the local legal matters. "Swamp country, then."

"What *isn't*, around here?" The doctor shrugged. "One gets used to damp earth under the boots."

"Just so the boots aren't under the damp earth," Matthew said, thinking of his last escapade through muddy water on Pendulum Island. "I lived here for several years, but I've never heard the Solstice River called the River of Souls."

"Witchcraft," Rachel answered.

"Pardon?" Matthew turned his attention to her, and the word he thought he would never hear issue from her lips.

"Supposedly," David Stevenson said, bringing up his bemused smile, "a witch cursed the river, for drowning her son. And cursed the entire swamp around it, as well. This was many, many years ago…if such really happened. So now the river's upper course remains largely unexplored, and according to the tale I heard it was said that…well… ridiculous indeed, but those who travel up it are destined to witness horrors that test the soul. And that the witch still lives and searches for a soul to trade the Devil for her son's." He had spoken these last two sentences with a quietly jocular air, worthy of a sophisticated distance between those who believed such poppycock and those who did not. He glanced up at the sun's progress. "Getting hot early, I fear. It'll be sweltering by noon."

"Yes, certainly," Matthew agreed, feeling the risings of sweat on the back of his neck even though they stood in tree-shade. In regards to the River Solstice, as he had spent much of his time in Charles Town either reading, plotting out chess problems, studying Latin and French or scribing testimony for the magistrate in cases that went on for hour after hour, Matthew had been primarily a single citizen of his own world. The selfsame for the Sword of Damocles Ball and all the other events meant for the town's elite; he'd existed far below their influence, and certainly would never have been in the rarified orbit as the Prisskitts or anyone at that damnable festivity. "You heard this tale from whom, and when?"

"An elderly negress, nearing ninety years, at the Green Sea Plantation only a few days ago. She told a very compelling story, also entertaining, as I worked. I was summoned there to apply a compress to a horse bite on an overseer's arm. It had become infected. While I was there I suggested an inspection of the slaves and house servants, thirty-four in all. I wound up pulling a few teeth and washing out some minor wounds."

"The whip?" asked Matthew, having had some experience with that particular pain.

"No, thankfully not. The Kincannon family restrains the use of that. The wounds I tended were snakebites—not poisonous, obviously—and others related to working in the ricefields. I *have* had to go there and amputate a hand mangled by an alligator, unfortunately."

"Dangerous work, it seems," said Matthew. "Very dangerous. And often deadly. But the rice must grow and be harvested, and the new fields carved from the swamps." Matthew checked the degree of the sun, and decided that if he were going he'd best get to the nearest stable, secure a horse and be on his way. An eight-mile trip would be about two hours, depending on the trail.

He reached out and took Rachel's hand. "I'm so pleased to have seen you," he told her. "Pleased also that you are happy, and have found a true home." He squeezed her hand quickly and then released it. "Sir," he said to Dr. Stevenson, "I wish you both a fine life and excellent health. If I'm in this vicinity again anytime soon, I'll surely accept a visit to your estate and dinner."

"Our pleasure, sir," answered the doctor, who reached forward again to shake Matthew's hand and give it another bone-crush.

"Goodbye, Matthew." Rachel dared to deliver a kiss to his left cheek, which was likely more scandalous here than in New York, and yet it was correct. "Good travels to you today, and I hope..." She paused, searching the chest of hope that Matthew had given her when he had freed her from her bondage. "I hope you find a solution to every problem," she finished, with a tender smile.

"Myself as well," he answered, and giving a slight bow to Dr. and Mrs. Stevenson, he turned away and walked in the direction of the stable from which he'd rented his chestnut steed a few days ago. He was very tempted to look back, and with each step forward tempted a bit more, but the point of going forward was progress and thus he was to all eyes admirably progressive. He continued on, following his shadow along Front Street's white-and-gray stones and thinking that he should be turning around and heading to the packet boat dock to secure his ticket and then going to the inn for his bags, and yet...

Matthew knew himself. When he was curious about a situation or a person, there was no retreat until he had satisfied his curiosity. He could not let this go. Thus his intended trip to the mountain Muldoon today, up the North Road into rice and Green Sea country, into the supposed realm of witches and devils on the River Solstice, into the future unknown...if only for a few hours, which suited him just fine.

He walked on at a steady pace, seeing the stable ahead, and readied his money for the rental of a noble horse to carry the warrior onward.

Five

"YA ain't from around here, are ya?"

An understatement, Matthew thought. But he said politely, "No sir, I am not. I am seeking the house of a—" He paused, because more and more people in this little town of Jubilee were coming forward along the dusty street to get a gander at the newcomer in his sweat-damp clothing. Matthew had removed his coat and tricorn hat in tribute to the oppressive heat, which seemed to not only be boiling from the hot yellow ball of the midday sun but also roiling off the huge willow trees that ought to be cooling the town, not inflaming it. Matthew felt like a wet rag. His chestnut horse, Dolly, was underneath him presently drinking from a trough at a hitching-post. He wished he'd had the sense to bring a simple water bottle on this jaunt. So much for preparations from someone who always considered himself well-prepared! Fie on it! he thought. He spied a well that stood at what seemed to be the center of this community of patchwork houses, and he said to the grizzled old man who'd first approached him, "Pardon me while I get a drink, please."

"He'p y'self," the fellow offered, and took the reins to tie Dolly to the post while she drank.

Matthew put on his tricorn, got out of the saddle and excused himself past many of the rather threadbare-looking citizens who had come to take the measure of his worth. Men, women, children, dogs and chickens had arrived on the scene. He felt the stroke of a few hands, not along his body but along the material of his linen shirt and the suit jacket he held over his shoulder. Eight miles north of Charles Town had brought him into a wholly different world. The structures here were ramshackle hovels, except for one larger building that seemed fit enough to stand against an evening breeze, with the title *Jubilee General Store* painted in white above its front doorway. A lean, rawboned man wearing a floppy-brimmed hat with a raven's feather in the hatband sat in a rocking-chair on the store's porch, a jug of something perched on a barrel at his side and his eyes aimed at Matthew, who nodded a greeting as he approached the well. The man failed to respond, but a couple of dogs and a few small children ran circles around Matthew and stirred up what seemed to the visitor the very dust of discontent.

He cranked the bucket up. He could look to the northeast and see—beyond several more houses and wooden fences—fishing boats and canoes pulled up upon a swampy shore. The River Solstice flowed past Jubilee, merging into the Cooper only two hundred yards to the southeast. It was notable in that it was a third as wide as its larger brethren, which was nearly a mile across in places, but seemed in what he'd seen of it so far through the trees and underbrush to be a nervous river, full of twists and turns in contrast to the Cooper's stately progress. Indeed, the North Road—a weatherbeaten trail, at its best description—had led him alongside the Cooper for a time before hiding it behind dense forest, and then had revealed it again near the point where the two waters converged.

Though the sun shimmered on the surface of the River of Souls in bright coinage, Matthew thought the water in its vault looked dark. Darker than the Cooper, it appeared. More gray in its belly, and fringed with the black of swamp mud where it agitated the earth. Across the river was naught but further wilderness, a whole country of it.

Matthew took his tricorn off and used his hand to scoop up some water. He drank first, then wet his face, hair and the back of his neck. The cloud of biting insects that had been swirling around him and darting into his eyes for the better part of the last hour retreated, but they would soon be back with—Matthew was sure—reinforcements. In this swampland, such a battle went on incessantly.

He saw that a large cornfield stood northward, and along with it a grainfield of some variety of wheat. Jubilee thus maintained itself as a farming community, but it appeared that visitors here were few and far between. And just as Matthew thought that and was taking another slurp of water from his palm, a wagon being drawn by four horses came trundling down the same narrow track he'd followed from the North Road, where the word *Jubilee* was painted on the trunk of a huge mossy willow. The wagon's wheels stirred up another floating curtain of yellow dust, people stepped aside to get out of the way for it seemed the wagon's driver had no qualms about running anyone over, and in another moment the wagon passed Matthew and the well and pulled up in front of the general store.

The rawboned man with the raven's feather in his hatband stood up in greeting, at the same time as four young black males—slaves, without a doubt—who'd been riding in the back of the wagon got out and stood obviously waiting for a command. They were dressed not in rags but in regular and clean clothing of white shirtings, black trousers, white stockings and boots. The driver was a white man, thick-shouldered and dark-haired, also wearing simple clothes. A second white man, who'd been sitting alongside the driver, climbed carefully down from the plank seat and he was the one to whom Sir Raven's Feather spoke. This individual was older, wore a gray shirt and a pair of dark green trousers with stockings the same hue, and had some difficulty with his right leg, for he limped and it seemed to pain him. After a quick conference with Sir Feather he motioned the slaves to go into the store. They obeyed, and a moment later were engaged in the labor of bringing out barrels and grainsacks to load onto the wagon.

Supplies for the Green Sea Plantation, is what Matthew surmised. The wagon's driver did not offer to help the loading process; he was content to light a pipe from his tinderbox, sit back and watch the slaves earn their keep. The distance between Matthew and the driver was not too far for Matthew to note on the man's right forearm a medical compress fixed in place by a wrapping of cloth bandages, as his sleeves were rolled up. So there was the overseer who'd suffered the horse bite, Matthew thought. And from Matthew's knowledge of medicine Dr. Stevenson's compress, to soothe the wound and draw out infection, would be a soft mixture of meal, clay and certain herbs wrapped up in cheesecloth, heated and applied to the wound. Matthew assumed that the doctor had left more of the mixture at the plantation and instructions on how to change the compress, for within a short time the application would be dried out and unworthy.

Some of the citizens came to watch the wagon being loaded, as the slaves worked quickly at their task. Dogs barked and scampered around, enjoying the activity. Other citizens edged closer to Matthew, still curious about his presence. And suddenly Sir Feather pointed toward Matthew, and with a puff of pipesmoke the overseer took Matthew in and the older gentleman in gray and green also turned his head to view the visitor.

Matthew nodded, as he was suddenly the center of attention. The older gentleman spoke to Sir Feather once more and then came limping toward the well. His right leg seemed to resist bending at the knee.

"Good day, sir," said Matthew as the man neared.

"Good day to *you*," the man rumbled. He was tall and slender but powerful-looking in spite of the recalcitrant leg. He was perhaps in his mid-forties, with dark brown hair brushed back from the dome of his forehead and just touched with gray at the temples. His was the face of a fighter, all sharp angles and ridges and the beak of a broken nose. His brown beard had been allowed to grow long down his chest and was also streaked with gray like the zigzagging of lightning bolts. A pair of deep-set, penetrating hazel eyes made Matthew think of a hawk sitting above him in a tree, regarding him with avian intensity to figure out what he might be made of: animal, mineral or vegetable? Or, rather, if he were worth the trouble of figuring out such, for this man carried with him a certain attitude like a hard push to the chest. One wrong word or motion here, Matthew thought, and this man would fly in his face like, indeed, the hawk in the tree.

He decided to announce himself. "My name is Matthew Corbett. I've come from Charles Town."

"Well," answered the other, "of *course* you have." This was said with nary a slip of a smile; the eyes were still measuring him, taking him apart here and there, examining, coming to some conclusion. "I am Donovant Kincannon, the master of Green Sea Plantation." No hand was offered. "*From* Green Sea Plantation," he added.

"I've heard of it," said Matthew. "I was speaking to Dr. Stevenson just this morning."

"Oh? You're a doctor?"

"No, not that."

"A *lawyer*," said Kincannon. His thick brown eyebrows went up. "I *thought* I could smell the odor of law books."

"No," said Matthew, now presenting a slight smile in spite of this jab, "though I do enjoy reading. I'm a problem-solver, from New York."

"A *what*?"

"I am hired to solve people's problems for money," Matthew explained.

Kincannon grunted, his eyes still hard at work darting here and there, putting the pieces of this young man together like a puzzle. "I'd heard people were insane in New York. I fear this proves it."

"I *am* good at my work, sir."

"And you've been hired to solve a problem *here*? In Jubilee?"

"No, sir. I am just passing through. I'm in search of the house of Magnus Muldoon."

"Hired by Muldoon? What's the problem?" Kincannon removed his attention for a few seconds to watch the slaves filling up the wagon with the barrels and sacks, while the horse-bit overseer continued to sit and puff on his pipe.

"No problem, really. I'd just like to speak with him."

"Makes no sense," Kincannon said. "No one comes up here to visit Muldoon. He's a solitary man."

"Yes. Well...that *might* be the problem, if there is such."

"Hm," was Kincannon's comment to this assertion. "I don't see him very regularly myself," said the master of Green Sea. "Only occasionally, when he comes to sell his bottles. He's a glass-blower, among other things. I've been to his house only once, to view his wares. My daughter was quite taken with his…as she calls it…artistry."

"I had no idea. I only met him last night, in rather…um… trying circumstances." Matthew was aware of the pipe-smoking overseer approaching them, perhaps bored watching the slaves work and curious as to the subject of conversation. The man had a stride like a cock-of-the-walk, thrusting his chest out before him and his chin also as if daring someone to take a swing at him. "So am I to understand that Muldoon lives somewhere *near* here?" Matthew asked.

"A mile or so past the entrance to Green Sea. But the road north is a bit more rugged than what you've experienced from Charles Town." Kincannon turned to take stock of the overseer, perhaps alerted by the pungent smell of the Virginia tobacco. "Griff!" said Kincannon. "Come meet a young wanderer who is very far from home. What'd you say your name was? Corbett?"

"Matthew Corbett, yes sir."

"Griffin Royce," replied the other, who was a short, stocky gent a few years older than Matthew, with thick dark brown hair that hung over his forehead in front and shot up in a cowlick in the back. He had a sunbrowned, pock-marked face with a square chin and high cheekbones that made him appear to be almost of the Indian breed. His green eyes quickly examined Matthew from head to foot before he spewed smoke and offered his hand. Matthew was prepared for another bone-crusher, but Royce went easy on him. "Pleased," said Royce, who held the grip only for a brief couple of seconds.

Matthew nearly mentioned the compress, but he decided not to. A horse bites a man not necessarily because the horse is mean, but because the man might be. Matthew thought there was much of the brawler in the big-shouldered Griffin Royce, who had a chest like a tombstone and clenched the black clay pipe between his teeth with the ferocity of a bulldog. Royce continued to stare at him through the shifting screen of smoke, even when Matthew returned his attention to Kincannon.

"So," he said, "you're saying just follow the North Road and I'll find his house?"

"It's up that way. You'll see it."

"Thank you. Very good meeting you, sir. And you as well," he told Royce, and then he turned away and began walking back to his horse.

"Mr. Corbett!" Kincannon called, and Matthew stopped to look back. "It's not too often I meet someone who's come all the way from New York. Also, I'm interested in your line of work. I've never heard of such before. Why don't you stop by the Green Sea on your way back from Muldoon's? Have a drink of rum with me. I know my daughter would be pleased to meet you." He offered a faint smile that Matthew figured for this man was the epitome of warmth. "She's a reader, too. Always has her nose in a book."

"I'd be glad to," Matthew said, "if it's not too late."

"Late or not, come by anyway. It would be an entertainment for Sarah."

Matthew nodded. He could not fail to notice that Griffin Royce was smoking like a dragon, his entire face almost shrouded by the fumes. "Thank you, sir," he repeated to Kincannon, and then he walked on to his horse and his continuance of battling with the wet heat and the swarms of insects that wished to suck his blood.

He rode away from Jubilee, with a last look at the little village that seemed to exist solely for the support of the Green Sea Plantation. Back on the North Road, he soon passed a low stone wall. There was an archway under which the road to the plantation proceeded across a grassy meadow where a dozen sheep were grazing. Weeping willow and oak trees stood aplenty. From this distance Matthew had no view of the main house or the river. The stone wall ceased, but the green meadows and the trees remained constant. Then, not fifty yards away, Matthew saw a white horse grazing and near it a group of gray boulders under a stand of willows. Upon one of these boulders, shielded from the sun by the tree-shade, was a young woman in a yellow dress and wide-brimmed yellow hat, sitting cross-legged and…

Of course that would have to be Sarah Kincannon, Matthew thought. She was reading a book, and nearly had her face in it. A small pond ringed with cat-tails glistened just beyond her, and Matthew wondered if she had found her particular place of peace and quiet in which to pursue whatever dreams her reading guided her toward. As Dolly continued along the road at a walking pace and Matthew was content to be on his way to Muldoon's abode, the young woman suddenly looked up from her book and saw him. She sat motionless for a moment, and then she waved.

Matthew took off his tricorn and waved it back at her. He intended for that to be all of the interaction, but Sarah Kincannon cupped a hand to her mouth and called out, "Where are you going?"

It struck Matthew that here might be a young woman in the mold of Berry Grigsby: a brightly-colored flower, adventurous and curious in her own way, intelligent and well-read and...yes, most likely quite bored with life on a rice plantation so far from Charles Town. He had a few seconds to make a decision, and he did. He turned Dolly off the road and across the meadow toward the young woman, who composed herself a bit by sitting in a more ladylike posture atop the boulder as he approached.

"Hello!" he said when he got nearer. "You must be Sarah!"

"I am. Do you *know* me?"

"I met your father in Jubilee." Matthew pulled Dolly up short of the boulder, not wanting to frighten the girl by getting too close. "He told me you enjoyed books."

"Oh, yes I do! They're very wonderful." She held up the volume for him to see. "This is poetry by Robert Herrick. Do you know his work?"

"Yes," said Matthew, "I do." The most famous of Herrick's poems being an urging for virgins to make the most of time, to gather their rosebuds while they may for time was fleeting; he decided not to bring that into the discourse. He noted that Sarah Kincannon had removed her shoes, her stockinged feet crossed at the ankles and hanging over the boulder's edge. The sturdy black shoes were lined up side-by-side. She smiled at him with a broad and very pretty face, her cheeks dimpled, her hair light blond and falling in waves around her shoulders. She had her father's hazel-brown eyes, but in her face they were soft and sincere and...really...a bit dreamy. Matthew judged her to be about seventeen years old, and again she reminded him of Berry for the direct way she looked at him, and there was an earthy and extremely attractive component in her makeup. In that moment he missed Berry greatly, and sadly replayed in his mind their last scene together.

"I don't see many strangers here," Sarah told him. "Who are you?"

"My name is Matthew Corbett." He felt as if he were introducing himself to half of the Carolina colony today. "And, as you may deduce, I'm not from around here. I'm from New York." He said this with a bit of puffery that alarmed him as soon as it was spoken, for it was offered to further pique the girl's interest.

"*New York?* But what are you doing here?" She gave him a sly smile. "Lost?"

"Not yet," he answered, "but the day is not over." He swatted at the air to drive away the nettlesome insects, and noted that none seemed to be bothering Sarah. In fact, the flesh of her face and exposed arms glistened with some kind of ointment that must be keeping the biters away.

She seemed to read his mind, for she reached into a small brown leather purse at her side and brought out a purple-colored bottle with a cork in it. "Oil of fennel seeds," she announced. "It does help." She offered him the bottle, which he was glad to accept. He dabbed some on his fingers and wet his face, throat and the back of his neck, and was pleased to find the mosquitoes and other angry darters retreating from its not unpleasant aroma. "There," Sarah said as Matthew gave the bottle back to her, "now they'll leave you alone for awhile."

"A little miracle," said Matthew.

"No, just something Granny Pegg taught me. Oh...Granny Pegg is a woman on the plantation."

"A slave?"

Sarah nodded. "We have many slaves. I mean...my father does." A little darkness passed across her eyes but it was a summer cloud and lasted only an instant. "Charles Town must have the rice. It goes up for sale all along the coast. That makes the work very important. Vital, even."

"I'm sure," said Matthew. He decided to change the subject, for talking about the slaves had spoiled her smile. "I'm on my way to see Magnus Muldoon. I understand he's a glass-blower?"

"Oh yes! He made this!" She held up the purple bottle. "He has a workshop where he makes the most beautiful things." Her eyes narrowed slightly. "Is Magnus in any trouble?"

"No. I simply wish to speak with him."

"I was wondering, because...pardon me for saying this, but... you seem a serious sort. Older than you look, I think. And you seem..." She searched for the right word. "*Official*," she said. "Like... the law."

"Well...not really," said Matthew, "but...in a roundabout way, perhaps I do represent the law. That's not my business with Mr. Muldoon, though. It's a friendly visit."

"I didn't know he had any friends. He keeps so to himself."

"As of last night," Matthew answered, "he has at least *one* friend." If he'll allow it and not break my neck before I've had a chance to speak, was Matthew's next thought. "I should be getting on. By the way, your father has asked me to stop by for a visit when I leave Muldoon's. Would that be suitable with you?"

"Please," she replied, "and say hello to Magnus for me."

"I'll do so." Matthew tipped his tricorn toward her again and then turned Dolly back to the road. In another moment he was heading northward once more, but he looked over his shoulder and to reward him for this Sarah Kincannon gave him another wave. He returned it, and then focused his attention on the way ahead.

Such attention was well-needed, for the road further along was nearly overgrown by the forest's weeds and thistles. Matthew had to beware lest Dolly step into a hole burrowed by some hidden animal. To his right through the trees and thick vegetation he caught occasional view of the Solstice River, twisting and turning, gray-green as a snake. And then rounding a bend he came upon a single house put together with white-washed boards and surrounded by willows. The place looked hardly large enough to house its builder. Off to the left stood a barn and a corral that held two horses, one black and one dappled gray. There was a pigsty with a few hogs wallowing in it, and beyond that a chicken coop. Next to the chicken coop was a shed about half the size of the house, also white-washed, that Matthew thought might hold the furnace where Muldoon did his glass-blowing. He was certainly no expert on the art, though he knew glass was heated to a molten state, blown into a bubble through usually an iron blowtube, and then fashioned into various shapes from that humble form. It was a complicated procedure and needed a steady hand and a strong lung, which it appeared Magnus Muldoon possessed.

As Matthew's Dolly approached the house, one of the horses in the corral nickered and snorted, and a few seconds after that the front door crashed open with a noise like the coming of Judgment Day and the mountain Muldoon himself appeared, wearing black trousers and a dirty white shirt with the sleeves torn off. His hair was wild, his black beard frenzied, and his iron-gray eyes flashed fire. He lifted the short-barrelled musket he held in his arms, aimed it squarely at Matthew's head and shouted, "Stop right there, dandy pants! Ain't you heard that a man with no head don't need a comb?"

Matthew reined Dolly in, perhaps a bit too hard, for the horse wanted to rear up and he had to fight her for a few seconds until she settled.

"Back away!" Muldoon said. "This is *my* land! Get off it!"

"Calm yourself, sir. I've come to—"

"Don't care! Not listenin'! You got yourself Pandora Prisskitt and I hope you choke on her! She can comb your damned hair every night, far as I'm concerned! Now get on away!"

Matthew kept his face expressionless. He said: "Sarah Kincannon."

"*What?*" came the half-roar, half-snarl.

"Sarah Kincannon," Matthew repeated. "She sends her greetings. And she says you make some very beautiful bottles. She showed me one, just awhile ago."

"Are you a fool, or just a plain idiot?" Muldoon demanded, the musket still aimed to part Matthew's hair and perhaps his brain as well.

"A little of both," Matthew answered. "Aren't you at all curious as to why I've ridden all the way here from Charles Town?"

"I know why. 'Cause you don't have the sense God gave a bumblebee." Now, though, he did lower the musket but his frown was as frightening as any weapon. "Corbett, ain't it? Well, what in the name of seven Hells *are* you doin' here? We had our duel, you won it fair and square—I reckon—and it's done. So *what* then?"

Matthew said, "I don't like being brought from New York to die for Lady Prisskitt because she wants to attend a fancy ball. You've killed three men for her, I understand."

"No more! I'm ashamed of that! Seein' her as she was last night...as she really is...I'm ashamed nearly to death!"

"I have some suggestions," said the problem-solver.

"Huh? What're you goin' on about?"

"Suggestions," Matthew repeated. "For you. Some ideas. Can I get down, tie my horse up and come talk to you?"

"You're talkin' *now*."

"Talking without a musket in the area, is what I mean. And, Mr. Muldoon, I think you'll find my suggestions very interesting."

"That so? Why should I?"

"Because you'll have a chance to get a little revenge on Pandora Prisskitt," said Matthew. "And I will too."

"How's *that*?"

"I think you have potential," Matthew replied, "to be a gentleman. I can start you out on that path, if you're willing to listen and learn."

Magnus Muldoon snorted so hard Dolly and even the two horses in the corral jumped. "Why the hell do I care to be a *gentleman*?" He spoke the word like describing something foul in a chamberpot. "So I can dance and prance like those fools in town?"

"No," said Matthew evenly, "so in time you will have your pick of any lady in Charles Town, you won't be living out here as a hermit, and...if you're as good at your craft as the example I've seen, you could set yourself up in business and make some real money. Becoming a gentleman doesn't mean you lose who you are...you just have more confidence in who you are. But first...the rough edges have to be smoothed."

"I think you've got moon sickness," was Muldoon's comment. "I'll bet you're one of 'em burns the midnight candle to a smokin' stub and ain't done an honest day's work in his life."

"Some might agree," Matthew said, with a shrug. "But at least hear me out. All right?"

"And if I say no?"

"I'll turn around and ride back to town. But bear in mind, Mr. Muldoon, that sweet honey attracts the female fly much more so than does angry vinegar. Lady Prisskitt has wronged you and myself as well. You know that by now. And I know you're not at heart a killer. Much of what you said to Lady Prisskitt last night... well, the poetry was right, but the package is wrong. There are many lovely women in Charles Town who would honestly desire to hear such heartfelt sentiments...without the murderous intent and threats of violence, of course...and I can't leave here, Mr. Muldoon, until I have at least tried to match the package with the poetry. Just so someday in the future Pandora Prisskitt may look into your glassblowing shop on Front Street and wish *she* were the one who had found you...instead of the woman who's *going* to find you, if you listen to what I have to say and act upon it."

Muldoon made another disturbing noise deep in his throat, like a shout that had been swallowed. "If my dear deceased Pap heard any of this," he managed to say, "he'd be rollin' in his grave!"

"If your mother heard it, would be she rolling in hers?" Matthew asked.

There was a long silence from Magnus, in which Matthew heard only the croaking of frogs in the direction of the river and a single crow cawing forlornly from a treebranch.

At last, the mountainous shoulders seemed to slump forward. Magnus held the musket down at his side, and he stared at the floorboards of his porch as if trying to read the future there. Then he rumbled, "Come on in. Speak your piece." He went inside before Matthew could reply or dismount, but he left the door open.

Six

EVERYTHING was going smoothly until Magnus pulled the cork from a long-necked bottle that was as red as holy fire and said to Matthew, "This is my own brew a' likker," before pouring some into a wooden cup for him. "Have a swig."

The little house was well-maintained and orderly, in stark contrast to the man himself. The furniture was simple and sturdy, the walls were pinewood pocked with numerous knotholes and the floor fashioned from broad pine planks. There stood a small hearth made of gray stones. On pinewood shelves were displayed some of the craftsman's creations, and upon first setting boots in the house Matthew was awestruck by something he never would've thought about Magnus Muldoon: the black-bearded mountain was a true artist.

The bottles were thin and tall, short and squat, rounded and squarish but no two were alike. They were colored dark blue, sea green, amber, bright yellow, purple, pale blue, and deep red. Some were banded with different colors, and some were of two contrasting colors, and some were grooved and fluted and as intricately executed as any chess problem Matthew had ever attempted to solve. A few stood out by being clear and as plain as gray rain, but even so their shapes were—to Matthew's eye, at least—perfectly formed.

"Excellent work!" Matthew had said when he'd found his voice. "How did you learn to do this?"

"My Pap was a glass-blower. He taught me. Then...I reckon... after he passed on, I decided to make some bottles that were in my head, but that hadn't come out yet. He sold a few to stores in Charles Town. I've been sellin' to the Kincannons. Miss Sarah's got nine or ten of 'em."

"I've never seen bottles like these," Matthew had said. "Not even in New York. You could make a *lot* of money there, I'd think."

"Don't do it for a lot of money," Magnus had said, as he'd lowered himself into a chair made of stretched cowhide. "Do it 'cause I enjoy it, and when I look at 'em...makes me feel good, like I've made somethin' worth the time and the heat." He put his dirty boots up onto a square piece of unpolished wood that served as a table. Upon entering the house he had deposited the musket in a rack on the wall, much to Matthew's relief. "*Now*," said Magnus, with a harsh note returning to his voice, "what's all this jollywhomp you've come here to tell me?"

Matthew had already noted the lack of bear-grease in Magnus' hair. In fact, it was still wild and uncombed but at least looked as if it had been lately washed and de-fleaed. Matthew reasoned Magnus had greased his hair for the occasion of seeing Pandora at the ball, as if that might help the mountainous one's chances to open a locked and rather cruel heart.

"Firstly," said Matthew as he stood at the center of the room, "never attempt to meet, see or speak to the Lady Prisskitt again. I can tell you that she is not worth the effort, and that any man you have killed in regards to her died a saint. Secondly, keep your hair washed. Bear-grease is not a suitable ointment. I can suggest something lighter in nature that you can procure in Charles Town. The idea is to attract, not to repel. Thirdly—and this may be a bit tough for you to take—I am going to also suggest that you shave off your beard."

Magnus had been staring at the floor during the beginning of Matthew's statements, but now the iron-gray eyes came up and stared holes through the problem-solver. "*What?*"

"Your beard," Matthew said. "Off with it."

"I've had a beard ever since I was a baby, seems like!"

"That may be true," Matthew admitted. "But now is the time is put it away with the toys and the rattles. How *old* are you, anyway?"

Magnus spent a moment counting on his dirty fingers. "Twenty-six years."

"Only two years older than me? Your beard ages you by many more."

"Not cuttin' the beard," came the defiant response. "My Pap and Mam thought it made me handsome. Told me so many times."

Matthew had the feeling that Pap and Mam had not necessarily wished their overgrown son to venture very far into the world beyond their guiding hands. He had no desire to criticize the dead, and felt that criticism here would result in a bootkick out the front door at the least. "You might then consider a *trimming*," he offered.

"The beard is left be, sir. And I'm listenin' but I ain't hearin' nothin'. I figure I'm good enough as I sit. What do I need anythin' else for?" He shrugged and settled deeper into his cowhide. "Damn me for a fool, chasin' a woman like that. And me thinkin' that *she* would make me better than I am. And damn me for pushin' those men into duels, and puttin' 'em under easy as eatin' sugar cake. Well, I *wanted* 'em to run! I just wanted 'em to get out of my way, so Pandora would see *me*." He looked up imploringly at Matthew and asked quietly, "Am I goin' to Hell?"

"I don't think so," Matthew answered. "I can tell you that many have done worse than you, and for worse reasons. Now: you say you wished the Lady Prisskitt to make you better than you are? Meaning you wish to advance in the world? My suggestions stand. Clean yourself up, cut—or at least *trim*—your beard, get yourself a new suit and take your craftwork to town. I'm sure you'll find an interested buyer in one of the shops on Front Street, who will likely ask for more. You may also find yourself with a sudden abundance of money, and though you may not create your work for that reason, money does help one advance in the world. Let me ask you this: why did your father and mother settle way out here? Why didn't they live in town?"

"My Pap was huntin' gold," said Magnus. "Heard before we came across the water that the gold was just layin' on the ground ready to be found. This place suited him, 'cause he and my Mam never did take to havin' close neighbors. He dug and dug for that gold, had me diggin' for it with him, but we never found a speck of it. I still dig for it once in awhile, just to please his memory." He motioned toward a wooden bucket on the floor in a corner. "Been findin' some of *that* hereabouts. Save it 'cause it's pretty. Tryin' to catch that color green in my bottlework."

Matthew walked over to look into the bucket. In it were twenty or so green stones of various sizes, the smallest a mere sliver and the largest maybe the size of Matthew's thumbnail.

"Dug those out of a hollow not too far from here. They cleaned up nice and bright," Magnus said, with a shrug. "No gold up there, though. Poor Pap, diggin' and diggin' as he did. And all for nothin'."

"May I ask a question?" Matthew bent down to have a closer look at the bucket's contents. He picked up the largest stone and turned it into the light that streamed through the nearest window. A streak of vivid green lay across the floor.

"Go on."

"Have you ever heard of something called an emerald?"

"A *what*?"

"Oh, mercy," said Matthew, who had to stifle a laugh. He had no idea of the quality of these gemstones, for some had black spots embedded in them and so were less than ideal, but it seemed to him that Magnus Muldoon's own shop on Front Street might already be paid for. Possibly a nice house in Charles Town lay in this bucket, as well. "These are *valuable*. How much they could be worth, I don't know...but you need to take these to town and show a jeweller. I think at least two or three of these are high quality stones."

"Valuable? Those little green *rocks*?"

"Raw emeralds," Matthew corrected. He put the gemstone back among its fellows, and he thought that if Pandora Prisskitt could see what lay inside this bucket she would be insisting she comb Magnus' hair and brush his beard herself. He stood up. "Yes, valuable. Maybe a hundred pounds' worth."

Magnus' eyes widened just for a second or two, and he frowned and scratched his beard as if it truly itched. "Have to think on that one. Never found any more, but figure if those are valuable as you say, and I take 'em to town to show somebody, then he's gonna want to know where I found 'em, and even if I tell him there likely ain't no more he'll tell somebody else and pretty soon I got strangers out here all over the place. Not sure I want that, now that I'm settled in my bottle-makin'."

"If you wish to be a hermit and continue the life you lead, then go right ahead," said Matthew, aware that he might well be talking to the wall. "If, however, you wish to—as you stated to the Lady Prisskitt—have things *change* for you, then you're standing on the threshold."

"The *what*?"

"Standing at the crossroads," Matthew amended. "I say remake yourself, beginning with a bath and clean clothes. Wash and trim your hair and your beard, take your emeralds and bottles to town and see what can be done. You might find your craft much in demand, and yourself as well by several ladies who are worth much more attention than Pandora Prisskitt. But...if you prefer this solitary life way out here, then by all means sink your roots deeper. Sink them until you disappear, if you choose. It's *your* life, isn't it?"

Magnus didn't answer. He was staring into space with the blank expression of a mountainous enigma.

"I've spoken my piece," Matthew said at last. "It would give me some satisfaction to know I had urged you out of this solitude and into a more congenial and gentlemanly role, if just to sprinkle a little pepper into the Lady Prisskitt's nose. But the rest is up to you, to decide or not, to act or not."

"You talk in riddles, don't you?"

"My talking is done. Good day to you, sir, and I hope you find great opportunity in whatever path you choose." Matthew started toward the door.

"Where are you *goin'*?" Magnus asked.

"Back to Charles Town, of course. I'd like to get there before dark."

"Hold on a minute. I was thinkin'...maybe...I want to hear more about these ideas. Maybe they make sense, even though I don't want 'em to." Magnus looked around the little room for a moment, as if measuring its space as a prisoner might measure a cell. "I'm goin' out to hunt some supper," he told Matthew, as he stood up and reached for the musket from the wallrack. A powder-horn hung nearby, and also a well-used brown leather bag that likely held the shot and other necessaries for use of the musket. "You want to come along, you're welcome. Shoot you some supper too, if you please."

⁂

Matthew's first response was to say no, that he had to get back to Charles Town, but something in Magnus' offer stayed his answer. It seemed to him that this was a rare and possibly first occasion, that Magnus had ever wanted anyone to share a meal with him. Matthew thought that the road to civilization might start here. He decided, in light of this, that it was worth staying for another couple of hours or so.

"All right," he agreed. "What're you hunting?"

"Squirrels," was the reply. "They fry up real good. Get four of 'em, you got yourself a feast."

Matthew nodded, thinking that this was the kind of feast Hudson Greathouse would heartily approve of. He followed Muldoon out the door, and in another few minutes was wandering through the forest alert for any sign or sound of their supper.

Thus it was, when the four squirrels had been skinned and cleaned and fried in a pan over a fire in the hearth, and Matthew had eaten this dish along with a roasted ear of corn and a piece of cornbread and the sun was starting to sink outside and the shadows lengthen, that Magnus got up, left the room into the next room beyond and returned with the bottle as red as holy fire. He was carrying two wooden cups, which he set down upon the table.

He wiped the squirrel grease from his mouth with his forearm, pulled the cork from the bottle and said, "This is my own brew a' likker." He poured some—just a small taste, really—into one of the cups for Matthew, who was sitting in a chair made from treebranches. "Have a swig."

"I'd best pass on that," said Matthew, as Magnus poured a drink for himself. "I think it's time I'm getting back."

"One swig won't harm you. Besides, I'll guide you back to town if you need guidin', I can ride that road in the dark. Go ahead, Matthew." He gave a sly smile. "Fella ain't feared of a deadly comb, shouldn't be feared of a little mild corn likker."

Matthew picked up the cup. The liquid was colorless. He sniffed it. It did have a strong aroma that promised a kick, but...he felt the challenge of another duel slapping his face, and it had been a good dinner and a good day and he really was in no hurry. All his concerns about Professor Fell seemed very far away, out here in these woods on the edge of the Solstice River. The same also about his concerns for Berry Grigsby, and his own future. He put the cup to his mouth and downed the liquor with a single swallow.

Muldoon had been correct. No harm was done, except for perhaps the instant watering of the eyes, a feeling of a flashfire searing down the throat and the speculation that a few hundred tastebuds had been burned off the tongue, but otherwise...no harm.

"Whew!" Matthew said when he'd gotten his eyes cleared and his throat working. "Quite potent!"

Magnus had taken his own drink down with seemingly no ill effect. He poured again into Matthew's cup and then his own. "Lemme tell you my story," he offered. "How we came across from Wales. Came through storms and seas as high as houses. How we got settled in here...and then, how I happened to see Pandora—I mean, *Lady* Prisskitt—on the street one day. You up for the hearin'?"

Matthew took a more careful sip of the liquor this time. Still, it went down the throat like a flaming torch down a well. "I am," he rasped, thinking that Muldoon was probably starved for company, and a couple of squirrels did not exactly fill the belly for that.

Sometime in the next hour, as the contents of the red bottle dwindled, the fire burned low in the hearth, the blue of evening claimed the world and Magnus' story began to go in circles, Matthew remembered the room starting to spin. He reached to finish off the last of his drink with an arm that seemed to grow ten feet long. He was sliding off his chair onto the floor. He thought he was falling out of a tree, therefore he grabbed at the branches and he and the chair fell together. He recalling hearing Magnus laugh, as if declaring himself the victor in this particular duel. Matthew tried to say something suitably witty for the occasion but all that came out was a frogcroak; he was well and truly stewed by Magnus' brew, and as he lost consciousness he realized he was not going anywhere anytime soon.

From the darkness he came to, groggily, with a boot prodding him in the ribs.

"Matthew! Wake up!" Magnus was standing over him, holding a lantern in which the stubs of two candles burned.

"*Whazzit?*" Matthew managed to say, just barely.

"Listen! Hear that?"

With an effort, Matthew sat up. His stomach lurched. For a few seconds he feared he was going to spew an awful mess of fried squirrels and fiery liquor everywhere. His head pounded as if being beaten by an insane drummer. The room was still spinning, slower now but enough to make him wish to lie back and enter again into the silent land of drunken sleepers.

And then he heard what Magnus was hearing, because Magnus had opened the door to let the sound in: the tolling of an iron bell in the distance, both mournful and frantic.

"Alarm bell's bein' rung from the Green Sea!" Magnus said, his voice husky with tension.

"Alarm bell? *What?* Why?"

"Callin' for help from Jubilee! Last time that happened there was a fire broke out over there!"

"A fire? On the plantation?" Matthew still couldn't get the liquor-sodden gears meshing in his brain.

"Sayin' that was last time I heard the bell ring! They're needin' some help! Come on, haul yourself up and I'll get the horses ready!" Magnus left the room, his boots making the floorboards whine.

Matthew had no idea what time it might be. Full dark had fallen, but how long the potent brew had laid him low was a question mark. In any case, his head was killing him. He tried to stand, staggered and fell back on his rear. Then he sat there for awhile trying to make the room further slow its spinning. What a laugh Hudson would be having at this moment, if the Great One could see him fighting gravity and heavy drink. One cup had become two, then three and four and that had likely been when he'd found the floor. Now it seemed the alarm bell was being rung with more force and frenzy, and though Magnus was revealing himself to be a good neighbor to the Green Sea's call for help, in truth Matthew wanted only to sit here until morning light.

But that was not to be, for Magnus had brought Dolly and his own black horse around to the front, and he called out, "Matthew! Come on, man, no time to waste!"

Matthew was able to get to his feet on the next try. Where were his coat and his tricorn? He found the hat, half-crushed where he must've landed on it when he slid to the floor, but his blurred vision couldn't find the coat in the gloom of the low firelight. He put the tricorn on as best he could, staggered out of the room to the porch and under the canopy of stars pulled himself up onto Dolly. The horse must've feared for her life with such a rider, for she rumbled and tried to sidle away from him, but he got situated and firmly took hold of the reins.

Magnus set off at a fast clip, Matthew following at a slower pace. He had to trust that Dolly would not break a leg between here and the Green Sea. The bell was still ringing, but there was no glow of a fire in the sky. The night was warm and humid, the forest alive with the whirrs and chitters and crick-cracks of a legion of insects. Now that he was directed somewhere, Matthew's head was clearing a little bit. The pounding had become an erratic drumbeat. He picked up Dolly's pace to stay closer behind Magnus. It occurred to him that Magnus' haste to get to the aid of the Green Sea Plantation might have more to do with Sarah Kincannon, and that turning his eyes away from the Lady Prisskitt had focused them on Miss Sarah. Whatever, Magnus was a man on a mission.

The bearded mountain and the young problem-solver wearing a half-crushed and lopsided tricorn turned their horses onto the road that entered the Green Sea. The dust of other hoofbeats hung in the air. The bell had been silenced, yet a feeling of chaos—or danger—lingered. Soon Matthew caught sight of many lights through the willows, and then rounding a bend he and Magnus came upon the plantation house and what appeared to be a mob of thirty or more men brandishing torches and lanterns. It appeared that some of the men had arrived on horses, in wagons and some on foot. Rising from the trampled grass like small flickering candles were dozens of fireflies, lured by the illuminations.

The plantation house was two-storied, fashioned of red bricks with four white columns standing out in front. Lights showed in most of the windows. The mob was milling about the house as if waiting for someone to emerge.

Magnus reined his horse in and swung himself off, and Matthew did the same though much less gracefully, for upon hitting the ground his knees crumpled and he nearly fell flat. He was composed enough to hear the response when Magnus clapped his hand on a man's shoulder and asked, "What's the commotion?"

"Sarah Kincannon," the man answered, as he held his torch aloft and sparks swirled above them. "She's been murdered."

Seven

BEFORE either Matthew or Magnus could utter another word, the plantation house's front door opened and out came the stocky overseer Griffin Royce, who lifted a lantern and shouted to the uneasy crowd, "Silence and bend an ear! I'm speakin' on behalf of Mr. Kincannon, who right now is in no shape to speak for himself!" He gazed across the mob until he got the silence he demanded. "As you may already know," he went on, "there's been a terrible tragedy! Miss Sarah has been murdered tonight, stabbed to death by the young buck slave called Abram! About forty minutes ago Abram, his father Mars, and Abram's brother Tobey stole a boat. They were last seen by Joel Gunn headed upriver. I'm offerin' ten pounds to the men who bring Abram, Mars and Tobey back… dead or alive. If the father and brother want to protect a killer, they'll have to pay too. I'll be joinin' the hunt soon as I can. I don't know how far up the Solstice they've gotten or where they're plannin' on pullin' out and headin' cross-country, but I—and Mr. and Mrs. Kincannon—want those black skins to pay for this crime, with their lives if they won't give up easy. Any questions?"

"Griff?" a husky brown-bearded man called. "That ten pounds for each skin, or ten pounds in all?"

"Make it ten pounds for each," Royce replied. "Ten pounds for a set of ears, a scalp, a dead body or a breathin' one in any condition."

"They got weapons?" someone else across the crowd asked.

"Don't know," said Royce. "Could have knives, maybe."

"Knives can't stop musket balls!" another voice nearer Matthew and Magnus called. "Shoot 'em where they stand with my Betsy!" That brought a rumble of nervous and eager laughter, and Matthew thought many in this mob would delight at a slave-hunt, particularly for ten pounds apiece. He had the feeling that most of the men were itching to go, thinking it would be quick and easy work.

"Griff!" called a sallow red-haired man who stood just a few feet away from Magnus. He had a hooked nose and a forehead marked with a deep scar over the left eye. "You say they went upriver? Joel Gunn seen 'em?" He waited for Royce to nod. "Then to the Devil with 'em!" he said, with a spit to the ground. "Let 'em rot up there! I heard the stories and I'm bettin' most of us have. I don't know if I'm needin' to go up that river and leave my wife and boys, no matter how much money Kincannon's offerin'!"

A small storm of hollers and catcalls passed over the mob, though most of the men remained sullenly silent. "Yellabelly, Jeb?" a caustic voice asked. "Or yella-striped?"

"Ain't yella," Jeb answered sourly, and from a sheath at his side he pulled a wicked-looking sword that Matthew thought could pierce three Magnus Muldoons. He held the sword out so the lamplight and torches reflected off its gleaming surface. "Got this to fight with and I damn sure know how to use it, McGraw! But I'm sayin'...swords and muskets might not be enough to fight what's up that Godforsaken river! Why not just let the skins *go*? They ain't gettin' nowhere, and they'll likely be dead by first light, up in that devil's country!"

"I'm for earnin' me thirty pounds!" shouted another citizen of Jubilee, a broad-shouldered man with a wild brown beard and a sweat-damp red kerchief tied around a bald scalp. He lifted his own weapon, a flintlock pistol with a small bayonet fixed beneath the barrel. "Zachary DeVey ain't afraid! Put me a ball through any spirit, ha'int or demon up that river, and I'll laugh when I do it!"

A chorus of assent followed this boast, with more pistols and swords lifted high. Matthew, still feeling a little queasy and blurry-eyed, thought there were enough weapons in this yard to start a small war, and possibly the mob had come here anticipating the possibility of trouble with the slaves...or indeed an uprising of the 'skins,' as the locals put it.

"Listen to *me*!" Royce bellowed. "Those stories some of you are feared of are just that...stories made up by slaves, Indians and damn fools!" He pointed toward the north. "You know why Miss Sarah's killer and those other two are headin' upriver instead of down? Because they're thinkin' those tales are gonna keep us rooted right here, feared to go up there and bring 'em back! Now...I've told you I'm joinin' the hunt, not because I'm wantin' the money but because I'm wantin' to see justice done! I've told you what Mr. Kincannon wants...and he wants it quick as possible. So any man who wants to serve Mr. Kincannon and avenge that poor girl's murder by the hands of a black buck, get your musket or your sword and whatever else you need, get your boat and start movin'. That's all I have to say. Either help or go home and to bed with you, but I'm expectin' ten or twenty *men* of you out there to remember that Mr. Kincannon *built* Jubilee, and you all owe him more than bein' afraid of ghost stories and a damn *river*!" He waited for a reaction to this, but there was none. "You decide!" he told them as a final statement, and then he turned away and went back into the house.

The assembly began to drift apart, breaking up into smaller groups to mutter among themselves. Pipes flared to aid the contemplation. A few of the men were obviously ready to go; without further hesitation they mounted their horses and wagons and rode off toward Jubilee and their fishing boats and canoes.

Magnus' voice was tight when he said to Matthew, "Come on," and started toward the house. He walked up the front steps to the porch, with Matthew following right behind, and pounded on the door with a heavy fist.

The door was opened by a young black girl in the dress and mobcap of a house servant. "Tell Mr. Kincannon Magnus Muldoon wants to see him," was the command, but the black girl shook her head. "Cain't see nobody," she answered. "He's stricken."

"Stricken? How?"

"He fell down when he seen Miss Sarah dead. Had to be carried up to his bedroom. Mizz Kincannon's up there with him now, but he can hardly talk."

"I want to know how this happened," Magnus insisted, putting a booted foot inside the door. "If I can't see Kincannon, I'll see—"

"You don't give orders around here," said Griff Royce, abruptly pushing the servant girl aside and staring up with glinting green eyes at the black-bearded mountain. "If you want to join the hunt, go ahead, but you have no business in this house." The eyes flickered toward Matthew. "*You?* Corbett? What are *you* doin' here?"

"It seems I…had a little too much to drink, and—"

"What's he babblin' about?" Royce asked Muldoon. "The both of you, go on!" He closed the door, forcing Magnus to step back, and a bolt was decisively thrown.

"Friendly sort," said Matthew, who had noted that the compress on Royce's right forearm had been removed in favor of a wrapping of regular bandages. "Not too good with horses either, I understand."

"I have to find out more about this," Magnus replied, his face stern and dark. "Sarah was a fine girl." He shook his head. "Can't believe it! Murdered by a slave? *Why?*" He watched the rest of the men getting astride their horses or climbing up into their wagons and heading out with a clatter of reins, wheels, swords and muskets. "There'll be a dozen boats on that river in a little while." He gave a quiet grunt. "Ain't nobody bringin' anybody back *alive*, that's for sure. Be three sets of black ears swingin' from somebody's sword, maybe three scalps too, but no skin's comin' back alive this night."

Matthew thought of Sarah Kincannon sitting on the boulder with her nose in the book of Herrick poetry, and her wave and bright smile and how much she reminded him of Berry. If Berry had been suddenly murdered, what would his first reaction be? Grief, of course. Bitter grief. And then…?

And then, he thought, his nature would take control, and he would wish to see the body and note the cause of death with his own two eyes.

"Where might Sarah's body be?" he asked.

"Maybe in the house or back in the dairyhouse. There's a chapel just beyond the house over that way. That's where the bell's rung from. Could be there."

"Let's find out," said Matthew, who descended the steps and began striding in the indicated direction, aware that Magnus had followed him and sounded like a horse stomping the grass at his heels.

The chapel was a small building made of red bricks, just as the plantation house. There was a steeple with a belltower, and lantern light showed through the windows. Matthew pulled the door open and entered, finding a half-dozen pews inside and a lectern at the front where perhaps Kincannon himself read the Scripture against the background of a tapestry of Jesus on the Cross. In the lamplight and the flickering of two candles on either side of her head was the body of Sarah Kincannon, lying on a table next to the lectern. Her corpse had been covered by white linens up to her chin, her arms beneath the covering, no inch of flesh showing except the face. She appeared to be peacefully sleeping as Matthew approached, but dark red bloodstains had surfaced on the linens at the hollow of the girl's throat. Her blond hair had been pinned up and gracefully arranged around her head. Matthew saw how pale she was from loss of blood, and how her eyelids were just barely open, the whites of her eyes showing, to defeat the image of a peaceful sleeper. He removed his half-crushed tricorn, in respect for the departed.

"*Sarah*," Magnus whispered.

He rushed past Matthew like a hurricane to stand beside the table and gaze down forlornly at the corpse. He stood motionlessly except for a pulse beating at his temple, his eyes shocked and watery. "Oh my God," he said, again in barely a whisper. "Why? *Why?*"

He reached out a hand to place his rough fingers gently against the dead girl's cheek. "*Don't touch her*," rasped a wizened voice from the furthest corner of the chapel.

Matthew and Magnus turned toward that corner. A small, slender figure was sitting in the pew there.

"I'm watchin' o're her," said the old woman, who was so black she was nearly made invisible in the gloom. "While I'm watchin', no one touches Miss Sarah."

She was wearing a gray dress with a stiff white collar. She had a dark brown scarf wrapped around her head and knotted at the front. Her face was a mass of wrinkles, her eyes deep-set and glinting in the age-weathered visage. Her white hair appeared to be almost gone but for a few fine wisps. Even so, her chin looked as sharp as a carving knife, and one might cut his fingers on the blades of her cheekbones. She stared impassively at the two men, her expression resolute no matter the difference in the color of their skins; she had been left in charge here, and in charge she was.

Matthew knew who she must be. "You're Granny Pegg?"

"Called that, yes'suh," she answered.

"I've heard of you," Magnus told her. "I'm Magnus Muldoon. Was a friend of Miss Sarah's."

"Ohhhhh." She nodded. "The bottle-man."

"And I met Sarah just today," Matthew said. "I was riding past, and—"

"The *reader*," said Granny Pegg. "Supposed to come by for a visit. She tol' me. Well…here you are."

"What happened?" Magnus asked. "I mean…*how* did it happen?"

"Knife goes in the hollow of the throat. Knife goes in the back six times…a person's gonna bleed to death." The ancient eyes moved from Magnus and Matthew to fix upon the body. "Miss Sarah was a slip of a girl. Must not have took her long to pass."

"A slave did this? Named Abram?" Magnus persisted. "*Why?*"

The old woman sighed. It sounded like the wind of doom moving through the headstones of a cemetery, and Matthew thought that behind it was just as much of a hidden world.

"I take it that's some kind of response?" Matthew asked.

Granny Pegg didn't speak for awhile. She looked down at her hands, knotted like pieces of dry bark in her lap. "Things happen here," she said at last, in a quiet and solemn voice. "Things go on. Like on any plantation, up any river. Not to speak of is the best thing." She lifted her gaze to Matthew's. "The *best* thing," she repeated.

Matthew turned his attention to the face of the dead girl. He had seen violence and withstood it; he had seen terrible things in his young life, but to think that this girl had been among the living today and then her flame snuffed out so suddenly…and so violently and bloodily. He could smell the blood and feel the pain of the untimely grave in this place. If the squirrels and hard liquor had not made his stomach churn, this surely did. "Do you know why Abram did it?" he had to ask.

Silence from the elderly slave.

"Surely you must," Matthew prodded, now staring directly at her. "I would think you know *everything* here. Nothing would get past you, would it?"

"Hm," she replied, her eyes half-lidded like those of a lizard lying in the hot sun. "Silver on your tongue don't make me cough up lead."

"Well, lead is going to be delivered to three men tonight. They ought to be brought back for a trial, but—"

Granny Pegg suddenly blinked and looked at Matthew as if seeing him anew and afresh. "Oh!" she said. "Oh, yes! Now I recall what Miss Sarah said about you. Said you seemed *official*. Said you were..." She paused, drawing it up from her well. "The *law*," she remembered.

Matthew recalled it, saying *perhaps I do represent the law*. It occurred to him that maybe he did, and just as much as what he had done to champion Rachel Howarth he should now do to see that the killer of Sarah Kincannon was properly brought to justice. But this wasn't his country anymore, he knew nothing of this plantation and the people on it, and anyway the slaves would be killed out there on the river or in the swamp once the mob caught up with them. So he ought to be quit with this, head home and mind his own business.

Granny Pegg stood up. She was barely as tall as Matthew's shoulders, and as slim as a shadow. "You're the law?" she asked him. "Got that power to you?"

"What power do you mean?"

"The power to do the right thing, and see it through."

"All men have that power."

"But all men don't use it," she said. "Do you?"

"All I want to know is," Magnus said, with an air of desperation, "*how* did this happen? Why would a slave kill Miss Sarah?"

"Why would *anybody* kill Miss Sarah?" Granny Pegg came forward from her pew to stand before them. "Not meanin' no disrespect to either of you fine gen'lmen...but things you hear said...ain't always how things are."

"I'm listening," said Matthew.

"But I cain't tell, suh, 'cause what I might say would be agin' the law...and you bein' the law...well suh, I cain't speak it."

Matthew was confounded by this, but he realized what Granny Pegg was telling him. Something had happened here in accordance with Sarah Kincannon's murder that was also a violation of the law, and therefore the elderly woman believed herself to be walking on dangerous ground by going any further. Still...she had something important to convey, and he had to find a way to allow it.

"Do you know why Abram murdered Sarah?" he asked.

"Don't know that Abram *did* murder Miss Sarah," was the reply. "Know Cap'n Gunn say he saw Abram standin' over Miss Sarah holdin' a knife, out back of the barn, and her lyin' still on the ground."

"Who is this Captain Gunn?" Matthew asked.

"Joel Gunn, the second overseer," Magnus supplied.

"Two overseers here? Joel Gunn and Griffin Royce?"

Granny Pegg nodded. "Peas in a pod," she said.

"This happened when? A little more than an hour ago, I'm guessing?"

"Happened after dark, yes'suh. Happened after the time we's forbid to leave our houses, down in the quarter. Ain't supposed to be no slaves nowhere near that barn or so close to the big house after that time."

"Yet Abram *was* there? Why?"

Granny Pegg simply stared impassively at him, and Matthew thought she knew why but could not tell.

At last she seemed to reconsider her silence, and she drew a long breath before she spoke. "Mars is my grandson. Abram and Tobey my *great*-grandsons. My son and daughter...long sold off, to another plantation in Virginia. They's old now...like their momma. Well, I wish I could die but I just keep on livin'. They tease me...say when I die they gonna roll me up like a piece of parchment, I'll be so thin. But I keep on livin'." She offered the faintest and most tormented of smiles. Her eyes gleamed in the candlelight. "If I can ask...what is your name?"

"Matthew Corbett."

"Oh yes, I remember Miss Sarah sayin' so. Matt'ew," she pronounced it. She came forward two steps more, now only a few feet away from him and Magnus. "If I told you that Abram did *not* kill Miss Sarah, would you believe me?"

"I don't know," Matthew said truthfully.

"Fair enough, suh," she answered, with a lifting of her sharp little chin. "If I told you them men the bell called are gonna go out there and hunt and kill three innocent slaves...and let the real killer hide behind more killin'...what would you say back to me?"

"I'd say...I need proof of that."

"Ain't no proof to be got. That's the trick of it. That's what he's hidin' behind."

"Who?" Magnus was confused and far beyond his depth. "The slave?"

"The killer," said Granny Pegg, still staring into Matthew's eyes. "Not my Abram."

Matthew asked, "And then, in your opinion, who *did* kill Sarah?"

"Somebody jealous as fury. Somebody wantin' her all for hisself, when she wanted nothin' to do with him. Somebody who misstook what Miss Sarah and Abram were doin', there in that barn, over many nights."

"You have an opinion as to who this *somebody* might be?"

"Cain't prove it. That's the trick."

Before Matthew could respond to this, the chapel's door opened and a man and woman entered. The woman came in first, was obviously startled by the presence of others than Granny Pegg in the room, and she drew herself up short. "Mr. Muldoon?" she said, and then with a wary look at Matthew through swollen and red-rimmed eyes, "And who are *you*, sir?"

Matthew introduced himself. The woman would have been very lovely if not for the suffering in her face. She was perhaps in her mid-thirties and had the same dimpled cheeks and light blond hair as her daughter, for this was surely Madam Kincannon. Her eyes had been tortured by tears and were as black as a tropical storm. She wore a dark blue gown with a ruffle of white lace at the throat, and she was trying very hard to comport herself with dignity and stand tall in this blood-scented chamber, yet her shoulders kept wanting to bend forward under the heavy weight of tragedy.

"I met your daughter today," Matthew explained. "I was passing by on my way to see Mr. Muldoon. I also met your husband, in Jubilee. May I ask what his condition is?"

"He is abed," the woman answered. "He lies still with his eyes open and is unable to speak. A rider has gone to fetch Dr. Stevenson. May I ask what you're doing in this chapel? This is private property."

"My apologies, but I wished to see the body."

"*Private property*," Madam Kincannon repeated. "Pegg, why did you let them in here? I told you…no one was to enter. I had my doubts about asking you to watch over her…since it was your blood who did this. But I thought you could be trusted as a good friend to Sarah!"

"I'se sorry, ma'am," the slave answered with her head lowered. "I think they was just leavin'."

"Get out, the both of you!" growled the man, who was maybe forty or so, was thick-waisted and corpulent and sported the red flush of anger in his heavy jowls. He had curly blond hair receding from a broad forehead and a small blond beard designed to hide the roll of fleshy dough beneath his chin. His eyes were dark blue and dangerous below wild blond brows that aimed sprouts of hair in every direction, and he carried at his side an equally dangerous-looking musket. He wore a plain white shirt, tan trousers, white stockings and brown boots.

"This is Joel Gunn," said Magnus casually, as if Matthew hadn't already guessed.

"*Get out!*" Gunn repeated, harsher still. He took a step forward and made a motion as if to raise the musket to a firing position. "*This minute!*"

"Surely," Matthew said to Madam Kincannon, "you wouldn't have Mr. Gunn defile this chapel and your time of sorrow with another killing, would you?" He kept his voice calm and his expression tranquil. "I did enjoy meeting your daughter today. She seemed a delightful young woman. It is a terrible shock to see her lying like this. But do you mind if I ask a few questions…if just to salve my own curiosity?"

"What are these questions?" Now some red was creeping into the woman's cheeks. "How *dare* you come in here and invade our time of mourning!"

"I will tell you that I am from New York, that I am an associate of a company called the Herrald Agency, based in London, and I am a…" Matthew paused for a few seconds, and then he went on. "I have experience in investigating crimes, madam. Including the crime of murder. I am possibly the closest representative of the law that you're going to find tonight. If you'll allow me, I'll offer my help to you in whatever way I can."

"We need no help!" Gunn said, with another step forward. "And you ain't the law! Are you a constable, or ain't you?"

"Not a constable, sir, but—"

"Then you ain't the law! Mrs. Kincannon wants you out of here! Now *move*!" This time the musket did come up, aimed between Matthew and Magnus.

Matthew did not move. His heart was pounding, but he levelled a cool gaze at Joel Gunn and stood his ground. "Sir," he said, "did Abram have the knife in his right hand or his left?"

"*What?*"

"I understand you saw the slave standing over Sarah's body, holding the knife. Was it in his left hand or his right?"

"His right hand! He's right-handed, I know that for sure!"

"And—pardon me for asking this, madam, but…how was Sarah lying on the ground? On her back or on her stomach?"

"Her stomach. She'd tried to run away from him and he'd stabbed her in the back a half-dozen times. But maybe she was on her side, I don't know. When I ran to get Griff and we came back, she was lyin' on her stomach."

"*Please*," said Madam Kincannon, who held up a trembling hand and had to lower herself onto a pew.

Matthew doggedly went on, though he knew the pain Sarah's mother was feeling; he was going by instinct and by what Granny Pegg had said. "So…you had a lantern with you? You could positively tell this was Abram standing over Miss Sarah?"

"I had a lantern. I shone it right at him when I came around the side of the barn, he wasn't standin' ten feet away. Took him by surprise. He looked at me, flung the knife aside and took off runnin' down to the quarter. I hollered at him and tried to give chase, but he's a fast one. Then I knelt down beside Miss Sarah, but she was…I'm sorry for stirrin' this up, Mrs. Kincannon…she was already dead, or near enough she couldn't speak, and…the blood was everywhere. I figured I needed to tell somebody quick, so I ran to Griff's house." The man glowered at Matthew. "What's the use of these questions? Abram stabbed Miss Sarah to death, and that's what happened." He glanced with disdain at Granny Pegg. "We're goin' up that river to get 'em, father and brother too. If they won't come back easy, it'll be all the worse for 'em."

Matthew wasn't done, and he didn't intend for Joel Gunn to push him aside. "How was Abram holding the knife, sir? By the blade? By the handle?"

"By the handle, of course!"

"So you assume he'd just finished his work a few seconds before you arrived?"

"Sir! *Please!*" The lady had pressed a hand against her forehead and squeezed her eyes shut. "Dear Lord...please spare us these questions!"

"I saw what I saw," said Gunn, with defiance in his fleshy face. "Abram killed Miss Sarah. He was standin' there with the bloody knife in his hand. Then he ran, and now he's out on the river with his kin tryin' to escape judgment. What more is there to know?"

"Well," said Matthew, turning his attention to the woman, "what was your daughter doing out there, after dark? Did she leave the house alone? Was she meeting someone? And what would've been the *reason* Abram killed your daughter? Do you have any idea?"

Suddenly Joel Gunn was in his face, and Gunn had sweat on his cheeks and showed the brown stubs of his teeth when he seethed, "They're *animals*, mister! If you don't have slaves, you don't know, but they've got to be watched during the day and kept away from the big house at night! They're the beasts of the field, and every man of them could be a killer if it lit his fancy! The women too! You can't turn your back on any of 'em, or you'll get what Miss Sarah got!"

"Settle down," Magnus advised, towering over Joel Gunn and Matthew as well. "And watch where you're aimin' that shooter!"

"Leave this place at *once*!" Mrs. Kincannon had regained her strength, if not her composure, and stood up. Even so, she wavered on her feet. "Get out before I shoot you myself!"

"As you wish," Matthew answered calmly. "But as I've said, I have experience in situations like this." He glanced quickly at Granny Pegg and then back to Mrs. Kincannon. "I have one request, and it's very important." He paused for a few seconds, to let that sink in if it would. "I know this is a difficult and terrible time. I know I've come in here—blundered in here, might be more accurate—in what seems to you to be the end of the world. I do have some…skills in this area—"

"What do we need *you* for?" Gunn growled. "Abram did it, pure and simple! When Griff ran up to the big house to tell 'em, I went down to the quarters and found out Abram and the others were gone. Then I got to the wharf and saw they'd broken into the boathouse! I seen 'em in their boat paddlin' up the Solstice! They had a torch lit, I could see 'em all! So you just step aside—and you too, Muldoon—and let justice be done!"

There was a moment of silence, in which Matthew thought he had lost the cause.

But then the quiet but determined voice said, "Thass why we does need this man, Cap'n Gunn. So justice *will* be done."

Gunn looked as if he'd been struck across the face. So too did Mrs. Kincannon. Matthew figured it was unheard-of for a slave—even a woman as elderly as Granny Pegg—to contradict a white man, and especially an overseer. He realized she had decided that it was time to speak up, if ever she was going to, no matter what the consequences might be.

"Say my great-grandson stabbed Miss Sarah to death?" she went on, both commanding the floor and tempting fate. "Say you saw him with a knife in his hand? But you didn't see him *use* that knife, did you? Couldn't he have just found it, and picked it up? And for the why of Abram bein' there, and Miss Sarah too…I'll tell you that it was agin' the law, as set down by Massa Kincannon." Granny Pegg stared fixedly at Matthew. "For some time…a month or more…Miss Sarah and my great-grandson been meetin' in that barn at night, after the forbidden hour. He say she always kind to him, and he say she always brought two things with her: a lantern and a book. She was teachin' Abram how to *read*. So why under the eyes of God would he kill her?"

"Because he's an animal like all the rest of 'em!" Joel Gunn sounded nearly choked with rage. "Because he wanted Miss Sarah for himself and couldn't have her! Who knows why? I just know she's dead and he killed her! And teachin' a slave to *read*? That's a damned lie!" He trembled, and for a moment Matthew thought the musket was going to come up to finish Granny Pegg's last day on earth. "Mrs. Kincannon's told you to get out! Now *get*!"

The lady of the plantation had been staring at the floor, supporting herself with both hands gripping the back of the pew before her. She spoke, in a ragged voice. "It's not a lie. Sarah *was* teaching Abram to read. She told me, two weeks ago. I said I didn't approve of it…that if her father found out, he would punish the entire quarter. Donovant does not like the whip, but he would've had a man from every house lashed for that crime. And punished Sarah too, in some way. At first I forbade it…but Sarah was going to do it anyway. I know her." She looked, anguished and red-eyed, at her daughter's corpse. "Sarah had talked to Abram before. Said she thought he was very smart, and could learn to read. She so loved her books…she wanted to share them. I didn't wish anyone to be lashed or Sarah to be punished…so I helped her sneak in and out of the house after dark without breaking her neck climbing out an upstairs window. I gave her one hour, from leaving to return. I told her to be very careful that she wasn't seen by anyone. That would cause problems. Tonight…when she didn't come back…I knew….I *knew* something terrible had happened." Dazedly, she shook her head from side to side. "I'm to blame for this. And for what's happened to Donovant too. Yes. I'm to blame." A sob came up from her throat, and she clenched a hand around her mouth as if to catch it before it was born ugly upon the world. "But *why*?" she gasped. "Why would he have killed her?"

"He didn't do it, Mizz Kincannon," said Granny Pegg resolutely. "No'm. Not Abram. He was too happy in her glow. She gave him somethin' to look forward to, ma'am. It was somebody else killed her, likely saw her one night and tracked her. Left that knife for him to find, and then—"

"I'm not listenin' to this!" Gunn exploded. "Listenin' to a damn slave? An old woman who hardly knows what's real? No! God help me, I'm goin' outside to get some air…hardly believe what I'm hearin'!" He turned away from Matthew and Magnus, stalked up the center aisle and then out the chapel door, which he closed behind him.

Mrs. Kincannon sat down again. She stared blankly ahead. "You gentlemen need to leave," she said listlessly. "Please. There's nothing more you can do."

"You haven't heard my request," Matthew reminded her, and he waited until she could focus on him. "I'd like your permission to look at the wounds on Sarah's body." He held up a hand to still her protest if it came, but it did not. "It will only take a few minutes. Wounds can tell a very interesting story...and sometimes much can be learned from them." He lowered his hand. "May I?"

There was a long moment in which Mrs. Kincannon simply sat staring at the tapestry of Jesus on the Cross. Tears were slowly trickling down her cheeks, dripping from her chin, and at last she whispered, "*Yes.*"

Eight

THE dead young woman was still wearing her yellow dress of the afternoon, now stained with dark red blood across the front from the vicious wound in the hollow of her throat. Matthew had lifted the fouled linens carefully and gingerly, braced for what he might find beneath. A brief look at the throat wound told him Sarah couldn't have called out if she'd tried; likely she'd been strangling on blood at the very first thrust of the blade.

Mrs. Kincannon shuddered and looked away. She drew a hard-earned breath and kept her head lowered.

"Has the knife been recovered?" Matthew asked.

The woman found a shred of a voice. "It's in the house. An ordinary knife, nothing more."

"Who brought it to you?"

"Griffin Royce."

Matthew nodded. He reasoned from the wound that the knife had about a six-inch-long blade. Ordinary enough, but he'd still like to examine it if he could push Mrs. Kincannon that far. He noted the thick red dampness of the linens beneath Sarah's body. He didn't wish to take it upon himself or Magnus to turn the corpse; that would certainly be going too far. "Are the stab wounds on the upper or lower back?" he asked.

"The upper," she said, with difficulty.

"Six wounds there?"

"I don't know. Yes...six...I think so."

The blade had pierced the lungs several times, Matthew thought. At least Sarah had not lingered very long. With all this blood loss, she had passed quickly. "I'd like to question Griffin Royce, if that would be possible."

"He was heading to the wharf the last I saw him."

"I'd be curious to know more particulars from Joel Gunn, as well." Matthew leaned over to examine the throat wound more carefully. Just one brutal stab here, face-to-face with her killer, and then she'd likely turned to run and taken the others in the back. It gnawed at his guts that Sarah had been so alive and bright this afternoon, and already the process of decay would have begun. He saw that her arms were crossed over her body, as she would be resting in her coffin.

"Who arranged her this way?" Matthew asked. "Who pinned her hair up and positioned her arms?"

"I did," said Mrs. Kincannon, and Matthew thought it was probably the most difficult task the woman had ever performed. "Royce and Gunn brought her in here. I asked Pegg to watch over her, while I went to see about my husband."

Matthew remembered the girl's hands clutching her book of poetry. He looked at her fingers, recalling how she'd offered him the purple bottle of fennel seed oil.

Wait, he thought. He leaned closer. And a little closer still.

Wait. What is that, right there*?*

There was something under the nails of the index and middle fingers of Sarah's left hand. Something...the crust of a whitish substance...like clay?

He was mindful of his manners and Mrs. Kincannon's suffering, but he had to carefully lift the left hand and use his own index fingernail to remove some of whatever it was.

"What are you *doing*?" Mrs. Kincannon asked, alarmed.

"Matthew?" Magnus also sounded quite uneasy at this display.

Matthew was able to get a small amount of the claylike substance in the palm of his hand. He smelled it and caught a faint bready odor. Meal? he wondered. Possibly mixed with clay? There were flecks of green in the mixture as well. Herbs of some kind, he thought. Perhaps of a medicinal nature?

"*Ah*," he said, as it came to him with a force like a blow to the heart.

"What is it?" Magnus asked, leaning over Matthew's shoulder to look.

"*It*," said Matthew, "is a scraping from the interior of a medical compress. At least that's what *I* think. A mixture of clay, meal and herbs." He gently lowered the dead girl's hand and also the linens. He asked Mrs. Kincannon, "You say you last saw Griffin Royce heading to the wharf?"

"Yes, just awhile ago. What's this about a medical compress?"

"Royce was bitten by a horse, yes? And Dr. Stevenson applied a medical compress to treat the infection? When I saw Royce this afternoon, he had the compress on his right forearm. Tonight when I saw him, the compress was gone and replaced by simple bandages. I believe we should find Royce, and ask why under the nails of Sarah's left hand is material from inside of that compress, which might have happened when her fingers tore through the cheesecloth."

"What're you saying? Why would *that* be under Sarah's fingernails?"

"It would be there," said Matthew calmly, "if she'd tried to grasp Royce's right forearm for some reason, and broken through the compress. And that reason might be...that she was trying to stop the thrust of a knife." He let that sink into the silence. "I'd like to examine Royce's forearm for scratches, as well." He turned toward Granny Pegg. "The story as you know it, please. Now is not the time to hold anything back."

Granny Pegg did not reply for a time, and Matthew thought that being a slave for likely a great part of her life had stolen her ability to be forthcoming with anything that might affect the others in the quarter. But then she seemed to steady herself, she closed her eyes for a few seconds as if either to pray or recall details, and then she opened her eyes again and spoke.

"Much goin' on here neither the massa nor his lady know," she began. "Massa Kincannon don't get down to the quarter or out in the fields like he should...his leg givin' him trouble. So he leave it up to them cap'ns to run things. Now we had a good or'seer with Cap'n Jameson, but he got on older and then they's hired Cap'n Royce to help him. Wasn't two month a'fore Cap'n Jameson's house caught on fire, and they sayin' he drunk in his bed and knocked over a candle into some clothes and that lit it up." She made a noise of disgust. "Wasn't how *that* been done."

The last time the Green Sea's alarm bell had been rung, Matthew recalled. *A fire broke out over there*, Magnus had said.

"Cap'n Royce got hisself to work gettin' in close with Massa Kincannon," the woman continued. "Tryin' to get in close with Miss Sarah, too."

"*What?*" Mrs. Kincannon asked sharply.

"Truth of it," vowed Granny Pegg. "From the first he was here and Miss Sarah was fourteen year old, Cap'n Royce was after that girl. After other girls too. Livy...Molly Ann...Long Jane...Macy. Molly Ann was near givin' birth to his child when all of a sudden she gone. You remember that, Mizz Kincannon? And everybody in the big house thought Molly Ann had run off, gone upriver?"

"I remember. You're saying Royce did away with her?"

"Cain't prove it. Just sayin' what I see."

"If this is true," Mrs. Kincannon went on, "then why didn't anyone tell my husband? He would've *wanted* to know!"

"Same reason Miss Sarah didn't say nothin' 'bout Cap'n Royce always doggin' her," said Granny Pegg. "She tell me...Cap'n Royce say funny how fire can get started in the quarter. How quick it can eat up a house and ever'body in it. He say, he don't mean no harm to Miss Sarah, he just funnin' with her, but if she took things wrong and told anybody how he tried to steal a kiss or grab at her when nobody was lookin'...then somebody was gonna pay for it. So she stayed as far away from him as she could, and she don't say nothin'. Now look what's been gone and done."

"*Royce* killed her?" Magnus rumbled. It was a dangerous sound.

"Didn't see it happen," was the answer. "Just know what Miss Sarah's been tellin' me. Wasn't long after Cap'n Jameson died that Cap'n Gunn came to work here. I heard it told from Vinia in the big house that Cap'n Royce wanted him here, told Massa Kincannon he was a hard worker and a good cap'n. They must'a worked together somewhere else. Like I say…Cap'n Royce and Cap'n Gunn are two peas in a pod. Whatever Cap'n Royce did, Cap'n Gunn made sure he did it too, and they's watchin' each other's backs. Likely did the same on more than one plantation. Not sayin' exactly I know what happened tonight, but I'm sayin' my Abram had no need to kill Miss Sarah. Look to the man who coveted her, and the man who say he saw a knife in Abram's hand."

"Abram shouldn't have run, then!" Mrs. Kincannon's eyes had taken on a feverish glint. "Why didn't he stay and defend himself?"

"Because Abram *was* breakin' the law, ma'am," said Granny Pegg. "He was out where he wasn't supposed to be. Might be he stumbled onto the body on his way back to the quarter, and he picked up that knife. However it happened, Abram must've figured there was not gonna be no defense between hisself and the noose."

Matthew said, "I think it's time I ask Mr. Gunn to step back in for some questions." The first would be: did a book happen to be lying on the ground along with the body? He went to the door and opened it, and found nothing but warm humid air and a cloud of gnats outside.

"Probably gone to join the hunt," Matthew reported to the others. "The faster Abram is found and disposed of, the better for Royce and Gunn."

Mrs. Kincannon shook her head back and forth, as this realization sank deeper. "My God…what would make a man want to possess a girl so much he would turn to *murder*?"

"Wantin' what you can't have," said Magnus Muldoon, in the hard voice of experience. "What you think is better than you are. What you think will make *you* better." He focused his fierce iron-gray eyes upon Matthew. "It can't be left like this. Sarah was my friend. I'm goin' out after Royce and Gunn. Get the truth out of 'em, maybe stop 'em from another killin'." He nodded, as if he had answered his own internal question. "Seems right, with what I've done in the past. Maybe spare myself a little bit of Hell's fire."

Mrs. Kincannon came forward. She stood between Magnus and Matthew and looked down into her daughter's pallid face. The tears welled up afresh. "She had so much *life*," the woman said softly.

She gently touched the girl's cheek. "Our only child. Dear God... this about Abram, Mars and Tobey...and Royce and Gunn...I can hardly believe it. I can't ask Donovant for help. What should I *do*?"

"You can fetch me a musket or a pistol, a powderhorn, some balls and fixin's," said Magnus. "A pouch of beef jerky and a torch would be appreciated. Then direct me to the wharf and a rowboat. I'll do the rest."

The woman looked into Matthew's eyes. "Will you go with him? Please...as a representative of the law? I can pay you whatever amount you like."

Matthew realized he was being asked to solve a problem, in his official capacity. It was not a task he relished, for he thought the runaways would be caught and killed before dawn, but it was a task he had been trained for and was expected to perform by both Madam Herrald and Hudson Greathouse. Also his own sense of justice demanded it. "I would ask twenty pounds," he answered. "To be divided between myself and Mr. Muldoon. Is that suitable?" He was asking Magnus, who grunted an assent. "Then," he told Mrs. Kincannon, "I would like to carry a sword, if you can honor that." He figured he needed a sharp edge, out where they were going. "And also...very importantly...don't move the body from where it is. All right?"

"All right. I'll get what both of you ask. Pegg, will you take them to the boathouse? I'll meet you there directly." She paused for only a moment longer to once more regard the face of her daughter, and then with a strengthless sigh she turned away and left the chapel.

"Come with me, gen'l'men," Granny Pegg instructed. "I'se old, but I can still walk fast. You two goin' up the River of Souls...there are things you ought to know about that country. Come on, then, and I'll tell you like I told my blood how best to keep y'selves alive."

Two

I Am Not Daniel

Nine

THE moon had risen. It was a lunatic's laugh short of being full, and it shone ghostly white upon the unquiet waters of the River of Souls.

In their boat, Matthew sat at the bow and held the torch aloft as Magnus manned the oars. They had left the wharf at the Green Sea Plantation a half-hour ago, and now followed the river's sinuous curves between the swampy wilderness on either side. They followed also what appeared to Matthew to be a floating carnival. Ahead of them were a dozen rowboats and canoes and more than a dozen other torches and lanterns lighting up the river. The boats held two, three, or four men, and some looked to Matthew's eye to be about to tip their passengers into the drink.

And strong drink there seemed to be, as well, for from this throng occasionally arose rude shouts and field hollers and bawdy songs born from the jugs that passed along. Looking back, Matthew saw a score of other torch-lit boats following. In the sodden, steamy air there was a cruelly festive mood and perhaps a mood of desperation too, for Matthew reasoned that many of the men on this hunt were hungry to get their hands on as much Kincannon money as a dead slave would buy them. The boats wandered from one side of the river to the other, the torches seeking an empty boat that Abram, Mars and Tobey would have abandoned to start cross-country, but yet no such boat or signs of a craft being dragged out could be ascertained. So the carnival wound on with the river, and under the lunatic's moon the brash singing of foolish men drifted out upon the thick green swamp. Swords caught firelight and threw it like a flurry of red sparks. A gunshot far ahead caused the merriment to go grim and silent, until the shouting passed back *Nothin' there, gents, nothin' there, ol' Foxworth is seein' hain'ts in the dark.*

"All right?" Matthew asked Muldoon, who labored steadily upon the oars and had not spoken since leaving the wharf.

Magnus gave a low grunt, which served as his *yes*. Then, to Matthew's surprise, the black-bearded mountain paused in his rowing and shouted toward the boats ahead, "Royce and Gunn! You within my voice?"

In another moment someone called back, "Not up here!" Matthew heard a distant fiddle start scratching out a lively tune, one of the occupants of the boats having brought his cat-wailer. Magnus began rowing again. They were catching up to a group of three boats that seemed to be travelling together, the twelve men in them throwing jugs back and forth, laughing at rough jokes about the 'skins' and acting in general as if this were the grandest adventure to ever lift them off their porch chairs. There was a little too much waving about of muskets and pistols for Matthew's taste. He thought the item of the Kincannons' tragedy was much forgotten already, and this was turning into a night of rum-fuelled sport.

There came a commotion ahead, some of the men hollering and pointing at the water. One of them hit at something with an oar, and another slashed downward with his sword. The water thrashed and churned, and then Matthew saw the dark mass of an alligator pass by their boat, having survived the oar and blade. It began to submerge itself and with a haughty flick of its thick tail the creature left the world of men for its own domain.

Matthew thought of a warning Granny Pegg had given them before they'd left the wharf: *If you fall into the water, get out quick.* He understood why, for now torchlight revealed the red glare of alligator eyes watching the procession of boats, and the scaly black bodies of the reptiles gliding back and forth between the vessels as if taunting the passengers. Singing quietened and jocularity ceased, in the presence of these river monsters.

Magnus rowed on, undaunted. He kept a steady pace, his eyes fixed ahead, past Matthew and the torch. He was, as Matthew had been today, a man with a purpose, and Matthew thought that part of Muldoon's quest was an effort to cleanse his soul of three killings under the sight of God.

"You want to watch the river," Granny Pegg had said, as they waited at the wharf for Mrs. Kincannon to bring what they'd asked. "It's wicked. It'll steal from you in a short minute, if you don't watch it."

"It's a river," Matthew had answered. "No more and no less."

"Oh, *no*, suh." The old woman's thin smile was nearly ghastly. "It's been cursed, as all the swamp and woods around it has been cursed, once you get up past Rotbottom."

"Rotbottom? What is *that*?" Matthew asked.

"The last town you'll find. Hardly a town, not even so big as Jubilee. They live off the swamp. Take their 'gator hides into Charles Town to sell 'em. I'se seen their boats passin' by, time to time."

"You told Dr. Stevenson about the witch's son being drowned, and the supposed curse," Matthew reminded her. "I can appreciate such tales for a midnight's telling, but there are no such things as witches and curses."

"I've heard some of this," Magnus said, as he leaned against a piling. The water lapped at the pier and frogs croaked by the dozen in the wet swampgrass. "Don't believe none of it."

"*I* didn't conjure it," Granny Pegg replied. "Heard it from an Indian woman elder than me, used to be the cook in the big house. She passed on last year. She come from Rotbottom, been married to a man up there a'fore a 'gator got him by the legs and dragged him down. She knew the tale, right well."

"It's nonsense," said Matthew, watching a pair of torchlit canoes being rowed upriver from the direction of Jubilee. He was, as he knew Magnus to be, in a hurry to get started but there was no going anywhere without weapons.

"I will tell you," the old woman said, standing before him under the sky full of stars and the slowly rising moon, "what I told my Mars, Abram and Tobey. How to stay alive up there, once you get to the cursed land. I told 'em, keep goin' past Rotbottom. Stay quiet and don't show no light. Indians up in there'll come to the river if they hear a commotion. They're dangerous, and you don't want to call their attention. I say keep goin' another few turns of the river. Find a place where you can pull the boat out and drag it into the brush. Then get movin' fast and quiet, but keep your knives ready."

"They have knives?" Magnus' eyebrows went up. "Thought that was against the law."

"Was and is. But Titus had one hid away, and so did Ash and Jacob. They give up their blades to their fellows. My boys took a leather bag full of whatever food was offered 'em, and I tell 'em to get to a boat and start rowin', 'cause ain't nobody gonna be listenin' to Abram's story when Miss Sarah is lyin' dead and Cap'n Gunn swearin' to his lies."

"Did Abram have a chance to tell you what happened?" Matthew asked.

"He did. I knew it to be a regular thing, Miss Sarah leavin' the barn first with her book and lantern. He was supposed to wait a few minutes. Then when he come out and around the barn, he said he near stepped on her. Knelt down beside her and called her name but she wasn't movin'. Didn't want to say this before Mizz Kincannon, but Abram tell me the knife was planted in her back. He pulled it out, said his heart was near to bust through his chest. Then all of a sudden he heard Cap'n Royce holler, 'Killer!', right close, and Abram looked up and saw him comin', with a lantern in his hand. Abram dropped that knife and took to runnin'. Said he could hardly think, his head was so full of the sight of Miss Sarah lyin' there all bloody and still as death."

"So Gunn wasn't even there, according to Abram?"

"Not there, as far as he knows. Couldn't say that before, in front of Cap'n Gunn."

"I'm guessing," Matthew said, "that Royce did this deed in a fit of passion, or jealousy. Then he went to alert Gunn, and get him to concoct the tale. Probably he needed to clean blood off himself too. The bloody clothes might still be in his house, it would be worth a search. I would imagine he and Gunn have between them a score of incidents they would rather not come to light."

"Find out when we catch 'em," Magnus rumbled, his flinty eyes following another boat being rowed upriver.

"Things to 'member," said Granny Pegg. "Keep your boat in the middle of the river. If you fall into the water, get out quick. Stay quiet goin' up, quiet as you can be. If you needs go cross-country, watch where you step for suckholes and quicksand. Snakes aplenty up in there, and poisonous as Satan's spit. And Old Cara told me this…if you hear a baby cryin', keep goin'. Don't try to find it…just keep goin', 'cause that's a spirit you don't want to see."

"Pah!" said Magnus. "Don't believe in *that*, neither!"

"Just mind what I say," the old woman insisted, and quite suddenly Matthew felt less of a champion for justice and more of a magistrate's clerk who found himself about to get into water over his head.

Mrs. Kincannon and the young black girl who'd answered Muldoon's knock on the door of the big house had arrived, the lady of the plantation grim-faced and beyond tears now, carrying a lighted torch and a leather bag that Matthew assumed contained food for a prolonged journey. The house servant carried a musket, a deerskin bag that likely held the tinderbox, powder and other arrangements for firing of the weapon, and a short-bladed cutlass. Magnus took the musket and both of the bags, while Matthew took charge of the torch and the cutlass. Within the boathouse, two rowboats were roped to the pier, and a pair of ropes trailed into the water where two other boats had been moored. One boat for the slaves, Matthew thought, and one boat for the hunters.

It was time to go. Matthew took his place at the bow of one of the remaining boats. Magnus untied it and climbed in, then fixed the oars in their locks. "Good luck to you," said Mrs. Kincannon, "and I pray to Heaven you are able to do the right thing."

"Watch the river, gen'l'men," Granny Pegg offered as Magnus pushed the boat away from the pier with a large, black-booted foot. "God be with you."

Matthew nodded his thanks. Magnus rowed them toward the middle of the river, and they were off upon its course. They rounded a bend where the grass waved in the water like the green hair of half-submerged nymphs. When Matthew looked back again he saw only star-strewn sky and dark river but for a few torches and lanterns gleaming in the distance.

Soon they had caught up to the floating carnival, and then the territory of reptiles. Matthew uneasily watched the passage of the creatures and saw their eyes glinting red in the rushes. One that glided by on the left side brought renewed agitation and hollering from the men just ahead, and when Matthew saw its scarred black body he thought it had to be as long as their boat. He caught sight of a hideous-looking snout and sunken eyes from a madman's nightmare, and why he in that moment thought particularly of Lord Cornbury, Governor of the colony of New York and cousin to Queen Anne herself, he did not know.

He looked back over his shoulder and said to Magnus, "I don't believe in curses. Or witches, either."

Magnus said nothing, but kept steadily rowing. They were almost upon the three boats ahead.

"I once had reason to be involved with the case of a supposed witch," Matthew went on. "It was the work of a human being... however evil, but human work."

"Hm," was Magnus' reply.

"Civilized men don't believe in such things." Matthew realized he was beginning to sound a little edgy for reassurance in this statement. "Because...they don't *exist*."

He turned away from Magnus to focus on their progress, and that was when he saw one of the men in the boat ahead and to their left miss the toss of a liquor jug from one end of the craft to the other. It splashed into the water, and another of the men shouted, "Jackson, you fool! Don't let that get away!"

The hapless Jackson, a wide-bodied man wearing a battered straw hat and trousers with patches on the knees, seemed already dazed by his drinking. He leaned over the stern and reached long for the jug, which was yet corked and floating. Jackson's fingers closed around the handle. Just that quickly, the river struck.

A massive black snout dappled with knotty gray growths rose from the water. A pair of jaws clamped their teeth upon Jackson's wrist. He gave a scream and, trying to pull free, reached to grasp the arm of the man nearest him, who a minute ago had been boisterous and heavy-voiced but now shrieked nearly in falsetto like a terrified woman. Then the alligator, a true leviathan, abruptly submerged with a twist of its body and slap of its tail. Jackson went over the stern and down under the water just a few feet away from Matthew, the straw hat spinning away. The second man pulled free but in so doing upset his own equilibrium and fell backward over the boat's starboard side. The boat rocked violently as the two men left in it struggled to keep their balance and not be thrown out.

Matthew saw more of the reptiles gliding in. The shouting of the other men in the surrounding boats had become hoarse and panicked. Someone in another craft fired a pistol shot that plumed blue smoke and did not hit an alligator but instead chopped a chunk of wood off the port side of the boat that was now missing half its passengers. The water churned and frothed. Before Matthew surfaced a distorted and agonized face that tried to gulp for air in the turbulent foam but was dragged down again with its mouth full of Solstice River.

The second man had come up and was trying desperately to climb back into the boat, making it rock even more precariously. "Help me, Briggs!" he pleaded, as he tried to haul himself over. "Help me, Briggs!"

But Briggs was evidently too busy trying to keep himself from going into the wicked drink, for no hand or help was offered, and suddenly the pleading man's voice was broken by a scream for he was being dragged down yet would not let go his grip. Alligators slid past on all sides and in between the boats like ships made of ugly iron. Magnus had ceased his rowing forward and was in fact rapidly backing them in an attempt to give distance between their craft and the boat in danger of capsizing. Perhaps Briggs was the one who did it, but Matthew witnessed one of the men there strike a blow for survival by slamming an oar across the top of his supposed friend's skull, which caused the fingers to immediately loosen and the body to be jerked down into the River of Souls as quick as one might say 'Dick Tuck.'

Though the water still thrashed with the activity of the reptiles, the second man did not rise from the depths again. The afflicted boat began to calm itself. Perhaps—or not—it was friend Briggs who gripped the oar, and who shouted into the descended silence, "I had to do it! He was already gone! I had to do it, or it would'a been the both of us too!" He looked around, his shoulders hunched as if for a whipstrike but his florid thin-nosed face crimped with anger. "You would'a done it! Every damned one of you!"

No one answered. Matthew had a reply in mind—*it seems not all the reptiles here are in the water*—but didn't know how the Jubilee men with firearms would take such a comment from a stranger. His heart pounded and his throat was dry, though here was surely not the place to cup a drink.

"I didn't kill him!" Briggs shouted to the world. "The 'gator took him, not me!"

A point to ponder, Matthew thought...but he had no time for that, for suddenly Jackson fought up from the river and grasped hold with his remaining hand upon the bow of Matthew's boat.

The contorted face was smeared dark with 'gator slime. One eyebrow twitched. The eyes were bright with near-madness. "Pull me up!" he gasped. "God's sake, pull me up!" The other arm rose up, and upon it the mangled stub of the crushed and bloody hand scrabbled to gain a grip. Matthew saw three or four alligators speeding toward the unfortunate victim. The reptiles struck one after another into the man's submerged legs. Jackson grunted with each impact, his body shook violently and yet his anguished eyes still looked to Matthew for some hope of climbing out of his fate. Matthew reached down to grasp the man's shirt. Before he could catch hold of it the free hand clamped onto his forearm and began to pull him over the side with frantic strength even as Matthew realized he was himself in danger and began to resist. Magnus threw aside the oars and reached for Matthew, but in the next instant...

...a bass-toned musket shot boomed. The top of Jackson's gray-haired head exploded from the force of the ball. Blood and brains flew into the air and spattered Matthew's shirt and face. Then Matthew pulled free, and the grimacing corpse slid back into the turbulence. The alligators hissed and snapped among each other as they sank their teeth into the flesh and rolled themselves over and over down into the murky depths.

It took Matthew a few seconds to comprehend what had just happened. He was standing in the bow holding his torch with Jackson's brains and blood upon his face. He looked dazedly around and saw a rowboat with three men aboard coming up from behind and to the left. A pair of lanterns hung from hooks at the bow. Standing up in the bow and holding a smoking musket was Sir Raven's Feather, the lean, rawboned man wearing the floppy-brimmed hat with the raven's feather in the hatband whom Matthew had seen at the general store in Jubilee.

Matthew managed to get his tongue working. His face flamed under its anointment of gory matter. "Are you *insane*? I could've helped him!"

"*No*," came the gravel-voiced reply, as hard as the heart of a stone. "Jackson was done. I saved your life, boy. Would've pulled you in with him."

"I say I could've pulled him up!"

"Say what you please, but his widow'll thank me for not sendin' him home to her in a basket." The man sat down in the boat and, placing the musket across his legs, began to reload the weapon from his alligator-skin ammunition bag. "Muldoon, you carryin' a damn fool as a torchboy?"

Magnus made no comment. He took his seat and the oars and continued to row steadily forward.

It occurred to Matthew that not only had he witnessed a murder, but he'd been directly in the line of fire. "I nearly had him!" he protested, though his voice was getting weak.

"No. He nearly had *you*."

"Sit down, Matthew," Magnus said quietly. "Let it go."

Magnus' tone of voice was final. The boat carrying Sir Raven's Feather slipped past, its rower a broad-shouldered man with a long brown beard and wearing a sweat-soaked gray shirt, his muscular arms working the oars like a machine. At the stern sat a third gent as straight-backed as a Sabbath preacher. He was also holding a musket. He wore a black tricorn hat and a black suit and he had a sharp-nosed, gaunt face as forbidding as three miles of bad road. The boat moved on past the area of troubled waters. Matthew sat down. His first instinct was to scoop up a handful of water to cleanse his face, but he noted that alligators were still gliding back and forth and so he decided to keep his hand out of the river.

"I could've pulled him up," Matthew said in another moment. The smell of blood was drawing a swarm of insects around his face. "I *could* have."

"Stamper put Jackson out of his misery and saved your hide too. So just let it go."

"Jubilee isn't a town that breeds a lot of brotherhood, I see," Matthew said bitterly.

"It's common sense," said Magnus. "Man falls in the water and gets tore up by 'gators ain't gonna be worth much no more, even if he survives it. So...the lesson is...don't fall in the water with 'gators. And don't put your hand in there like you're wantin' to, neither. You can clean up later."

Matthew had no intention of moving himself from his present position. He swung the torch from side to side, inflaming the red eyes of a score of reptiles that still waited in the shallows of the River of Souls for more unfortunate victims. When Matthew had regained his senses and wits, he asked, "Who was that...the man with the raven's feather...who?"

"The big man in Jubilee. Owns the general store. Name of Baltazar Stamper. Man rowin' is Caleb Bovie, works for Stamper. Fella in black is Jubilee's preacher, Seth Lott."

So even the town's holy man was out here after his share of blood money, Matthew thought. And it seemed to him, after witnessing Jackson's head be blown open and friend Briggs send his companion to the alligators by way of an oar across the skull, that perhaps life had become cheap on the River of Souls, and that there were some out here—possibly many—who would gladly commit a 'mercy killing' if it meant removing the competition for the fortune of thirty pounds of gold.

He had to wonder if the muskets and swords might start finding other ways to cut down the competition, if this hunt went on for any length.

Perhaps Magnus Muldoon had the same thought at the same time, for he let the boat drift and hollered upriver with the full force of his mighty lungs, "Griffin Royce and Joel Gunn! You up there?"

This time no one amid the forward rowboats and canoes answered.

"Shall I row?" Matthew offered.

"I'll get us where we're goin' faster," said Magnus, as he took a moment to stretch his arms out, twist his head from side to side and then stretch his back. He took up the oars again and powered the boat onward.

Matthew had no idea of the time. The sky was still inky black, the moon still high. Huge willow trees met overhead and their branches hung over the river. The noise of men had quietened in the aftermath of violence. The chirrups and croaks and chitters of the swamp's thousand-and-one creatures held sway. Matthew had the sense of a monstrous presence out there amid the wilderness, beyond the range of his torch. It was not one monster but many, waiting tensed in the dark to spring forth. It was the swamp itself, he thought. It was the alligators, the sinkholes, the quicksand, the snakes, and…what else?

It was Griffin Royce and Joel Gunn, somewhere far ahead, searching for the three runaways in order to silence the truth. It was men like Briggs, and Baltazar Stamper, Caleb Bovie and Seth Lott, hungry for money and ready—perhaps eager—to kill for it. It was a whole mob of desperate men from Jubilee, drunk on liquor and the thought of bringing back a pair of slave's ears for a sum that might lift them up from the impoverished dust.

Matthew realized he had one hand upholding the torch and the other hand on the grip of his cutlass. The insects swarmed around his face, darting and biting. He knew that in spite of his best intentions he had nearly lost his balance and gone into the river with Jackson. So…it *was* true that a musket ball had saved his life this night, even though a murder—two of them, in fact—had been committed in front of his eyes. He wished for the comfort of his little dairyhouse, and with it the familiar town of New York with all its traffic and horse figs and complications and…yes…even the cold winds that swept his way from Berry Grigsby.

A disturbing thought came to him, though he had no use for tales of witches and curses.

I will not leave this river the same.

Well…who would? Already the deaths had begun. But Matthew had this feeling deep in his soul, and he could not shake it.

I will not leave this river the same.

He had a feeling of intense dread that surpassed even his experiences with Professor Fell. It lasted only briefly, but it was enough to give him a chill shiver on this steamy, sullen night. He gripped the cutlass harder. Little good that might do, but it was something.

And now onward...onward...following the quietened flotilla of torch-and-lamplit vessels, following the grim blood-hungry men with pistols and muskets and blades, following the twisting course of the Solstice River into the witch-cursed country, and Matthew Corbett with damp brains and blood upon his face, and carrying deep within himself a primal fear for the sanctity and survival of his soul.

Ten

"I HAVE to clean myself," said Matthew when the smell of the dried gore on his face became stronger and the swarm of insects more maddening. Still, he resisted putting his hand over the side or even cupping water in his half-crushed tricorn, for his torchlight revealed here and there the slowly-gliding shapes of the alligators yet seeking another bite of the human breed. "Will you guide us to shore for a minute?" he asked Magnus, who after a pause to deliberate this request nodded and aimed their boat toward the northern bank. As soon as he'd asked the favor, Matthew recalled Granny Pegg saying *Keep your boat in the middle of the river.* But surely a minute's pause on the shore for him to wash his face in shallow water would not bring a curse down upon his head, he thought, and anyway it had to be done. There were lights of boats both ahead of them and behind; Matthew figured he and Magnus were probably somewhere near the center of the floating carnival, and so far there'd been no shouts of anyone finding an abandoned boat, no gunshots, and no answer when Magnus called for Griffin Royce and Joel Gunn.

The rowboat's prow slid onto mud amid a tangled thicket. The water here was only a few inches deep, and the torch showed no red-eyed reptile waiting in the high weeds. Matthew leaned over the bow...

"Careful," Magnus cautioned. And explained to Matthew's jittery start: "Don't fall in."

"Thank you," Matthew answered, as he wet his face and wiped the bloody matter off his cheeks, forehead and chin with his shirt. He made out what appeared to be the meager light of candles through the woods ahead. Light through windows? he wondered. Ah, yes...the town of Rotbottom, according to Granny Pegg the last stand of civilization on the River of Souls. The thrum of frogs was like a constant drumbeat, the noise of crickets and night-insects a rising and falling cacophony. It seemed that a hundred nasty little humming and buzzing flying things were circling his head and trying to drink the liquid from his eyeballs. He waved them away with his torch and kept scrubbing his face in an attempt to get every bit of human debris off himself. He had had time to think, between the attack of the alligators and his request to head for shore, that it was certainly not a sure thing that the trio of runaways could be found—or could be saved from being killed by any of the other men. In fact, it was a high chance that they could *not* be saved, if they were indeed found, and all of this would be for naught. Still... what would he be, if he did not try?

"Have to pick up our pace," Magnus said. "Try to get to the front of the pack. Way back here, we can't do anything."

"I know," Matthew replied.

"How we gonna stop those skins bein' murdered?" Magnus asked, as if in the past few minutes this question had suddenly dawned on him. "How are we gonna prove Royce killed Sarah? Seems like all you've got is some clay under Sarah's fingernails, and Granny Pegg's story. That won't send a man swingin'. Anyhow, Gunn'll stand up for him. Hell, they'll kill those slaves and cut their ears off before we ever *see* 'em...then what're you gonna prove?"

"That...I don't know," Matthew admitted. "The first thing we have to do—if we *can*—is to stop any murdering of Abram and the others. Royce and Gunn want to silence them, but they don't trust the river or the swamp to do it for them. So if we can find the slaves first, so much the better." And good luck with that effort, he thought. He swung the torch again at the multitude of swarming insects. "Damn these things!" he fumed. "They're everywhere!"

Magnus scratched his own cheek where a biter had landed and left a swelling. "Before he settled in Jubilee," said Magnus, "Baltazar Stamper made his livin' trackin' down runaway slaves. He and Bovie both. If anybody can find 'em, it's those two. And that preacher's half-crazy and hot on the trigger. I wouldn't turn my back on any of those three."

"It seems we have excellent company on this jaunt." Matthew had finished cleaning his face to his satisfaction, and now he waved the torch again to ward off the hungry congregation. He started to slide back into the boat.

"*Mud*," someone said.

The voice made Matthew freeze, though it was spoken so softly it might nearly have been only the sultry breeze searching through the rushes. It had been a feminine voice with a low, smoky quality. Matthew knew someone was standing there amid the underbrush, but his torchlight could not find her among the shadows of shadows.

"What?" he asked, as if proposing his question to the swamp itself.

"Mud," came the repeated reply, and then she moved forward from the wildness of vines and thorns and lifted her own punched-tin lantern. The torchlight fell upon her. "Mud keeps them away," she said. She came toward him without being invited, and she looked into his eyes as if trying to spy the essence of his soul. He felt himself being probed in every hidden place, which caused him to want to draw back and away from the young woman...but he did not. Then, also without being asked, she leaned down, scooped up a handful of dark river mud, and held it out for his approval. He smelled in it the strong odor of the swamp, a heady and earthy aroma that might have been repellent for its many layers of decay and rebirth, and yet Matthew caught within it a strangely medicinal whiff as well, as pungent as camphor. He wondered how many thousands of dead trees and riverweeds and passage of years were in that handful of mud. It was if the young woman was offering him a salve formed from the River of Souls itself.

Matthew understood, and he took some of the mud on his fingers and streaked it across his chin, cheeks, forehead and across the bridge of his nose like warpaint in his battle against the bugs.

"More than that," she urged, and he obeyed her.

"Thank you," he said, when the job was done and the insects began to whirl away from their interrupted feast.

She stood before him, staring at him with dark blue eyes that seemed luminous in the light, and sparkling like the star-strewn sky. "Pleased," she answered at last, in her quiet, smoky voice.

Of course she was a citizen of Rotbottom, Matthew thought. But she was not what he might have expected to find out here in this country, this last gasp of so-called civilization before the true wilderness began. For one thing, she was very lovely. Matthew might even have considered her beautiful, and far more so than Pandora Prisskitt for she was natural and unadorned in her loveliness. She was perhaps seventeen or eighteen, small-boned and slim, wearing a dress sewn from some kind of coarse gray cloth but adorned at the neck with a ruffle of indigo-dyed lace. Her hair was black and lustrous, not pinned up or prepared in any way popular in Charles Town, but allowed to fall casually about her shoulders in thick waves and in bangs on her forehead. She had beestung lips and a thin-bridged nose that turned up slightly at the tip, like the slightest disdain for her own state of ragamuffinry. She had a firm jaw and high cheekbones and in no way appeared weak or impoverishered in spirit; in fact, she faced the two journeyers with what Matthew thought was a stately air of what might have been great confidence, as if to say this was her world and these two men were strangers upon it.

"My name is Quinn Tate," the young woman said. "What is yours?"

"Matthew Corbett. This is—"

"Magnus Muldoon," came the rumble. "Think I can't speak for myself?"

"Matthew Corbett," she repeated, still staring intensely at him. "I've seen the boats goin' upriver. What's happenin'?"

"A hunt for three runaway slaves from the Green Sea Plantation. But...it's more than that."

"I heard gunshots. Others were out here, callin' to the boats, but the men wouldn't answer."

"They're in a hurry. We only stopped because...well..."

"You wanted to wash your face," said Quinn, with a faint smile that seemed to say she knew more than she was telling.

"We need to be on our way, miss," Magnus told her. "Thanks for helpin' my friend." He pushed the oars into the mud in preparation to back the boat off.

Quinn Tate let the boat start drifting backward before she spoke again. "You need more help, I'm thinkin'."

"We'll manage," said Magnus.

"No," she answered, "you won't. Neither will most of those men ahead of you. Those goin' first...without knowin' what they're goin' into...they likely won't come back."

"Uh-huh," said Magnus, pushing them out toward the middle of the river.

"Just a minute." Matthew wished Magnus to slow their retreat, because of something in the girl's voice...some note of surety, or knowledge, or warning. "What exactly are they going into? The ones up ahead," he clarified.

"First thing they're gonna run up on soon," said Quinn, standing in the mud with her lantern upraised, "is the village of the Dead in Life." She was speaking quietly, but her voice carried through the sultry air and across the water.

Magnus ceased his rowing. "*What?*"

"The Indians call it somethin' different. A name I can't get my tongue around. It's like...their little piece of Hell on earth. Not far up the river, maybe a mile or more."

"All right, it's an Indian village," said Magnus, though he rowed in closer to Quinn by a few strokes. "What makes it so different from any other?"

"The warriors only come out at night," she replied, matter-of-factly. "To hunt. They don't care what they catch. They have a game they play. This is what I hear, from some who've seen and gotten away. I wouldn't want to be caught by any of 'em, because that village is where all the tribes for miles around put their bad men and women and their... what would you call 'em?...ones who aren't right in the head."

"It's a village of exiles?" Matthew asked. Or an Indian insane asylum? he wondered.

"Whatever it is, it's up there, and those torches are gonna draw 'em to the river like flies to..." She shrugged. "Dead meat."

Magnus sat with the oars across his knees. He rubbed a hand across his mouth, and Matthew saw him beginning to wonder if

Abram, Mars and Tobey were worth going any further upriver, especially since—if the girl was right—they might have been already taken by the Indians. But the moment and the hesitation passed, and Magnus took up the oars and squared his shoulders again.

"We'll go on," he announced. A few more boats were coming up the river behind them, still distant yet close enough to be heard the drunken shouting and laughter of their passengers, who obviously had not seen any body parts floating in the water and were too inflamed by liquor to be rightly frightened of the alligators.

"Are *you* the one?" Quinn suddenly asked. She was speaking to Matthew.

"Pardon?" he asked, not understanding. The moon floated between them, cut into pieces by ripples.

"Are you the one?" she repeated. She held his gaze. "Yes, I think you are. I think...you wouldn't have come to me, where I was standin', if you weren't. I wouldn't have been there, waitin' for you, if you weren't. Yes." She nodded, and she reached out as if to draw him closer. "I know who you are. Who you really are, I mean."

"You know me? *How?*"

"You had another name, and now you call yourself Matthew Corbett...but that's not your real name."

"She's out of her mind," Magnus muttered, low enough only for Matthew to hear. "Swamp fever's got her."

Matthew thought Magnus was right, and yet...he had to ask the questions: "What do you think my real name is? And where do you know me from?"

"Oh," she answered with a small, sad smile, "I can't bear to speak it yet. And I know you from *here*." She put her free hand over her heart. "This is where you live. You may not remember me...not just yet...but I have not let you go."

"Swamp fever," Magnus repeated. He began to work the oars and the boat glided forward.

The young woman followed them along the muddy shore. She was wearing leather sandals, which sank into the muck with every step. "I can help you," she repeated. "Up the river. I can go with you."

"Pity," said Magnus. "She's a beautiful girl, to be so addled."

"Don't go!" Quinn called, as the boat pulled away from her. "Don't leave me again! Do you hear?" A note of panic surfaced. "Please don't leave me!"

"Don't listen." Magnus put his back to the rowing and the boat gained speed. "No use in it."

"Matthew!" Quinn swung her lantern back and forth with the strength of desperation. "You said you'd come back to me! *Please!*"

Though Matthew tried not to listen, he couldn't help but hear. He didn't look back at her, though it took an effort. The mud was drying on his face, but he felt the rising beads of sweat on his forehead and at the nape of his neck. He had never in his life met that young woman before, as far as he knew. How could he have? He'd never been on this river before, had never even heard of Rotbottom. *Matthew!* he heard her call once more, and then she stopped calling.

After Magnus had rowed on a little further and some distance had been put between them and the dark shapes of the houses of Rotbottom, Matthew said, "I don't know what to make of that. Yes, I suppose you're right. About the swamp fever. She thinks I'm someone else."

"Maybe you look like somebody she used to know," Magnus offered. "Damn shame. Out of her head, for sure."

They rounded a bend on the serpentine river and found they were catching up to a small group of rowboats and canoes. Torchflames and candlelight flickered on the water. Matthew saw that once again the jugs were being passed around, and rough voices were slurred as they shouted back and forth. Up ahead, a man in one of the boats stood in the bow with a jug in one hand and as he drank from it he slashed his sword from side to side as if fighting invisible foes.

Matthew had a very clear memory of Sarah Kincannon sitting on the boulder beneath the willows, reading her book. How fast a life could be changed, he thought; how fast a life could be extinguished. He recalled how her brightness had clouded over when speaking about the slaves. But, however one might consider the subject of slavery, it was a fact that slaves were necessary on these plantations, for only slaves had the endurance to work in the swampy fields, under the harsh sun and conditions that pale skins could not tolerate. Of course there were many slaves in the town of New York; it was again a fact of life. The difference between the slaveholders of the northern colonies and those of the southern had to do with the land itself. In New York the slaves usually lived in the attic or basement of the main house, whereas the plantation had enough space to create its own slave quarters. Was the work more full of hardship in the south as opposed to the north? Certainly the northern slaves were used as laborers, in the fields or on the docks as well as in the households, and so it was difficult to say. Matthew knew that whips bit flesh the same in the north as they did in the south, depending only upon the mercy and motives of the master.

Magnus' rowing was smooth and efficient. He was working harder than the rowers in the vessels ahead, and so they were steadily catching up and would soon pass them.

"Sarah seemed like a very fine young woman," Matthew said. "You certainly impressed her with your artistry." When Magnus didn't respond to this, Matthew continued on: "Your glass-blowing," he explained. "She liked your work."

At first Matthew thought Magnus was too lost in either his own reverie or the pattern of the rowing to answer, but then Magnus shrugged his massive shoulders and said, "Glad of that. She paid me for 'em, but that wasn't why I done 'em. Happy to make things she liked. Happy to go visit her and talk for a spell."

"You spent a lot of time with her?"

"No, not a lot." He gave Matthew a quick, sharp glance that said he was still proud and determined to continue living in his hermitage. "But when I *did* go visit her...she was always kind to me. In the summer, offerin' me a cup of lemon water. Cider in the winter. And she wanted to hear about me. The glass-blowin'...that too...but she wanted to know about *me*. How I got where I was, and what I was thinkin'. I started makin' bottles I knew she would most like...usin' the colors she favored. Greens and purples, they were. When I took her somethin' I knew she would like...you should've seen her face light up. Seen her eyes shine. It made me feel good inside, knowin' I was bringin' her somethin' she thought was pretty. I tried to take some bottles to Pandora once, but Father Prisskitt wouldn't let me in the door. Said if I came back, he'd have a musketball ready for me." Magnus stopped rowing and let the boat drift for a moment. "It's a kind of Hell to think you're in love with somebody who don't care if you live or die, ain't it? Who don't show you no care a'tall...

and yet you keep on 'cause you're thinkin' you can make it happen, like knockin' down a door or breakin' through a wall. Then it gets to where you *have* to make it happen, or you think you're no damn good. It gets to where it's a thorn in your head, and ain't no other rose can catch root there." He began rowing once more, his gaze fixed past Matthew toward the river. "You must think I'm a poor piece a'work. don't you? To be so tranced by such a woman?"

"I think all men have been tranced, by some woman or another," Matthew replied. "And women the same. We men don't hold the only key to that particular vault."

"Reckon not," Magnus agreed. "You have a woman?"

"Good question. I'm not quite sure."

"If you don't know for sure…then you must not. You livin' in that big town…maybe you wanted to come see me and give me some advice you oughta be takin' yourself."

"Oh?" Matthew's eyebrows went up. "What would that be?"

"Climbin' out of the hole you dug for yourself. I know I dug a deep one, 'cause I didn't have use for people I thought was laughin' at me and my folks. What hole are you in, and why'd you dig it so deep?"

Matthew had to ponder that one for a moment. "Someone else is digging it for me," he replied, thinking of the image of the masked Professor Fell working tirelessly in a windblown cemetery, shovelling out a grave meant for a young man from New York. "I don't intend to be pushed into it before my time," he said. "Neither do I wish anyone I care for to find themselves in it, and dirt thrown into her face."

"*Her* face?" asked Magnus.

"Hey, Sipsey!" shouted one of the men in the boat just ahead. "Play us a tune!"

The voice had been ragged and slurred. Up further along the river, the man with the fiddle obliged by beginning what at first was a slow, sad and gray song that suddenly with a scrape of the bow blazed itself up into a conflagration of notes. The man with the jug and the sword was standing in his boat, twisting his upper torso to the music and slashing at the air; he let go a wild holler that seemed to reverberate across the wilderness and for a moment silence all the night-things that chattered and chittered for a space of their own.

In another boat, someone who was obviously also not only a music-lover but a lover of the jug fired a pistol into the air, and Magnus muttered, "Damn fools."

Matthew caught sight of something, but he wasn't quite sure what it was.

It was something sliding into the water from the righthand thicket.

He thought at first it was another alligator, but it moved so fast and so smoothly he was unable to tell for sure. He caught other quick movements from that direction, maybe three or four dark shapes submerging themselves. Something was definitely in the river that had not been there a moment before. Matthew felt the flesh prickle on his arms and at the back of his neck.

The man with the sword and jug was still cavorting to the fiddle player's tune. Matthew said, "Magnus?"

Before Magnus could answer or Matthew could determine what he was going to say next, there came a high thrumming sound nearly masked by the fiddle music.

The swordsman suddenly dropped his jug to clutch at his throat, which had just been pierced by an arrow. He fell backwards into the river, his sword now ineffectual and the liquor in his blood not strong enough to overcome a sharpened flint through the windpipe.

In the next instant, the boat from which the swordsman had fallen was overturned by a pair of mud-dark figures that burst up from beneath, spilling the craft's other two passengers into the water. The same also with a boat to the left of that one, even as a musketball shrieked off into the sky, and two more unfortunates tumbled into the Solstice. A torch hissed as the water drank its flame. Arrows came flying from the thicket on the right, one lodging itself into the shaft of Magnus' oar on that side and another passing by Matthew's face so close it nearly shaved his cheek of the day's whiskers. Up ahead, three more boats were overturned, including the one that carried Sipsey, the fiddler. Pistols flared and swords struck down at the river from those boats still upright, and in answer to those insults more arrows flew from the wilderness to strike wood and flesh alike.

Matthew felt a *thump* beneath their boat, and then another. His heart hammered in his chest. An arrow passed through the flame of his torch and threw a firestorm of sparks. Suddenly they were going over, and as Matthew fell across the side of their boat he felt an arrow strike him in the meat of his left shoulder. The pain stole his breath, and in the following second he was in the river holding his cutlass and a dead torch. He was underwater one instant and the next could stand on a muddy bottom, the river up to his collarbone. The attackers had chosen a shallow place in which to devise this assault, using the river's foundation to propel themselves upward against the hulls. This fact did not linger long in his brain, because the mud-smeared figures were everywhere around him and so were flailing white men who found themselves, like Matthew, very suddenly much too far from home.

Eleven

MATTHEW was painstricken and dazed, but he knew he must get out. In the moonstruck darkness he had no idea where Magnus was, or if the figure to the left or to the right was an Indian or a citizen of Jubilee, as water thrashed and foamed and men cried out in either their own pain or their own terror. Matthew made for the swamp on the lefthand side, away from the attackers. He had gotten only two strides through the turbulence when an arm like iron grasped him around the throat and began to pull him toward the opposite shore. A flint blade was put to the side of his face, daring defiance. He heard flesh being struck nearby and thought that Magnus must be fighting for his life with either an oar or his fists. Then Matthew was hauled out of the water into a dense thicket where thorns grabbed at his trousers and shirt, and he stumbled and fell and yet the arm tightened about his throat and the blade began to dig at his cheek.

He still had hold of the deceased torch and the cutlass. With no desire to be strangled or sliced, he did what he had to do; he brought the cutlass' business edge up sharply between his legs and into the crotch of the Indian who'd seized him. There was no cry of pain, just a muffled grunt of it as if between gritted teeth, and the blade scrawled blood from Matthew's cheek but suddenly the arm was gone from around his throat. Without thinking of direction or what he might do to help Magnus or anyone else he tore through the nightblack woods before the warrior could recover, and fighting through thorns and vines he was aware of other figures running around him, but whether they were Indians on the hunt or white men being hunted he did not know.

He just ran, with the mud of the River of Souls clotted on his boots and the dank smell of the river up his nostrils.

There was no light. Here the roof of trees was thick enough to obscure the moon. Vines caught at his legs and nearly toppled him. "Oh my God! Oh my God!" he heard someone half-shouting, half-sobbing to his right, but he could see no face to go along with the pleading. He ran on, fighting through the brush, and suddenly he tripped over a fallen limb or tree root and fell to the ground, losing his grip on the doused torch and twisting his body to one side to avoid driving the arrow in any deeper. The impact with the sodden earth knocked the breath from his lungs. He lay on his right side, his lungs heaving and his teeth clenched with pain. He still had hold of the cutlass, and no power in this haunted swamp would make him let it go.

He heard distant screams and, nearer, the noise of men tearing their own paths through the wilderness. When he was able he forced himself up on his knees, and he sat there thinking that he should get back to the river and cross it to the other side, which seemed the safer. But what about Magnus? Shouldn't he try to find Muldoon and give whatever aid he could? That was laughable, Matthew thought. He could find no one in this wild darkness, much less give aid with an arrow sunken in his shoulder and blood running down his face. But he still had the cutlass, and thank God for that blessing.

He was aware of stripes of moonlight streaming through the trees to illuminate in deep blue the woods before him, and he was aware also of figures moving through that light.

Except they were not human figures. They were skeletons in motion, skulls and bones that glowed with faint green luminosity.

There were six or seven of them, hunched down and creeping slowly through the foliage, and in that moment Matthew doubted the strength of his own sanity.

A man came running past Matthew from the direction of the river. He evidently saw the green-glowing skeletons—too late!—and with a hoarse cry of terror tried to turn away from them. One of the nightmare figures leaped forward with an eerie howl. A scythe-shaped weapon at the end of a long shaft swung out. In another instant the runner's head was nearly removed from the neck. With a gush of black blood the man's body danced a macabre jig as the head flopped back and forth, and when the body collapsed two of the skeletons leapt upon it with drawn flint knives and finished the job of hacking head from bloody neck.

In that moment, Matthew Corbett of New York did perhaps take a jolt to his mind, for he fell unto his right side and curled up, knees to chin, and he thought that if he did not move from this place until daylight he would be safe, for surely the sun would frighten away these evil spirits of the night. Looking up he saw two more of the skeletons run forward in pursuit of a man who burst from the brush and fled like a terrified rabbit. This unfortunate's head was likewise nearly cleaved off by the scythe. One of the skeletons picked up the head by the hair and, swinging it round and round with malignant glee, ran off with it held high into the woods as if offering the swamp its greatest trophy.

Screams and cries echoed through the night. Matthew realized he was in the middle of a battleground...or, more correctly, a slaughterground, for the skeletons were taking the heads left and right of men who had escaped from the Indians at the river. He let go the cutlass for a moment to grasp the shaft of the arrow lodged in his shoulder, but the slightest pressure on it was enough to make the pain shoot down his arm and freeze his left hand. He gave that up as a bad job and once more found the cutlass, which was at present his best and only friend. Sweat had beaded on his face and his heart was racing. One of the skeleton men came very near to where he was lying, but then pulled back just short of stepping on him in the thicket.

If he thought he was safe in this little patch, Matthew suddenly found himself gravely mistaken. A body landed on his back, his hand was hammered to release the sword, his head was yanked back by the hair and a leather cord was wrapped around his throat. The weight slid off him and he was hauled to his feet by rough hands. A knife was placed against his neck and he suffered a slap to the face that must be, to the Indians, a supreme insult. He found he would much rather be insulted than dead, for no weapon swung at him to remove his head. At least, not yet. His vision was blurred by the force of the blow and by the pain in his shoulder, but he saw several of the skeletons ringing him. Through the abject terror that thrummed through him, a cooler part of himself realized that these were only men painted with some kind of black pigment and then the images of skull and bones applied with a phosphorescent agent...likely an elixir made from a swamp plant. But Matthew realized that though they were only men, they were most certainly Indians from the village the strange young woman in Rotbottom had foretold, and thus the lopping off of heads might be only the beginning of this deadly ordeal.

The skeleton men hopped and leaped about Matthew, gibbering in what might have been their own language or the language of the mad. He was pulled along by the leather cord, and though he tried to address them in both English and French his voice was half-choked by the binding and no good came of it.

By the moonlight he saw a few other white men, dripping wet from the River of Souls, similarly neck-bound and being dragged along through the swamp. "God's mercy! God's mercy!" one of them croaked, but no mercy was shown and Matthew thought God kept His distance from this accursed place. Was there any purpose in fighting the cord? In dropping to his knees and trying to scrabble away into the thicket? He decided no, if he wished to keep his head...and in so keeping his head, he might yet have time to think himself a way out of this.

Someone sobbed brokenly, like a woman, to Matthew's right. Matthew's mind was inflamed with both terror and the need to plot some kind of escape, but as he was being pulled roughly along he wondered how many boats and canoes from Jubilee had gotten past this village of the damned before the torchlight had alerted the Indians and brought them, as Quinn Tate had said, to the river like flies on dead meat. Most likely Abram, Mars and Tobey had gotten past, and the first group of boats as well. Would that have included Royce and Gunn? Probably the Indians hadn't been waiting too long before they attacked, which meant that many of the boats further ahead had gotten through.

He didn't have much longer to ponder such questions, for suddenly he and the others were pulled from the wilderness into a clearing where multiple torches burned and a bonfire illuminated dwellings that obviously had been constructed by members of different tribes: some made of stones, some of logs, some of woven grass and treebranches, and some of stretched animal hides. The commonality among these dwellings, Matthew noted, was that they were all decorated with alligator skulls and bones, as if these elements from the River of Souls bound the outcasts—the criminal, the insane, and possibly both, if Quinn Tate was correct in the questionable lucidity of her own mind—together as one tribe.

Came the inhabitants of these huts out to watch the arrival of the hunters, and to themselves dance and caper around the white men stained by river mud. They were young and old, male and female, nearly naked, their bodies painted with garish hues of red and blue but scarred in some way or deformed by a hunchback or with withered arm or leg...outcasts, all. Matthew was brought by the skeleton men into a parade of eight other whites being pulled, poked and prodded along a dirt path toward another area ringed by torches. It was a grassy field, Matthew saw. At each end there were open nets fashioned of river reeds, and it seemed that the entire populace of this damned village were gathering around the field as if to watch a sporting exhibition.

Two of the skeleton men passed by on their way to the field carrying between them a basket that dripped blood. Matthew had an instant to see what he wished he had not seen, that the basket held several of the heads that had been lopped from their necks. One of the other white men saw it, too, and instantly gave a cry of horror and fell to his knees. Matthew recognized him as the broad-shouldered, brown-bearded Zachary DeVey, who wore a sweat-damp red kerchief tied around his bald scalp and who had lifted his pistol and declared himself able and willing to put a ball through any spirit, ha'int or demon up the river for the promise of thirty pounds. His pistol was now lost, probably to the belly of the river. DeVey looked up with renewed horror, his face puffed by insect bites and blood gleaming at his nostrils, as one of the skeleton men swung the scythe-like weapon and the edge of sharpened flint sliced through flesh and cracked against neckbone. A second swing finished the job. Blood sprayed into the air. The body remained, trembling, on its knees as some of the other Indians rushed up to catch the gore in their hands as if from a fountain and smear it over their faces and bodies with cries that could only be the joy of destruction. Then the body collapsed and the head with its sightless eyes and open mouth was picked up by the beard and put into the basket along with the others. The parade, including the dazed and arrow-struck Matthew Corbett, was pulled onward.

They were made to stand still while the cords around their necks were tied and knotted together, captive to captive, and then they were pushed down to sit along one side of the field, where they received the taunts and spittle of both their captors and the audience. The Indians shrieked with delight when two teams of five skeleton men were daubed with blood, one team upon the forehead and one upon the chest. The teams took up short but stout wooden poles with oar-like paddles on the ends. They ran to opposite ends of the field and waited there, all down on one knee, as a corpulent Indian covered with black tattoos plucked a head from the basket and waddled out to plant it at the field's center. Then he waddled back again, and when he held his fleshy and tattooed arms up the audience did the same, and they all clapped their hands together with a noise like rolling thunder.

To the blast of excited screams and chattering that followed, the two teams leapt up and ran for the head at the center of the field. One of the chest-daubed warriors reached it first and gave it a smack with his paddle toward the opposite net, but it rolled only a few feet before the paddle of an opposing player stopped its progress and struck it a blow for the bloody foreheads. Back and forth the head was struck, as Matthew and the men from Jubilee watched in dreadful fascination.

It took perhaps fifteen minutes for the tattered head to be struck a keen blow by a cunning bloody forehead who got it past an opponent's gory paddle and into the net. Then both teams retreated to their sides to take their knees again and the corpulent Indian repeated the ritual, this time with Zachary DeVey's head. After the communal clap of thunder, the game went on.

It was a quick round, the brown-bearded and battered head rolling into the net guarded not too well by a bloody-foreheaded skeleton man after about six minutes of play. A third head was selected, as the other two heads were allowed to remain in the nets. The game continued, with much joyfully deranged noise.

Matthew, fighting pain and shock, knew what would happen when all the heads from that basket found their way into a net, for behind the captives were positioned two skeleton men wielding the deadly scythes. His arms were unbound and his legs free, but the leather cord knotted one man to another made escape if not impossible then highly unlikely. The arrow in his shoulder was taking its due. To remain still and frozen in this posture of defeat, though, meant certain death. To stand and fight...certain death. So for the moment Matthew was caught between deaths with no way out except to Heaven or Hell, according to the will of his Maker.

To emphasize the predicament, the wizened and mud-splattered old man to Matthew's right gave a cry of either panic or desperation and tried to fight to his feet. Before he got there, he was knifed several times in the back by one of the skeleton men while the other one used his scythe to create another bloody ball for the game. Much to the delight of the Indians who viewed this decapitation, the grizzle-bearded head was placed into the basket and the body dragged away so that a number of children could use their child-sized flint knives on the still-shuddering torso.

Matthew realized the leather cord between himself and the next man on his right was now unconnected, having been severed by the scythe. The game was continuing on with a new head, and presently both teams were being thwarted by the other. Matthew figured there were perhaps forty or fifty Indians here in this mad village, almost all of them shouting and screaming for their team of favor, their attention fixed on this gruesome game.

Matthew thought he might be able to unwind the loosened cord from his neck and at least try to run, but as soon as this idea came to him one of the skeleton men dragged the next man on the right over to him and tied and reknotted the cord and his hopes collapsed.

He needed a sharp edge, something to cut the binding. There was no way he could get hold of a knife, but...

If he could get to it, he *was* in possession of *one* sharp edge. It was insane, yes...but perhaps this was a night where insanity must rule, because...there was the sharp edge of the arrowhead buried in his shoulder. His only weapon, and only way out. The skeleton men were watching the game, but were also ready for any sudden moves from the prisoners. Thus...if it was to be done...it had to be done slowly...but the pain was going to be unbearable. He was going to have to probe with a finger along the arrow's shaft and into the wound. It was the only way.

He bent forward, as if to be sick. Touching the shaft sent a shiver through him. If the arrowhead was imbedded in bone, he could never get it out. And if the shaft broke, so much the worse. He closed his eyes, sweat glistening on his face and the delighted screams of the audience ringing in his ears, and he swallowed hard and pushed the forefinger of his right hand into the wound.

Somewhere in Charles Town the palm trees along the harbor stirred in the night breeze, their fronds clattering together softly over the white stone streets. In New York, Berry Grigsby might have been awakened from a slumber by a disquietening dream that she could not fully recall, but that she thought concerned Matthew Corbett. Not far from Berry's dwelling, Hudson Greathouse might have sat up in his own bed and thought with a start of alarm *Matthew is in danger* until the hand of the widow Abby Donovan rose up and brushed along his backbone and he decided that Matthew was likely enjoying a Charles Town vacation in spite of himself, God help the boy.

And somewhere in the world a slender man in an elegantly-cut tan suit whose face was streaked by shadow sat at a desk with pen in hand and a small candle burning before him to illuminate the papers he was executing, and he thought that the next time he saw Matthew Corbett he would show no mercy, for no one lived who had done to his plans what that boy had done, and vengeance would be slow and cold and very, very satisfying.

In the Indian village of the damned along the River of Souls, as another noggin went into the net from the now-empty basket and the first man in the line of the doomed lost his head to a scythe,

Matthew was bent forward with eyes squeezed shut in his sweating face, his forefinger searching for the arrowhead. The pain was sickening, nearly making him pass out, yet he had to hang on to his senses. One of the skeleton men walked past and struck him across the back with the shaft of the scythe, and Matthew winced but paid no heed; he had to get this task done, for he'd realized two more heads into the net and his would be the next offering.

Blood was oozing from the wound, wetting his shirt. Matthew got his thumb into it, to widen the aperture. *Follow the shaft*, he thought. He clenched his teeth; the sounds of the crowd ebbed and swelled as his consciousness wavered. *Fight it!* he told himself. It was either this or he was dead, and he could well be dead even if he got the arrowhead out for he might be too weak to use it. He probed deeper into the torn tissue of his shoulder, and perhaps he steeled himself even more to overcome the pain when the crowd screamed with ecstacy as another head was netted.

His forefinger touched the arrowhead's hard edge. He remained bent forward, as if either sick or sobbing with terror, as the skeleton men hacked the head off the next unfortunate victim in line and dragged his body away for the children. The head entered the game. Matthew worked feverishly to get both forefinger and thumb in position to pull the arrowhead free, but it was a bloodslick and brutal job and he felt his will to live leaving him like a candle being slowly extinguished. His face felt swollen and pressured by currents of blood. He thought he couldn't hang on any longer, that it was all for naught and he would die here anyway, but suddenly the arrowhead came loose between his forefinger and thumb and there was not as much pain as he'd feared because the arm and shoulder felt dead. Now the task of getting the arrowhead out was before him, and he thought he should do this quickly before he lost heart and too much more will and strength. He began to withdraw the arrow...slick fingers on the flint...lost his grip on it...found it again and touched something that shot pain not only through his arm but down his side. He nearly wept, but for that there was no time.

Matthew drew the arrow out. At the very last a wave of sickness and agony passed over him and he very nearly lost his senses. He might have, had not a great hollering and tumult from the audience indicated the netting of another dead brainhouse. Matthew put the arrowhead's edge to the cord around his throat and began to saw at it, his own skin be damned. The remaining man on his right was doomed; the skeleton men were coming up behind him. Suddenly this citizen of Jubilee, who had been struck mute with shock until now, gave out a scream and tried to stand but the knives plunged into his back and drove him down to his knees. The action upset Matthew's focus and intent, as well as his balance. One of the scythes was upraised to cleave head from neck.

Just as the scythe was falling, Matthew felt the arrowhead cut through the cord. As it loosened he ripped it off his neck and with a burst of desperate energy scrambled to his feet. Emboldened by Matthew's success, two of the other white men also tried to stand. One of the skeleton men whirled toward Matthew, knife in the left hand and the scythe gripped in the right. The warrior's eyes in the skullface were black holes of madness. Before either blade could come at him, Matthew plunged the arrow into the Indian's upper chest with as much strength as he could summon, and then he could do no more for anyone else. He turned and ran for the swamp. He was aware that almost instantly the second skeleton man was after him, the deadly scythe seeking his head. Matthew kept his head tucked into his shoulders as he ran along the dirt path, and behind him he heard a screaming and shrieking that might have raised the dead from their graves, for the Indians in this mad village of the damned were delirious with joy in what seemed a sudden new twist of the game.

He ran among the huts in the direction of the bonfire, seeing no other Indians because they were likely all at the field. A glance back showed the skeleton man almost within swing of the scythe. Matthew stumbled; his legs were weak, he was about to fall. He felt death about to take him.

He was nearly to the bonfire when he heard the crying of a baby from the woods beyond. It was a wail that rose up and became a soft sobbing, went on for perhaps three or four seconds and then ceased altogether.

Matthew passed the bonfire. He glanced back and saw with amazement and pure relief that the skeleton man had stopped; not only that, but the eerie figure was backing away, the scythe still held high to deliver a blow. Matthew tore into the wilderness, fell onto hands and knees, got up again and kept going.

The baby's cry did not repeat itself, but as Matthew struggled through vines, thorns and muck toward the river he recalled what Granny Pegg had said: *Old Cara told me this...if you hear a baby cryin', keep goin'. Don't try to find it...just keep goin', 'cause that's a spirit you don't want to see.*

And evidently a spirit the skeleton man had not wanted to see either, Matthew realized. He tripped and fell again, and once more struggled up. The left arm of his shirt was wet with blood. He was trying to make his way through the utter dark, his strength ebbing away and possibly the most dangerous spirit of the River of Souls somewhere near him. If one believed in such things, and in spite of his rational mind Matthew was beginning to become a believer.

Twelve

At the edge of the River of Souls, Matthew sank to his knees in the weeds. He was almost done. He saw that the moon had fallen toward the horizon and was being consumed by the gray tendrils of clouds. He thought of Professor Fell's octopus, slowly wrapping its tentacles about the world.

He had decided first to cross the river, here at a shallow point, to get the Solstice between himself and the hunters. He'd not seen any following him, and perhaps the cry of the so-called spirit would keep them from venturing out beyond the firelight of their sanctuary, but still...

There had to be bodies in the river—and maybe that of Magnus Muldoon—that might be attracting the reptiles. Possibly they weren't nesting in this area of the river, since the Indians hadn't been afraid of swimming, but Matthew wished not to take that chance with all the blood on his shirt and a thick matting of it on his left shoulder. His left arm felt dead, yet at least the rest of him was still alive and he still wore his head.

Were there any of the overturned boats floating? He could see none of them by the darkening moon. The sullen heat lay like a black cloak upon him and the swamp on all sides was a buzz and thurrup of the noise of insects fighting their own constant war for survival. He could see no stars, and not a glimmer of light yet from the east.

He was weary. He wished only to lie here in this mud and these weeds and be lulled by the cursed swamp, for better or for worse. Morning would come soon, he thought. Morning had to come soon. And then he would walk his way out of this swamp...but what of the runaway slaves? Gone, most likely. Either already captured and killed or disappeared into the wilderness. By all reason, Royce and Gunn had won. The murder of Sarah Kincannon—most probably rooted in the same kind of jealousy that had caused Magnus to kill three men for the dubious admiration of Pandora Prisskitt—would result in the deaths of Abram, Mars and Tobey as well...but possibly the slaves would escape this swamp, and keep going. To where? Matthew wondered. Where did they think they were going to find refuge? On another plantation? The custom was to brand slaves on the back or chest with a mark of ownership; another plantation owner would return them in chains to the Green Sea. Either that, or the three would eventually perish in the swamp. Royce and Gunn could not take the risk of them getting out, though; neither man knew the questions and accusations waiting for them when they returned, but in their minds they wanted the three runaways—and especially Abram—dead and silenced. *I pray to Heaven you are able to do the right thing*, Mrs. Kincannon had said. "Ha," Matthew said quietly. "The right thing." His voice was wan and hoarse. "And what *is* the right thing?" he asked the starless night.

"The right thing," came a harsher voice, from only a short distance away, "is first to get your ass out of that mud, Sir Gentleman."

Matthew at once sat up. A mountainous black-bearded figure, dark with mud, towered over him.

"Saw *somebody* come out of the woods," said Magnus. "Didn't know who it was 'til I heard you. Anybody else comin'?"

"No," Matthew answered when he could find his voice again. "I don't think so."

Magnus knelt down beside him. "Indians got you?"

"Yes."

"How'd you get away?"

"Not easily." *They're using human heads in their ballgame*, he almost said, but to revisit all that was a torture in itself. "What happened to *you*?"

"Fought a couple of 'em off with an oar. Then I went underwater, grabbed hold of a rock and near drowned down there, tryin' to keep my breath. A pair of boots stepped on me, that didn't help. When I could, I crawled into the thicket. Was gonna stay there 'til first light, then I saw somebody come out...turns out to be you." He was silent for a moment, as the swamp spoke around them in its unintelligible chattering. "Lot of men dead, I'm figurin'."

"Yes," said Matthew.

"It was bad," said Magnus, a statement rather than a question, and he waited for Matthew to nod. "Well," said the muddied mountain, "we lost everythin' when the boat went over. The musket...the black powder...the tinderbox...the food. Figure your cutlass is gone?"

"Gone," Matthew said.

"Maybe we can find a boat and get it uprighted. Moon's near dark," Magnus said, noting the change in the lighting. "Clouds rollin' in, maybe get some rain in the mornin'." He stared without speaking into Matthew's face for a time. "Smellin' blood on you. Hurt bad?"

"I had an arrow in the shoulder. I had to pull it out. My left arm is...less than perfect."

"Hm," said Magnus. He scratched his muddy beard. "Could've been worse, I'm thinkin'."

"Yes," Matthew agreed, feeling as if he were in the midst of a bad dream that had no beginning and no end, one of those that set upon you and caused you to think the night was without time and the world without form. "Much worse."

"Look here," Magnus said suddenly. "Somebody else is comin'."

Matthew saw for himself. Approaching from downriver was a rowboat with a pair of punched-tin lanterns set on a hook at the bow. Behind the boat was nothing was dark river; this was obviously the final journeyer from Jubilee. Matthew tried to stand but found he hadn't yet the strength, so Sir Gentleman remained with his ass in the mud. Magnus stood up and waded out to meet the boat, and in so doing bumped against a body floating faceup with an arrow through its throat. When he pushed it aside, something slithered underneath his hand and he jerked the hand back as if it had touched a hot griddle.

In another moment the boat had drawn close enough for both Magnus and Matthew to see who was handling the oars. Matthew got to his feet; the world spun around him a few times, but he held firm to his senses.

"You know," said the young black-haired girl, staring at him with her dark blue eyes in the dim lantern light, "that I couldn't let you go again. Not when you're so close."

Matthew had no idea how to respond. Quinn Tate thought him to be someone else, of course. Swamp fever or not, she was out of her mind.

"Stepped on somethin'," said Magnus, and he reached underwater. He came up with a short sword...not Matthew's cutlass, but good enough to fight with.

"What happened here?" Quinn asked. She scanned the lefthand riverbank, and then she caught sight of the floating body with the arrow in its throat. She answered her own question. "I told you they'd come when they saw the torches."

"They might still be creepin' about," Magnus said. "They took Matthew, but he got away from 'em. Time we were gettin' out of here too." He laid the sword down into the boat. "I'm gonna climb in. Just sit still and keep the oars out and flat."

She nodded. Magnus pulled himself over the side and helped Matthew over as Quinn held the boat steady. Matthew noted that she looked at him with wonder and near adoration, as if he were a spirit sent to her from God. He sat at the stern, clasping his wounded shoulder, and at once Quinn abandoned the oars and sat on the plank seat next to him, pulling the torn shirt open to look at his injury.

"Arrow," he told her. "I was lucky. Didn't hit a bone."

She touched the clotted mass of blood with gentle fingers. "Got to get somethin' on that, Daniel. It'll fester if you don't."

"*Matthew*," he said quietly but forcefully. "My name is *Matthew*."

Quinn seemed to catch herself drifting in some memory of the past. She blinked, a shade passed over her features, and she said, "Yes. I meant to say...Matthew."

Magnus had sat on the center plank and taken up the oars. He hesitated, and Matthew realized he was trying to decide to go on or not. "What's up ahead?" Magnus asked the girl, his voice a harsh rumble. "More Indians?"

"No. But other things."

"What other things?"

"Spirits," she said. "They wander, lookin' for peace...or revenge. The river leadin' you on and on, and the swamp takin' you in and makin' you lose your way. The quicksand pits and the snake nests, trickin' you to step in 'em. I know from hearin' tales...it's a bad place."

"*Tales*," scoffed Magnus, yet his voice wasn't as strong as it had been a moment before. A flicker of heat lightning shot across the sky to the west. "Matthew, what do you say? Do we go onward or back?"

As soon as this uncomfortable question had left Magnus' lips, there came the sound of a distant gunshot. The noise rolled to them through the weeping willows, the gnarled oaks and along the river's flow. In a few seconds another gunshot—likely a pistol this time, the sound a little higher register than the first, which was probably a musket—rang out. Following it almost immediately was a third shot, from another musket.

Then silence, but for the voice of the swamp.

Magnus waited. He glanced back at Matthew. "Three shots. Three runaways. Maybe got 'em all."

Matthew looked for the red wash in the eastern sky that would be the coming of daylight, but it was not there. Time seemed to have slipped its boundaries. His shoulder had begun to throb with deep pain that radiated up the side of his neck. He had no idea what to do with the girl; she had to be taken back to Rotbottom, but still...he couldn't be sure the three shots had killed the runaways, and there was yet the chance to save them.

"I say we go on," Magnus decided. "Come this far, we should go on. You bear with that?"

Matthew didn't like the idea of taking the girl any further upriver, but it seemed that the die was cast. "I bear with it," he said, and Magnus began rowing them onward with strong strokes.

"Brought some things," Quinn said. She reached down into the bottom of the boat and brought up a small yellow gourd topped with a cork and equipped with a leather strap. "Fresh well-water," she said, and sloshed the liquid around for them to hear. She uncorked the gourd and offered it to Matthew, who drank gratefully and then passed it to

Magnus, who also drank. The gourd was recorked and hung around her neck by the strap, and then Quinn brought up a paper wrapping of what, unwrapped, revealed several chunks of dried meat.

"Alligator?" Matthew asked before he took one.

"Surely," she answered. "Go ahead, it was a big fat one."

In spite of what he'd witnessed this night, he was hungry enough. He ate a piece, but he couldn't help wondering what had made this particular reptile so fat. It had a taste somewhere between chicken and fish, with more gill than cluck. Magnus took two of the chunks and put them down his gullet as if they were from the finest steak in Charles Town. "Obliged," he said.

Quinn reached down and brought up a third item to show Matthew: a rusted-looking pistol that likely would explode at the pulling of the trigger. "Got a tinderbox, a bag of powder and some shot too," she said, holding up a deerskin bag.

"This belongs to your father? Or your husband?" Matthew asked.

She stared into his eyes for a few seconds before she replied. "It was *yours*," she said. "I thought...maybe...you'd know it."

"Listen to me," Matthew told her. "I've never seen you before. Who do you think I am? Someone named *Daniel*?"

"Your name is Matthew now." She gave him a small smile that held within it both a great grief and a heart of hope. "But you've done what you said you'd do. What you swore. I don't want to rush it on you, 'cause I figure you might not remember. But you *will* remember, in time."

Matthew thought the girl was beautiful—a flower among the swamp weeds—but she was surely mad. As Magnus rowed, Matthew closed his eyes and tried to find some rest, aware that Quinn was pressed against him as tightly as a new waistcoat. He was wet with sweat in the humid night, and the insects were back with a vengeance around his face and the shoulder wound. Behind his closed eyes, the cutting scythe rose and fell and the headless bodies jerked and shuddered beneath the children with their knives. He had known horror before, many times, through his dealings in the case of the Queen of Bedlam, the vicious killer Tyranus Slaughter and just lately his meeting with Professor Fell on Pendulum Island, but that scene of bloody celebration at the gamefield had nearly unhinged his already-shattered door. It had been the knowledge that he was waiting for his own head to be delivered to the game paddles that had been the worst, and everything he had wanted to do or planned to do or expected to do in this world would have been ended with the slash of the scythe.

He felt Quinn's hand, gentle upon his cheek, and he opened his eyes to see her face very close to his own, as if inhaling the essence of him. "Daniel was your husband?" he asked.

"*Is* my husband," she said. "Always will be, 'til the stars fall out of the sky."

"He's dead?"

"Alive," she answered.

"In *me*, you think?"

"You'll remember, soon enough."

"I am not Daniel," said Matthew. "No matter what you believe, I'm not him."

She smiled, ever so faintly. Her fingers traced the line of his jaw, which was stubbled now with a day's growth of beard. "You'll remember," she replied. "Soon enough."

Magnus ceased his rowing and let the vessel drift. "Boats pulled up on shore ahead," he announced. "Looks like...five or six of 'em. Shots likely came from here. I'm puttin' us out."

"All right," Matthew agreed, as Magnus aimed the boat toward the others pulled up in the brush and weeds. When they were lodged upon the bank, Matthew took up the sword and Magnus accepted the rusty pistol and the powderbag from Quinn. Magnus spent a moment loading the thing. Quinn gathered up the water gourd and the rest of the 'gator meat. Matthew's head spun a little upon stepping onto the slimy shore, and he stumbled a step but Quinn was quickly there to keep him standing.

The glow of a fire could be seen through the trees not far ahead. Magnus went first, leading Matthew and Quinn through the tangle. Soon the voices of men could be heard, talking quietly. Magnus eased into the firelight, causing some of the fifteen or so men who sat around the fire to jump to their feet as if being visited by a bearded and muddied giant hai'nt of the swamp. Swords, muskets and pistols pointed in the direction of the new arrivals.

"Ease up, boys," said the gravel-voiced Baltazar Stamper, who sat on a length of rotten log. Under his raven-feathered hat his hard-lined face was placid and unconcerned, but his musket was close at hand. "Just Muldoon and...well, look who's joined the party." He was staring past Matthew at the girl, and he smiled thinly and tipped his hat to show a mass of unruly black hair with tendrils of gray on the sides. "Where'd *you* come from, young miss?"

"Rotbottom's my home," she answered in a tentative voice, as she came fully into the firelight beside Matthew.

"Ah, Rotbottom!" This was spoken by the black-garbed and gaunt preacher Seth Lott, who remained on his feet and gave Quinn a slight bow and a sweep of his ebony tricorn. His hair was cut close to the scalp, like a sprinkling of dark sand. Matthew noted that the man's keen-eyed gaze covered all of Quinn's body from head to feet and then travelled upward again, with a couple of joyously wicked stops on the journey. "I am told much sin abides in Rotbottom, since you have no preacher there?"

"We have some who read the Good Book," Quinn replied, with more strength. "I'm one of 'em."

"Blessed are you, then," said Lott, offering a quick smile. He returned the tricorn to his head. "Come join us, friends. We are cooking up some snakes over this bountiful fire."

Matthew saw that many of the men held sharpened sticks upon which were pierced pieces of white meat. He recognized the broad-shouldered, brown-bearded and husky Caleb Bovie, who regarded the three additions to the 'party' with an impassive expression that might have been tinged with dull-eyed contempt. The others he'd probably seen before, maybe in the boats or in the crowd at the Green Sea. They were mostly lean examples of men who had labored hard and long for very little, and wore in the lines upon their faces the tales of lives of quiet desperation. It was easy to see how any of them would be out here hoping to earn money for the ears of a runaway slave, particularly one who had murdered Sarah Kincannon, for such might lift them up at least for awhile from the common clay, or serve to buy a wife a nice piece of cloth for a new dress, or a playtoy for a child. A few of these gents, however, were intent on passing the jugs back and forth; their ruddy faces, glazed eyes and occasional giggling displayed the fact that they were out here, indeed, to join the 'party.'

"Lord, boy!" said a man with a crown of white hair and a face seamed by many summers of burning suns. "You got blood all over your shirt! What happened?"

"Indians," Matthew answered. He felt like he needed to sit down before he fell. "From that village back there. They came up from underwater. Threw some of the boats over, and—"

"You got away from there with your *head*?" Stamper was roasting his piece of snake over the flames. "We made sure we got past that place quick. Never been there—thank God—but I know what it is. The Catawba, Creeks, Yuchi, and Chickasaws put the people there they call 'Dead in Life'...the outcasts. We figured the skins had already gotten past, without attractin' too much attention. Yeah, all those torches on the river...all that singin' and such...sure to draw 'em out." Matthew thought the gunfire on the river might also have alerted the Dead in Life to trespassers in their realm, but he said nothing. "Heard tell of the game," Stamper said. "You see it?"

"A part I want to keep," Matthew answered, "was almost *in* the game."

"Lost a lot of blood, looks like. Took a knife?"

"Arrow."

"Broke off the shaft?"

"No," Matthew said. "I pulled the arrowhead out."

There was a moment of respectful silence, even from the drunken gigglers. Then Stamper called out, "Halleck, pass that jug over here! Let's give this boy a drink. I think he needs one more than you do."

The jug was passed. Matthew had a swallow, which burned hot going down and brought tears to his eyes but he welcomed the sensation. Then Quinn took the jug, said to him, "Draw a breath," and when he did—knowing what she was about to do—she splashed some of the liquor onto his shoulder wound.

Comets and fireballs whirled through his head. The pain almost broke his teeth. He thought for a second his tormented flesh in that area had burst into flame. Then he was aware of being helped to the ground by Magnus, because his legs had collapsed. He sat in the firelight with his hand clasped to his shoulder and the beads of sweat glistening on his face.

"Thank you," said Quinn, giving the jug back to Stamper, who began its passage back to Halleck and the other drunkards.

"Heard three shots," Magnus said. "Killed three snakes?"

"Snakes were killed by the sword," Stamper answered as he chewed on the blackened meat. "Whetters, Carr and Morgan fired those shots." He motioned toward three men on the other side of the flames. "Tell the man why you're wastin' gunpowder, Morgan."

"Wasn't no waste!" said the wild-looking red-haired man with a hooked nose and maybe four or five black teeth in his head. "Somethin' was stalkin' us! We all heared it!"

"Scared it off, whatever it was!" said one of the others, thin and balding and red-eyed from either his experiences of the night or sips from the jug. "Somethin' *big*...followin' us through that thicket. Didn't make a lot a'noise, but it cracked a twig or two. Gettin' closer and closer. Thought it might've been one of the skins, slippin' up to cut our throats!"

"Those skins are a long way from here, I'm bettin'," said Stamper, with a nostril-flare of disgust for either the runaways or the three shooters. "And no *one* of 'em is gonna try to cut anybody's throat. They want to run, not fight."

"Just tellin' you what we heard," Morgan insisted. "Out there lookin' to scare up a rabbit or such...then we all heard it prowlin' through that brush. Couldn't see it, not even with the torch. Keepin' well-hid." He turned his attention from Stamper to Magnus. "So we took our shots and to Hell with whatever damn devil it was."

"Indian, maybe?" Magnus asked. "The Dead in Life?"

"Maybe, but I don't believe they'd roam this far from their village," Stamper said. "Whatever it was, you boys are damned poor shots. Wasn't a drop of blood in that thicket." He reached over and gave his musket a loving pat. "We'll find out before dawn whether you hit an Indian or not."

Matthew looked up at the sky. Had it ever been so dark before dawn in his life? Quinn settled herself beside him and pushed the sweat-damp hair back from his forehead.

Magnus reached down. He took for himself a stick of burnt snake meat from the hand of a long-nosed man who seemed to think just for an instant of defying Fate, but then regained his senses and sat with his knees pulled up to his chin. Magnus chewed on the meat and surveyed the group of men. He was a formidable beast, with his hair and beard matted and filthy and his face darkened by Solstice River mud. "Why'd you pull off the river here?"

"I don't know who got here first and started a fire," Stamper said, "but it's a good place to camp. High off the mud. Eat some food and wait 'til daylight. Get started again in a couple of hours."

Magnus nodded. "I'm lookin' for Griffin Royce and Joel Gunn. Anybody seen 'em?"

"I seen 'em," said a man leaning against a tree on the other side of the fire. He cradled a musket, was thick-bodied, had a neck like a bull and a square-jawed face that looked like he could crush stones between his teeth. Even so, his blind left eye was stark white. "About an hour ago. They was rowin' ahead of me, Ellis and Doyle. Movin' fast. Rounded a bend, and they was gone."

"Hm," said Magnus, still chewing on the reptile.

"Why you lookin' for *them*, Muldoon?" Caleb Bovie had snake meat in his teeth and a voice that sounded as if his throat had been scraped with a razor. "You're out after the skins just like the rest of us, ain't you?"

Magnus was suddenly at a loss for words. He looked to Matthew, who took up the banner even though he was still nearly insensible. "We wondered...if those two might've found the runaways yet. They started off...before everyone else. So..."

"And what the hell are *you* doin' here and who are you?" Stamper asked, his eyes narrowed. "I saw you in Jubilee. Wearin' fancy clothes with fancy manners. You're from Charles Town, am I right? What are you doin' out here on a slave hunt, boy?"

Magnus got his jaw unlocked. He had realized, as Matthew knew, that telling these men what Granny Pegg had said would carry no weight, and might work against their aim. "Matthew's a friend of mine. Was at my house when the bell started ringin'." He offered a crooked, muddy-faced grin. "Don't hold it against him that he's from Charles Town. Wantin' to help me start a business. Ain't that right, Matthew?"

"Yes, that's right."

"*Business?*" Stamper snorted and a few of the others dared to laugh, but quietly. "Muldoon, only business you can do is spreadin' a stink wherever you walk." His hand touched the musket, just in case. "And it's news to me that you *have* a friend. Boy," he said to Matthew, "you must be as poor a soul as *he* is."

Quinn leaned toward the man. Her face was tight, her eyes dark, and she said in a voice of fire and ice, "Don't you talk to him that way, mister. I won't have it. You hear?"

"Is that so?" Stamper replied, with a quick glance at the other men, for Matthew saw he enjoyed not only being the center of attention, but also being a hornet in a chamberpot. "Why? What's he to a sad-eyed young wench from Rotbottom?"

"He's my husband," Quinn said calmly, "and he's come back to me from the dead."

THIRTEEN

THERE followed a long, frozen silence.

It was broken when Baltazar Stamper said, "That explains it, then. Fitzy, cut me off some more snake and put it on here!" He held up his sharpened stick toward a thin young man who obediently knelt down and started slicing the meat from a dead brown snake that lay across a rock next to two already well-carved carcasses. Stamper's deep-set eyes glittered as he appraised Matthew and Quinn. "Mr. Matthew," he said, "you got yourself one there, it seems."

Seth Lott wore a grin like an ugly gash. "My services are yours, sir, for a Christian wedding. Or might I say...a renewed marriage."

"Then you can do the deed to her," said Caleb Bovie, peeling some skin from his chunk of snake. "Do her good and proper. Right here by the fire, kinda..." He struggled to find the word, his mouth working but no sound being produced.

"Romantic," said Stamper, who received his portion of reptile from Fitzy and put it over the fire to burn.

"Thank you for your interest and comments," Matthew replied, taking them in one after another with a hard-edged glare. "Perhaps in Jubilee you have little respect for women...particularly one who might be...confused...but I'd ask you to restrain your jocularity."

"Big words," said Bovie, with a frown. "What do they mean?"

"They mean...shut your damned mouths," Magnus answered, and he rested the rusted pistol against the bulk of a shoulder. "Stamper, I hear you put two wives in the grave. Lott, you got a fifteen-year-old girl with child a couple of years ago and she's still wanderin' the alleys of Charles Town, lookin' for Jesus. And Bovie...you wouldn't know the backside of a woman from a horse's ass, would you?"

Bovie flushed red and started to stand up, but Stamper gave a harsh laugh and held out his stick of smoking snake meat to prevent Bovie's rise. "Let him talk, Caleb. Entertainin' to hear a fool prattle on. Oh, you men ought to hear what's said about our friend Muldoon in Charles Town. Speakin' of a certain society lady, who goes to balls and fancy dances with young handsome men. And then Magnus shows up, like a little boy with a broken heart. Beggin' himself on her. Oh yes, I've heard it told in more than one tavern. How they laugh at him in that town! Our hermit Magnus Muldoon, tryin' to..." He paused, and took a slow bite of snake. "*Be* somebody," he went on. "When ever'body knows, and he knows it too...that he won't ever in his life amount to any more than the pile of walkin' shit he *already* is." Stamper smiled faintly, with a bit of meat in the corner of his mouth. "But let Magnus reach high, I say. Let him reach up as far as he can. He ain't goin' nowhere, and he ain't gonna catch no star, if that's what he's after. Let him reach up, and try and try to get away from what he is by grabbin' the skirts of a—"

"That's enough."

It had been Matthew's voice. Delivered as strongly as a pistol shot, but with better aim and elegance.

Bovie stared holes through him. "Just 'cause you been arrow-shot, boy, and lived to tell the tale don't mean nothin' to me. You better watch that smart mouth."

"Oh, let's be friends," said Stamper, with a shrug. "Comrades, out here on the River of Souls lookin' to do the *right* thing. Get us some black ears to take back with us. Avenge Miss Sarah's murder. That's what it's about, ain't it?"

Magnus had said nothing during all this. His face may have tightened and his glowering become more fearsome, but Matthew thought he was admirable in his solidity. The jugs began being passed around the fire once more, the other men began talking back and forth, and after a moment Magnus lowered his pistol and sat down with one side toward the party of avengers and the other toward the river.

"Your husband," said Seth Lott to Quinn. "As a man of God, I am interested in your story. Of life and death, rebirth and resurrection. What happened to him, dear child?"

Many of the men were listening, though some had started a game of cards to go along with their taste from the jug. Quinn shifted uneasily, perhaps taking note—as Matthew did—of the rapacious eyes upon her.

"My Daniel died last summer," she said, speaking to the reverend. "It was a hot summer. Dry, like this one. Thunder and lightning, but no rain. You know how it can happen here, all of a sudden. The lightning strikes, and a tree catches fire. Then another one, and one after that, and then the whole woods starts burnin'. It can happen so fast, if the wind is dry and the thicket's parched. So it was last summer."

"Wildfires," said Lott. "Yes, they do start quick. They move fast, until they burn themselves out. It's God's will."

Quinn nodded. "Maybe it is. But it's a hard will, I think. God must be a long ways from this place. Must be thinkin' of other things, and helpin' other people."

"God helps those who help themselves," said the preacher. "That's His mysterious way."

Matthew wondered if—taking into consideration that Magnus had been more truthful than spiteful—Lott had dismissed his young pregnant mistress with those exact words.

"Could be," said Quinn, her expression impassive. "When that fire takes hold and starts movin', nothin' can hardly stop it. Animals run from it and get caught when the wind jumps the fire from place to place. Happens to men, too. Last summer fire was ragin' toward Rotbottom. We ain't much, but we're *somewhere.* Got lives and houses and families just like in any place. My Daniel and some men went out to chop down trees and dig firebreaks, stop it from gettin' any closer to town."

"I saw the smoke," said Stamper. "Looked a long way off, though. Happens just about every year."

"You got the swamp and the river to keep Jubilee from burnin'," Quinn went on. "We got our picks and shovels and wantin' to keep what's ours. Maybe twenty men went out there, to fight the fire that was comin'. Lightin' up the sky at night like the Devil's grin, and throwin' sparks onto anything that would burn. And the wind pickin' up, and moanin', and rushin' those flames on. Gettin' closer all the time, gettin' stronger, and startin' to catch even the swamp trees alight. My Daniel went out there, to help save our town...and he was one of three who didn't come back, when it was all said and done."

"Burned up, was he?" asked Stamper, indelicately.

"Not burned," the girl replied. "*Taken.*"

"Taken?" Matthew frowned. "How do you mean?"

"By the beast," said Quinn. "It came out of the smoke. Nearest man saw its shadow...couldn't tell much of it...but it fell on my Daniel, and he was gone." She reached out and put her hand on Matthew's. "You said before you left me...you had a feelin'...a *fear* that day. But you looked in my face, and you told me how much you loved me, and you said, 'Quinn...don't you worry, 'cause I'll be back.' Said the child I was carryin' was too important for distance to come between us...not the distance between our town and that fire, or the distance between life and death. Don't you remember that?"

Matthew was silent, but he felt an arrow pierce his heart as two tears ran from Quinn's eyes in her terribly-composed and solemn face. It was a mask, he thought, that hid tremendous suffering, more than a young girl could stand without creating a desperate fiction.

"You're Daniel, returned to me," she said. "I *know* it. I feel his spirit in you. And maybe you don't remember everything of us...how things were...but as he gets stronger, he'll tell you. And someday, maybe soon, you'll remember all about Daniel Tate, and you'll let Matthew Corbett go...because he's just a suit of skin over the heart of my husband." Her hand squeezed his, and she managed the saddest of smiles that drove Matthew's arrow deeper. "I can't ever let you go again...and we can have another child, Daniel. I'm so sorry...so sorry...I was so tore up I lost our baby. I just cried our baby's life away, and for that I am so sorry." She leaned toward him, her eyes glistening. "It was a boy. They told me, before they wrapped him in white linen and buried him. You remember that white linen, Daniel? For our weddin'? And how much you paid for it at the store in Jubilee?"

"White linen is expensive," was Stamper's comment. "Pity to bury somethin' as expensive as that."

Someone across the fire laughed, and Matthew saw Quinn wince as if struck by a slap across the face, and he took hold of his short-bladed sword that had likely belonged to a man now beheaded and lost to the world, and with every ounce of strength he possessed he struggled to his feet and stood in the leaping firelight with the young madwoman at his feet.

"One more word of disrespect to *her*," said Matthew to Baltazar Stamper, "and I'll run you through or die trying."

"Let's test that out, boy," answered Caleb Bovie, who reached beside himself to grasp a wicked-looking sword that had probably twice the blade of Matthew's weapon. He stood up, grinning and wild-eyed. His chest swelled out as he inhaled the swamp air, bugs and all. "Muldoon," he said, "I'll be on you 'fore you cock that pistol, so if I were you I'd just stand real still."

"Don't need to cock it." Magnus held it up to use as a club. He took a single step toward Bovie. "Come on, let's see if you've got any brains in that damn ugly head."

Before anyone else could move, something moved in the thicket beyond.

A torchlight could be seen approaching. "Hold your tempers and everyone keep their brains in their heads," said Stamper, as he got to his feet. Most of the other men stood up as well, and brandished firearms or swords toward the advancing unknown.

"*Who comes forth?*" Stamper called. A faint tremor in the man's heavy-lunged voice told Matthew that the tales of this haunted swamp must not be fully lost on even the hardest of these men.

There was a few seconds' pause, in which the crackling of the fire and the humming of insects were the only sounds.

Then a voice came: "*Stamper?*"

"I know myself, but who are *you*?"

More movement sounded in the thicket. The torchlight spread wider. A few of the men cocked their muskets. "Stay your triggers!" Stamper hissed. "I think I recognize that voice." He spoke to the distance again: "*We have some nervous men with guns in here, gentlemen*! *Kindly tell us who you are*!"

"Oh, for the sake of Christ!" replied the man, much nearer now and still coming. "It's Griff Royce and Joel Gunn! Hold your fire!"

Matthew and Magnus exchanged glances. Bovie's attention, a short-lived beast, had turned from the approach of violence to the approach of the two Green Sea 'captains.' Quinn stood up, but grasped onto Matthew's arm as if fearful the spirit of Daniel would again fly away from the body it supposedly inhabited.

In another moment the two men appeared through the tangle of vines and brush, both of them looking hollow-eyed and weary under the torchlight. Gunn was carrying the torch. Both men were armed with muskets and had knives in sheaths tucked into their trousers at the waists. They came into the circle of the fire, as the other men visibly relaxed and lowered their weapons.

"No ears yet?" Stamper asked.

"Not yet, but we'll get 'em," Royce answered. He and Gunn scanned the assembly, and both of them stopped at Matthew, Quinn and Magnus. "*Well*," said Royce, in a voice that held a knife's edge of tension. "What do we have *here*?" The pock-marked face with its square chin and high cheekbones showed the hint of a cruel—perhaps cunning—smile. The green eyes seemed full of flames. "The young man from Charles Town...Matthew Corbett, isn't it? Magnus Muldoon the love-struck hermit and...*who* is this?" If his eyes indeed *were* full of flames, the fires reached toward Quinn. "A beauty in rags?" he asked. "Or a ragged beauty? From Rotbottom, I'm thinkin'?"

Gunn had no interest in Royce's focus of attention; he was fixed on the sight of Matthew Corbett. "*You!*" he said, with a curl of contempt on his fleshy lips. "Not enough that you came in where you weren't wanted, you had to come *here*?" He saw the bloody shirt. "Looks like you paid a price for it, too! I could've told you not to come on this hunt!"

"And Joel would've been *right*, Corbett," said Royce, as he walked forward to stand only a few feet away from Matthew. "Dangerous place out here. Things can happen mighty fast." He eyed the gory shirt. "I see you found that out already. What hit you?"

"Boy got himself taken by the Dead in Life," Stamper supplied. "Accordin' to him they came up under some boats and took quite a few Jubilee men. Boy caught an arrow but kept his head."

"Bad wound, looks to be," Royce went on. "Best head back to the Green Sea, you and Muldoon both."

"I'll live," said Matthew, grimly. He looked at the cloth bandages on Royce's right forearm, where the medical compress had been yesterday. To his dismay, he saw that both of Royce's forearms were scratched and bloody, and so too were Gunn's. If there was any evidence of scratches from Sarah Kincannon's fingernails, they were lost amid the others. "You went through some thorns?"

"A heavy patch. There was no easy way around." Royce held Matthew's stare for a few seconds, and then he visibly dismissed the younger man and turned toward Stamper. "We're not too far ahead. Saw your fire back here. Knew it couldn't have been the skins, they wouldn't be that stupid, but we had to come take a look. No offense meant."

"None taken," said Stamper. "But why'd you two leave the river?"

"We found their boat," said Gunn, who kept spearing Matthew with his hard blue eyes. "Tried to drag it out and hide it, but the mud told the tale."

"They're on foot now," Royce said. "They had a choice to make. Either swim back across and head through heavy swamp, or go northeast through the woods to the grasslands. I think they'll likely take the easier way."

"May I ask this question?" Seth Lott ventured, his voice mannered and quiet. "Where do they think they're *going*? To freedom from the crime? Where would they ever hope to find refuge out there?" He motioned broadly toward the wilderness.

"Wild animals run 'cause it's in their nature," Royce answered. He had spied the snake upon the stone, and kneeling down he drew his knife and began to carve himself some meat. "They don't know where they're goin'. All they're tryin' to do is run from justice. And that damn buck Abram...drawin' his blood into it, and makin' them pay too." He took a stick from one of the others, pushed the chunk of snakemeat upon its sharpened end and began to roast his meal. "I'll tell you, if I had my way that damn Granny Pegg would be swingin' from a rope right now, too. Seems to me she should've stopped Abram from runnin', should've told him to face up to what he'd done. Saved us all a lot of trouble."

Matthew couldn't help it. It came out of him before he could stop it, and maybe it was because of his loss of blood or weariness or lightheadedness, but he spoke the words: "Mr. Royce...how many knives do you own?"

Royce looked up from the business of snake-cooking. His expression was untroubled. "Three. How many do *you* own?"

"None. But I was wondering...have you lost a knife lately?"

"Not that I know of." Royce gave Gunn a quick, dark glance before the calm expression returned. "Matthew...can I call you such?...you ought to sit down before you fall down. I think the swamp's workin' on that wound right now."

"I was wondering," Matthew went on, in spite of himself, "where Abram might have gotten the knife he used to kill Sarah." He paused to let that circle Royce's head. "I mean to say...could Abram have stolen one of *your* knives? He had to get the knife from somewhere. Or from *you*, Mr. Gunn." Matthew turned his face toward the other captain. "My question is...how did Abram get hold of that knife?"

"Easy answer." Royce's teeth began to tear at the meat. "A servant in the big house likely stole a knife and got it to him. Those girls are always stealin' things to take down to the quarter. One of 'em slipped a knife up her skirt and Abram got hold of it. That's how it happened."

"Bet Abram slipped somethin' else up the bitch's skirt in exchange," said Gunn, and he laughed a little too loudly and harshly, which a few of the others echoed with dumb humor.

"A lady's present, gentlemen," Stamper cautioned, with a sly grin.

"Where?" asked Bovie. "All I see is Rotbottom trash." He aimed his eyes not at Quinn, but at Matthew. "Cracked in the head, too. Thinks this boy here is her dead husband come back to life. Ain't that a crazy thing, Royce?"

Royce made a noise of affirmation while he consumed the snakemeat.

Matthew thought he should say something in Quinn's defense, yet he knew not what to say. Suddenly Quinn let go of his arm and stepped forward, and she lifted her chin in defiance of the rough-hewn men around the fire and she said, "I pity you."

The three words, quietly spoken, brought down silence.

"Where are your women?" she asked them. "Where are your wives? Why aren't they here with you? Because you didn't want 'em, or because they don't care whether you come back home or not? They know what's said about this river...this swamp. They must not love you very much, to let you come out here...and them not with you, to see you through this. Well, I'm here with Daniel..." She hesitated, struggling inwardly. "*Matthew*," she corrected. "And I am going to see him through. You will never know what *real* love is. You will never touch it, or hear it spoken in a voice. That's why I pity you...every one of you poor wretched men."

To this, one of the men across the fire—Matthew thought it was the red-haired Morgan—lifted his leg and let utter a reply from between his buttocks, which brought a gale of laughter from the gallery. But the laughter did not last very long, and afterward the silence seemed as heavy as a gravestone.

Quinn said nothing else; she backed away from the fire, and her arm found Matthew's. He was perplexed and unsure of what to do about this girl. It was a problem he didn't know how to solve. But in the meantime he was glad she was beside him, for he did have to lean upon her lest his legs weaken.

"Daylight soon," said Royce. He wiped his lips with the scratched and bloodied left forearm. Matthew noted that the day was indeed coming, faintly, but it was going to be a gray morning. "An hour's rest, then I say we move out together. Comb the woods better that way. Should get 'em 'fore they make the grassland."

"Fine with me," Stamper replied. "But I'm still plannin' on gettin' me some ears...*and* some of that Kincannon money."

Matthew couldn't stand up any longer. As he sank down, both Quinn and Magnus kept him from a hard fall. He settled with his back against a tree, and Quinn sat close beside him. His head was spinning, his focus blurred. He knew that Gunn had surely told Royce the whole story of what had happened in the chapel. *If I had my way that damn Granny Pegg would be swingin' from a rope right now.* Yes, if Royce had his way. Royce and Gunn feared the slaves might be captured, their brands read, and then returned to the Green Sea. If Abram had a chance to defend himself before Mrs. Kincannon, and with Granny Pegg's story plus the evidence of the broken compress…it wouldn't go well for the two captains. Yet out here, Matthew could prove nothing.

Matthew was further perplexed by something Quinn had said, and he pondered this as he slipped away from the world.

Something about Daniel. His death.

Taken, she'd said. *By the beast. It fell on my Daniel*, she'd said, *and he was gone*. Matthew slept, as heat lightning streaked across the dark gray sky above and the River of Souls ran its ancient, twisting course.

FOURTEEN

THE searchers, twenty in all including the girl from Rotbottom, moved through the wilderness in a long row so as to cover the most ground. Quinn carried her water gourd and stayed close to Matthew, who still staggered and felt lightheaded after barely an hour's sleep. Beside Matthew walked Magnus, the bearded bear keeping an eye on him if he started to fall. Matthew carried the short-bladed sword, which felt as heavy as an anvil to his weary arm.

The early morning sky was plated with thick gray clouds, cutting the light to a grim haze. Every so often thunder would rumble and lightning flared, yet no rain fell. The woods were a tangle of vines, thorns and underbrush, the ground sometimes swampy and sometimes hard, and the going was slow. The torches had guttered and started to burn down to blue flames, but Stamper was carrying a leather bag strapped to his shoulder that held a supply of rags soaked with his own mixture of flammables, and from these the torches were revived. The more light to pierce this gloom, the better. From where he was positioned in the row, Matthew could see only Joel Gunn under the torch the man was carrying, Seth Lott and Magnus to his left, Quinn right beside him, and then through the thicket on his right the red-haired Morgan and an older man with gray hair and a full gray beard streaked with white. This man was armed to the teeth, with musket, sword and dagger. The other men on either side were obscured by the woods and the low light, though occasionally the glint of another torch could be seen through the trees.

Matthew spoke to Quinn as they walked. "You think Daniel's spirit is in me? That he's become some *part* of me?" He waited for her to nod. "*Why*?" he asked. "Do I look like him? Is there something about me that reminds you of him?"

She took a moment in answering. Then, "You do look like him… some. But there's more to it than that. There…was a knowin'. A feelin' that I should leave my house and get to the river, because…*you* were comin' back. Because after all my waitin'…finally…this was the night. I brushed my hair out and tried to make myself pretty for you. I didn't know what you would look like…or what your name would be, or if you'd remember me at all, but I knew when I saw your boat pull over…I thought…*this* must be him. And then I heard your voice, and I saw your face. Yes, you do look like him. In the eyes. The way you carry yourself. With dignity, like he did. With a purpose, like he did. I knew he was going to come back to me, if he had to break out of Heaven and use the body of another man to do it. I knew this, deep in my heart." She looked at him and gave a lopsided little grin. "You think I'm as crazy as a two-headed dog, don't you?"

"I think you've wished for something so strongly that you believe it's true," Matthew replied. "What do your mother and father think about this?"

"They don't. I never knew my pa. My ma liked her drink strong and her men wild. A few years ago she got full of one and ran off with the other. Goin' to Charles Town, she said. Be back directly, she said. And him in his wagon full of 'gator skins, 'cause he was mighty good with a spear and a knife. Said she'd be back directly, but she never came back."

"You were married to Daniel by then?"

"No, not then. I was left on my own. But soon after that, Daniel came to Rotbottom like any outsider does…to hunt the 'gators. Get their skins, get paid for 'em in the big town. We met at a dance, on a night in May. But Daniel was an educated man, and soon after we met he decided his callin' was to start a school for the young ones—teach 'em readin' and such—and give up the huntin'. You'll remember, in time. I know he'll bring the memories back."

Matthew sighed. Her conviction that he had been 'possessed,' if that was the correct term, by the spirit of her dead Daniel was—for the moment, at least—unshakeable. She was desperate and out of her mind. He couldn't go any further along that route, but as they pushed onward through the woods he decided he needed to ask about one more thing that had piqued his interest.

"The beast," Matthew said. "You said Daniel was *taken* by a beast that came out of the smoke. What did you mean by that?"

"I meant what I said," was the firm reply. Lightning speared through the clouds to earth and distant thunder rumbled like a bass drumbeat. "It's called the Soul Cryer. Sobs like a little child."

Matthew said nothing for a moment, as he had run into thornbrush and was picking his way carefully forward even as the thorns pricked at his shirt and trousers. He was recalling Granny Pegg's warning and the sound he'd heard at the village of the Dead in Life. "All right," he said. "But what *is* it?"

"Nobody's ever really seen it up close and lived. Just glimpses from a distance. Seems to be about the size of a man. Mottled colors, brown and black. Can run on four legs and walk upright on two." She glanced at him to make sure he was listening seriously, which he was. "First heard about it killin' a man when I was ten. Took him from a huntin' party. They found his bones couple of months later. Brought 'em back to town in a sack. They were all broken and had teeth marks all over 'em, I remember that. But sometimes they never find the bodies or bones. They never found my Daniel. And they *have* found bodies with just the throat ripped out, or the face chewed away or the heart gone. The Soul Cryer's a meat-eater, but it kills for pleasure too."

Magnus had been close enough to hear most of this conversation, and now he came a little closer. "You talkin' about the demon thing supposed to live up in here? Somethin' the witch made and let loose? That would be a good story, except what I hear is that the thing wasn't around until six or seven years ago. It's just an animal, is all. Likely a panther."

"Could be," said Quinn. "But the colors aren't right. Not brown *and* black. They say its skin looks scaly...like a snake's. And walkin' on two legs, which somebody from Rotbottom swore he saw at a distance? There are plenty of deer and wild boar in these woods. Why does it want to hunt men?"

"Because men can be more careless than deer and wild boar. They get out here huntin' and they forget to look at what's comin' up behind 'em."

"The Soul Cryer's as much part of this swamp as the river itself," Quinn said. "It's a cursed thing too, born of pain and bound to give pain. Whether a witch made it or not, or where it came from, I don't know, but I know what sufferin' it can cause. When you hear that thing cryin', you'd best guard your life."

As much as a short-bladed sword could do against a man-killing predator of supposedly supernatural nature, Matthew thought, but then again...he didn't believe in such things. Did he?

The searchers moved on. Overhead in the turbulent sky the lightning flared from clouds to earth and the sound of thunder seemed to shake the ground. No rain fell, and there was no relief from the stifling heat. Within the next hour a man on the left side of the row from Matthew and three beyond Magnus stepped into a bog that looked simply like a large puddle of grainy mud. He let out a series of shouts for help when it quickly took him down to his knees and like a viscous paste held him trapped there. Then it began to draw him downward still, and though the man panicked and fought against the thick embrace he could not pull free nor stop his slow submergence. The others ringed around to watch, keeping their distance from what Matthew realized was a quicksand pit. Stamper somewhat redeemed himself for the killing of Jackson by taking command of the situation, ordering Bovie, Magnus and a couple of others to find the largest fallen treelimb they could handle, drag it over and throw it into the pit for the unfortunate citizen of Jubilee—whose name was Tom Coleman, Matthew learned—to grab hold of and therefore pull himself up to solid ground. This endeavor, which took the weakening Coleman another half hour to complete before Magnus reached out and pulled him fully free, was a hard-earned lesson to all not to walk so confidently—or foolishly—into any body of standing water in these woods, no matter how shallow it seemed to be. Many small branches suddenly were in use to probe the treacherous earth. Matthew found his own and both Quinn and Magnus also acquired them, and then as the storm above continued to throw fireworks from the clouds and sharp rebukes from what seemed the angry voice of God someone asked a question:

"Where's Doyle?"

"What'd you say, Ellis?" Stamper asked the man who'd spoken.

"Doyle," the man repeated. He was thin and brown-bearded, his eyes sunken in nests of wrinkles, and he held an axe at his side. He scanned the assembly, which included Royce and Gunn, Lott and Morgan and all the rest…except the one he sought. "John Doyle. He was walkin' to the right of me. Know he must've heard Tom's shoutin'. Where is he?"

"Maybe takin' a shit in the woods," said Bovie. "Who gives a care where he is, anyway?"

"*I* care," said the other. "John's my friend. He was maybe thirty feet away from me." He turned to the right and faced the wilderness. He cupped his free hand to his mouth. "*John!*" he shouted. "*Where are you, man?*"

There was no reply.

"*John! Holler back!*"

Still nothing.

"We've got to move on." Royce swiped his hand through the air to ward off the biting and humming insects, of which there were legion around every man and the one female. "Doyle's got himself lost, maybe."

"He was right *beside* me," Ellis said, as if explaining this fact to either an infant or an idiot. "Saw him through the trees. Then I heard Tom and I came over here. Figured John would follow." He shouted once more into the thicket: "*John Doyle! Answer me!*"

John Doyle did not answer.

"Maybe we should look for him?" Magnus asked.

"You do that," was Royce's response. "Take your boy and his girl and whoever else wants to waste time, and go lookin' for that damn fool. Gunn and me are headin' on. Anybody else?"

The voices to head on were almost unanimous. But Ellis, Doyle's friend, stood his ground. "You go on, then. All of you. I don't know what's happened to John, but I'm goin' to find him. You won't at least *wait* for me?"

Stamper said, "You can catch up. Royce is right. We need to keep movin'."

"All right," Ellis answered, resignedly. "But I'd sure think that if any of you was lost...or maybe stepped in another of those suck pits, you'd want a friend to come help you."

Matthew was close to saying he would help, but his task demanded that he stay with the larger group. Ellis turned away, and as he did Quinn said, "Mister? Don't go."

The man hesitated. "What?"

"Don't go," she repeated. "It's not safe."

"Oh, she's talkin' about that *thing*," Stamper said. "The Soul Cryer." He spoke it with the sarcasm of a twisted lip. "Everybody who believes in *that*, believes in every ghost story told about this damn country. You believe in that, Ellis?"

Ellis paused a little too long, but then he said, "No, course not."

"Beggin' your pardon," said Quinn, "but either of you men even been this far up the river? I know those who have. I know what they say they've seen, and I know they're not liars. So...Mr. Ellis...I wouldn't go out there alone. It's not safe."

"Let's move!" Royce demanded. "Oh, hell with it! Gunn, come on!" He forged ahead into the brush and Gunn followed. Stamper and Bovie strode forward, and the other men also continued on, only Matthew noted they seemed not so quick to spread out as they'd been before.

Ellis looked from the girl to Matthew and Magnus. "Either of you gimme some help?"

"We've got to move on, too," Magnus answered. "Sorry."

Ellis nodded. He stood for a moment as if at the crossroads of decision, watching the torches of the men move away through the trees and then staring off into the dark woods that had taken his friend. Finally, he leaned his axe against his shoulder and walked off into the thicket, and he called, "*John Doyle! Gimme a holler!*"

Magnus, Matthew and Quinn left him. In another few minutes they caught up with the rest of the group, who'd run into another barrier of thorns. It was slow and painful going, and suddenly Matthew found himself side-by-side with Royce as they picked their way through.

Royce glanced at him with what might have been a sneer. "Shouldn't be out here, Corbett. Should've gone back to Charles Town. That wound you've got might cost your arm."

"I'll have it tended to when I get back," Matthew replied. And he had to add: "I'm sure Dr. Stevenson can put a compress on it."

There was no visible reaction from Royce. His voice was silky. "You know him?"

"I do." Matthew winced as thorns plucked at his shirt and bit his sides. Quinn was right behind him, and he was doing his best to cleave a path for her but it was impossible for her not to be bitten as well. "I saw him in Charles Town yesterday morning. He mentioned...*ouch!*...having come to the Green Sea to put a compress on a patient's forearm. I'm guessing that was you?"

"It was. Horse nipped me. Whipped her good, too, taught her a lesson she won't forget."

"You must have a way with females," Matthew said.

Royce stopped in the midst of the sharp-edged thorns, which boiled up black and green all around. He turned toward Matthew, his smile cold. "Gunn tells me you were where you didn't belong, askin' questions. Y'know, you're *still* where you don't belong. In pretty damn bad shape, too." He pushed at Matthew's wounded shoulder with a thick forefinger, which caused Matthew to flinch and draw back. "Just what're you *doin'* out here, anyway? Why is this your business?"

"I want to see justice done."

"So do I. And I intend that it *be* done."

"I'd like to see the slaves captured and returned alive," said Matthew. "Is that your aim as well?"

"It is. Abram should hang for his crime. The others too, for helpin' him run." Royce began picking his way forward again, and Matthew followed.

"The problem *is*," Matthew said, "that very few of these men you've enticed with the promise of Kincannon gold share that view. They'd rather kill the slaves out here and take the ears back. Does that not bother you?"

"What *bothers* me are fool questions." Royce's voice had become tight, his entire body like a charge about to explode. He grasped the thorns with bloody fingers and shoved them aside. Above the dangerous earth the dangerous sky flashed and muttered. "I needed men to help me. Sure wasn't gonna come out here, just me and Gunn. *Never* find 'em that way."

Matthew was silent for awhile, as they worked their way through. He heard Magnus give a curse, a distance off to his right, as a sharp edge or two pricked the mountainous man. "You *do* know," Matthew continued on, "that Sarah was teaching Abram to read in that barn, over many nights? I'm supposing Gunn told you?"

"Don't matter," was the quick response. "I don't know *why* that damn buck killed the girl, but he did and he's got to hang for it."

Matthew was formulating his next question—*What happened to your compress, Mr. Royce?*—when a shout came from the left.

"Hey! Hey! Over here! *Quick!*"

They made their painful way in that direction and found six other men already there, including Stamper, Bovie and Gunn. The old bearded man who was armed to the teeth was showing something that had gotten caught by the thorns. A small piece of gray cloth, Matthew saw it was. Most likely torn from a shirt.

"They've been through here!" the old man said excitedly. "Look how them thorns are broken! They been right through this way... prob'ly not too long past!"

"Steady, Foxworth," Stamper said. "Mind your heart." He pulled the bit of cloth free and smelled it. "Fresh skin stink. Maybe an hour old. Gunn, give me your torch." He took it from the Green Sea captain and angled it toward the ground. The earth was hard here, but it was evident the underbrush had been crushed by bodies passing through. "On their trail," Stamper said. He knelt to examine the brush more closely. "Hm," he grunted. "One of 'em's draggin'. Slowin' 'em down." He stood up but did not return the torch to Gunn. "That's good for *us*. I'll take the lead from here on. Bovie, get a torch and move on out to the left maybe forty feet. Royce, you do the same on the right. Everybody else, spread out as you please. Not far behind 'em now. Move quiet. Keep your guns and swords ready, we may come up on 'em anytime."

Matthew could keep silent no longer. "Mr. Stamper, I want you to know that I've been empowered by Mrs. Kincannon to make sure the runaways are returned *unharmed.* It's important to her—and to *me*—that these men aren't killed out here. Do you understand that?"

Stamper fixed Matthew with a narrow-eyed stare. Bovie gave a short, sharp laugh and even Seth Lott, standing nearby, grinned as if this were the ravings of a pure lunatic.

"Ain't *men*," said Gunn. "Told you. They're animals."

"I ain't takin' nobody back!" Foxworth said, coming up beside Matthew. "Takin' ears, is all. The swamp can keep the bodies!"

"Killed that girl," said Morgan, "they all deserve to die."

"Hold on, hold on!" Royce had gotten a torch from another man, and now he added its glaring light to the scene. "Matthew, we all want to do the right thing. We *know* Abram killed Sarah. Gunn caught him with the knife, standin' over the body just after he'd stabbed her. Now...Mr. Kincannon has been laid low by this, and Mrs. Kincannon is near out of her mind. We *want* to take the skins back for a proper hangin'...but an awful lot can happen before we get 'em there. That's just how it is."

"I want 'em taken back alive too." Magnus had taken a position at Matthew's side, with Quinn behind him. "Mrs. Kincannon's got some questions she needs to ask Abram."

Matthew wished Magnus had not said this, but the cat had jumped from its bag. "She wants to know *why* Abram killed Sarah," Matthew clarified. "She can't rest until she knows."

Royce stared forcefully into Matthew's eyes. "Well...maybe we can find out *for* her, if it comes to that. But *you* rest easy, sir. We know these animals and you don't. We know what they would do to us, if they could. So...we'll do our best to obey the lady's biddin', but the reality of it is...we're out here in these thorns, and she's there in that big house. A long way off. And sometimes even the rich folks in the big house can't always get what they want." He dismissed Matthew with a shrug of his shoulders. "You leadin' the way, Stamper? Let's get movin', then."

They pushed on through the thorns, following the crushed track of the runaways. Several of the men gave Matthew and Magnus jeering looks as they passed, as if daring them to step between a musket, a sword, and a slave.

"We ought to go back," Quinn said, clutching at Matthew's good arm. "Let them go on, find those slaves and do whatever they're gonna do. You can't stop 'em."

Matthew thought that by now he couldn't find his way back, even if he wanted to. "I have to *try*," he told her quietly, though what he truly desired was a bed of moss and another two hours of sleep. His vision kept blurring in and out and his legs felt near collapse. But he had to keep going, and that was that. The Great One would be proud of him...or else be telling him to get the hell out of this situation because he was an addle-pated fool.

He followed the others, and Quinn followed her Daniel, and Magnus snorted flying insects from his nostrils and also pressed onward.

Fifteen

NOT ten minutes after passing through the last of the thorns, Matthew heard the *crack* of a gunshot.

It was over on the left, in the storm-darkened woods. "Who fired that?" Stamper hollered in the echo of the shot. Beside him stood Royce and Gunn, both with their torches and secrets.

"Seth Lott!" came the shouted answer, from maybe sixty feet away. The voice was raw and tremulous, had lost its smooth Christian sheen. "Come over here, quick!"

"You get a skin?"

"Just come over here! *Now*, for the love of God!" A note of panic flared.

"Got his codpiece on too tight," Stamper muttered, and then he headed in the direction of Lott's voice. Royce and Gunn followed, and behind them Matthew, Magnus and Quinn. Other men emerged from the woods to see if Lott had earned his ten pounds. But when the group reached Lott, where the smell of gunpowder was thick in the air and wisps of blue smoke still roiled, the black-garbed and sweating preacher was standing with Caleb Bovie, who shone a torch upon something lying in the green underbrush.

"What is that?" Stamper asked.

It was a body, Matthew saw. The boots were muddy and the soles nearly worn through.

"Who is it?" Royce stepped forward for a closer look with his own torch, and then when he got it he immediately stopped in his tracks, his mouth hanging half-open.

"It's Fitzy," Bovie rasped. Matthew recalled the thin young man who'd obediently sliced a piece of snakemeat for Stamper. Except now the lower part of his face had been ripped away, and most of his throat. The eyes were open in a frozen stare above the mass of bloodied flesh. Quinn saw what Matthew had seen, and pulled back. "Christ Jesus...somethin' tore him up!" Bovie looked at Lott and then to Stamper. "He was between me and Seth! I didn't hear nothin', 'til that shot went off!"

"He was walking ahead of me and to the side. Maybe twenty feet away." Lott's voice was shaking. "Had his pistol in his hand, but...it happened so *quick*."

"What happened?" Stamper demanded. "What'd you see?"

"I don't know. Just...something was all of a sudden *there*, where the dark is. I couldn't make it out, but it jumped on Fitzy. I heard..." The preacher had to pause a moment, with a trembling hand to his mouth. "I heard the bones break. It shook him...hard...like a rag-doll. I shot at it...all that smoke, and it was gone. Fitzy...he gave a shudder and a...a strangling noise...and that was all."

"Well what in hell *was* it?" Royce asked. "A panther?"

Lott's eyes were watery and dazed, and he struggled to speak. "Maybe. I don't know. It was big. And...it did not move right, to be a panther."

"What does that mean?" Stamper's voice was harsh. "How did it move?"

"I...can't say. Like...a jerking motion. Unnatural." Lott stared at Quinn before he returned his attention to Stamper. "It was... brown and black. Streaked...blotched. Its head...also unnatural. And...Stamper, whatever it was...Soul Cryer or—"

"Stop that!" Stamper said. "Hear me? Stop it! There's no such beast!"

"Whatever it was," the preacher went on, "it came at Fitzy on two legs...like a man."

"You don't know that for sure!" Royce's face had reddened, and he was nearly shouting it. "You didn't see enough to know that! Now stop your ghost stories, preacherman! A panther got Fitzgerald, is what I say! That's all!"

"Ain't that enough as it is?" asked Morgan, with a quick, flinching glance at the body. "I told you me, Whetters and Carr heard somethin' stalkin' us! I say we were lucky to get past that damn Indian village with our heads...but a panther out here...and maybe somethin' that's *more* than a panther?" He shook his head, as distant thunder rumbled from a sky that seemed to Matthew to be as dark as a coal mine. "More than I want to handle, no matter the money."

"Then don't handle it!" Royce shot back. "Get on your way! Course, a man alone tryin' to get back to his boat...that's a long walk, Morgan! But go on, we don't need you!"

Morgan looked to another man, standing beside Bovie. "Carr, you with me?" His gaze moved. "Whetters? Halleck, how about you? Not enough liquor in the world's worth your life."

The men Morgan had spoken to shifted in their tracks, their faces downcast.

"*I* shall go with you, Morgan," Lott suddenly said, his face glistening with sweat beneath the black tricorn. He managed another look at the body. "Yes. I'll go."

"Me, too," said a second citizen of Jubilee, who Matthew thought was the man named Whetters.

"I'm for it," said a third man—Carr, most likely—and the muddied Coleman, who carried a torch, announced, "Ain't worth dyin' for thirty pounds of gold. I'll go, too."

"Then *get*!" Royce snarled. "All you fools...and you're the biggest fool, preacherman! Yes, you go lead this flock of cowards home, and good riddance to you!" He swung his fevered gaze upon Matthew, Magnus and the girl. "Aren't you goin' with 'em? Now's your chance!"

"I'll stay," said Magnus. He regarded Matthew with his iron-gray eyes. "You ought to head on back. Both of you. I'll do what I can."

"Come on, Matthew." Quinn gripped his hand. "Come on, let's leave this place."

Matthew was torn. He was ready to head back, yes...but to leave was to let Royce and Gunn win this particular duel. He knew why Royce wanted him gone. Could Magnus with a rusted pistol stop the execution? Could he, himself, armed with only a short-bladed sword? One of the men—the bull-necked one with the blind left eye—was gathering up Fitzy's pistol and ammunition pouch, though he already carried a musket.

Matthew couldn't leave. Not even with the wound in his shoulder, his head still dazed and his spirit weary. It was against his nature to give up, to retreat to safety while danger threatened a friend... and he did consider Magnus Muldoon a friend. He couldn't leave without seeing this task through, however it might end. "I can't," he told Quinn. "You go, but I can't."

"I won't," she told him resolutely, and her hand tightened on his. "Not leavin' you. Not lettin' you leave me. Not this time, no."

"To Hell with fools and cowards!" Royce shouted at the other men as they started off, now eight in number. "You'd best watch your backs, that Soul Cryer'll be on you before you know it! Preacherman, I thought you trusted so much in *God*!"

Seth Lott turned from his path. "I do, Mr. Royce," he replied, trying to maintain his dignity in retreat, "but I trust Him also to tell me when it's time to go *home*. Let the slaves go, they'll likely die out here if they're not already dead. Let God deliver the justice, in His own way."

"Fuck that," Royce answered, and spat on the ground between them.

"Blessings on you," said the preacherman, and then he and the other seven men moved away into the thicket, with the torch-bearer in the lead.

"Let 'em go," said Stamper quietly, his face grim under the raven's feather hat. "Maybe whatever that thing is, it'll follow *them* instead of us. A panther, it's got to be. But...still...I don't like it."

"You thinkin' about goin' back, too?" Royce asked, his face flaming up again. "*You*, of all people? Runnin' from a ghost?"

"Mr. Royce," Matthew spoke up, "a ghost may have the power to frighten, but it doesn't have the power to tear a man's lower jaw and throat out, plus most likely have broken his neck before he fell. Would you want to look at that corpse again?"

Before Royce could respond, the one-eyed man who'd retrieved the pistol and ammunition bag asked, "We puttin' Fitzy under?"

"With what, Barrows? Our hands?" Stamper asked. "No. Sooner we move on, the better. Likely that thing'll come back to eat the body...and a full-bellied panther won't bother us. But we'd best stay together, much as we can. We string out too far...well, let's just don't do that."

Nine remained, including the girl from Rotbottom. There was Matthew, Magnus, Stamper, the aged and trigger-happy Foxworth, the one-eyed Barrows, Bovie, Royce and Gunn. They started off again with Stamper and Bovie in the lead under Stamper's torch, followed a few feet to the left side by Barrows, behind him Foxworth, then on the right side Royce and Gunn, Matthew and Quinn and Magnus. Lightning shot across the sky and the dark clouds roiled, but the wind was hot and dry.

Matthew found himself pushing through the woods beside Gunn, separated a short distance from Royce. He said in a guarded voice, "Granny Pegg tells a fascinating story."

Gunn gave no response. He stared straight ahead as he labored forward, his torch moving back and forth to penetrate the shadows, though he only succeeded in moving them around.

"About what goes on at the Green Sea," Matthew continued quietly. "About you and Royce, in particular."

Gunn gave a brief, harsh laugh but offered nothing else.

"I understand there was another captain at the Green Sea before you got there. His name was Jameson, I believe. Burned up in his house one night, it seems. How long have you and Royce known each other?"

Gunn's face was impassive. His lip might have curled, but that was all.

"Granny Pegg thinks you and Royce have worked together before," said Matthew. "At another plantation? More than one? Where did you two happen to meet?"

"Shut your hole, boy," came the muttered response. "Move away from me."

"I'm just asking," Matthew went on, as they worked through the green foliage. Vines trailed down from the branches and here and there fallen trees lay rotting like the bones of giants. "Seems you and Royce understand each other. What I mean to say is, he tells you what to do and you do it. A man could get in some serious trouble that way."

"I'm gonna give you three seconds to move," Gunn hissed through gritted teeth. "Then I'm gonna knock your goddamned head off."

"I'm not sure my friend Magnus would like that. But...very well, I'll move away. Give you room to breathe, sir. Room to *think*, too."

"Think about *what*, Corbett? Granny Pegg's made-up *tales*? Sure, she'd make up any kind of damn story to save her blood!"

"Possibly," Matthew agreed. "But think on this. I examined Sarah's body, with Mrs. Kincannon's permission. I found something interesting, Joel. It has to do with your good friend over there."

"Empty talk. That wound of yours is gettin' to your brain."

"I know about Molly Ann, too." Matthew ventured, still quietly. "He's probably told you? Bragged, I'm guessing."

Gunn gave Matthew a look that would've turned Medusa to stone, and then he veered away and crossed the distance between himself and Royce. Matthew watched as Gunn said something to his compatriot. Royce tilted his head toward the speaker, but gave no expression of concern. Gunn kept speaking for a few more seconds, and then Royce nodded but spared not even a glance at Matthew.

Was it possible to turn those two against each other? Matthew wondered. Gunn might be the weaker of them, and obviously the questions had rattled him. So...maybe Gunn's trigger could be pulled?

They continued on, as the sky above remained as dark as a witch's dream. As another hour passed and Stamper led them along a trail only he and Bovie could make out, Matthew felt his strength leaving him. He began to stagger, and as much as he fought it that quicker was his strength depleted. At last he took a step and the earth denied him balance, and as he fell he heard Quinn cry out behind him. He twisted his body so that he did not hit on his wounded shoulder, but even so the breath was knocked from him and he lay gasping amid the weeds and brush. Quinn knelt beside him to put a comforting hand to his forehead, and Magnus knelt down on the other side.

"I'm all right," Matthew said when he could get his breath back. His vision was blurred, but he saw that the others had stopped too.

"I can stand up, I'll be all right." But he couldn't stand, he couldn't get his legs under him, and he realized that without rest he could not go on.

"Leave him," Royce said to Stamper. "Let's keep movin', the skins can't be much further ahead."

"Let's go!" Gunn urged. "Wastin' time standin' here!"

With Magnus' help Matthew managed to sit upright, though his shoulders sagged and even the stubble on his face felt heavy. "Joel," he said. "Granny Pegg told me...Magnus and myself... *everything*."

"What're you goin' on about?" It was Royce who'd asked the question.

"She told Mrs. Kincannon, too," Matthew continued, with an effort. "There in the chapel. Joel...Mrs. Kincannon is waiting for some answers. It has to do...with what I found on Sarah's body."

"You found a half-dozen knife strikes, is what you found!" Royce said. "What else was there?"

"I'll let Mrs. Kincannon ask that question, when we get back." Matthew directed his blurred gaze to Stamper. "You may be hunting an innocent man. I don't think Abram did the killing. That's why they have to be brought back alive. Anything else would not be justice, but murder."

"I'll stand for what Matthew says," Magnus added. "More questions to be answered."

"Sarah's killer is yet unproven," Matthew said. "But...that will be remedied, when we get back to the Green Sea."

"Abram killed Sarah!" Royce almost spat it. "It's proven! Damn buck must've gone crazy! You think somethin' like that's never happened on any other plantation?"

Matthew smiled faintly. "Ah! Did it happen on another plantation where you and Joel worked?"

"Hold on, now!" Stamper frowned. "Boy, you're sayin' it was somebody *else* killed the girl? But Joel saw that buck with the bloody knife, standin' over the body!" He looked to Gunn. "Ain't that right?"

"A good question," Matthew said when Gunn's reply didn't come. "Did you see him with the knife, or not?"

"He did!" Royce spoke up. "If he says he did, he did...and he's already *said* it!"

"I'd like to hear it from Gunn again," said Magnus. "Go ahead, everybody's listenin'."

Gunn's mouth opened and then closed. He stared at the ground as if the stones and weeds might guide him in his speech. Matthew knew what he must be thinking: he could swing for helping conceal a murder, if he was found out...and he had no way of knowing what Matthew had discovered on Sarah's body, or what Mrs. Kincannon's questions were. Gunn was a man in a very precarious position, and he knew Griffin Royce had put him there.

Still, Gunn did not—could not—speak.

"Hey!" Bovie suddenly said, and he sniffed the air. "I'm smellin' *smoke*!"

Indeed, a breath of dry wind brought the odor to all. Stamper narrowed his eyes and looked ahead. Matthew followed his gaze; there was no sight of a fire through the trees, yet the smell was certainly wood burning.

"Campfire?" Royce asked.

"Strong smell," said Stamper. "Could be lightnin's hit a tree, set it afire. Whatever it is, it's not far away."

"We should be movin'," Royce prodded. "Leave Corbett here, if he can't go on. Muldoon, you and the girl want to stay with him, that's fine by me. I think we're gettin' close to the skins, and I won't be slowed down."

"Mr. Stamper," said Matthew, "I would remind you...that the reward is for the runaways...dead or *alive*. Mrs. Kincannon wants them returned alive, as I do...for Abram to answer some questions. Is that too much to ask?"

Stamper thought about it. He ran a hand across his grizzled chin. "No," he said at last. "Not too much. All right then, we'll take 'em alive. No ears cut off, no harm done 'em."

"Ha!" was Royce's response. "Those animals won't go back so easy! You'll see!"

"Go with them, Magnus," Matthew urged. "I'm used up for awhile. You *have* to go."

"Leave you and her with that *thing* out here? No, I'm stayin'."

"You have to go," Matthew repeated, with some force behind it. "To make sure, Magnus. You have to." He lifted his sword. "I've got this."

"Little of nothin'."

"*Better* than nothing."

"Losin' time," said Barrows. "Let's move."

Bovie turned away and started off. Royce followed. Gunn hesitated only briefly before he went, and then Barrows and Foxworth. Stamper gave a long weary sigh, and he said, "Sorry to leave you, but we've got to go on. We'll come back this way, soon as we get 'em. Muldoon, you comin' or not?"

Magnus nodded. "I'm comin'. Matthew," he said, "you two stay right *here.* Don't move, and keep a sharp eye out. All right?"

"We will," Quinn answered. "You be careful."

"Always," said the bearded mountain, and he followed Stamper into the dark woods.

"I'll just rest a little while," Matthew said. His voice was becoming slurred. "I'll be all right...soon as I rest."

"Put your head in my lap," Quinn offered, and Matthew accepted. He stretched out upon the ground and his eyes closed. He felt Quinn's hand running back and forth through his hair. *I am not Daniel,* he thought as he sank into the silence. Then he felt her lean forward and very tenderly kiss his forehead, and he let go of this world and fell away.

SIXTEEN

HE was standing in a room in which there were five doors. They were all ordinary doors, with ordinary handles, yet Matthew sensed that behind each was something extraordinary... and perhaps terrifying.

For better or for worse, he was compelled to open the first on his left, which opened onto a scene he remembered well: Rachel Howarth in the dirty cell in Fount Royal, throwing off her gray cloak and hood to reveal her naked body, and saying defiantly to the world *Here is the witch.*

Suddenly Matthew's hand was on the next door, and opening it displayed the Prussian swordsman Count Anton Mannerheim Dahlgren, he of the blond hair, gray teeth and deadly command of the rapier. He whom Matthew had bested, broken his left wrist and sent him reeling into a fishpond. He who had seemingly vanished from the world, and was yet out there somewhere in the shadows. In this instance, however, Dahlgren had the use of both arms and was coming at him, teeth bared, with a rapier. Matthew slammed the door in his face.

The third door showed a wagon travelling under a sky threatening rain, and a man with a patchwork beard sitting in the back with his eyes closed, his arms and legs confined by irons. A fly landed at the corner of the man's mouth. The man did not move, nor did his eyes open. The fly began to crawl across the lower lip, unhurriedly, and when it reached the center the man's mouth moved in a blur. There was a quick sucking sound, and then Matthew heard the faintest *crunch*. The eyes of the killer Tyranthus Slaughter opened and fixed upon Matthew, and when the man grinned there was a bit of crushed fly on one of his front teeth.

Matthew also slammed that door.

The fourth door opened upon a dining hall, and sitting in a chair before the assembled guests was a man who was not a man, but appeared to be an automaton, a wiry-looking construction of a man dressed in a white suit with gold trim and whorls of gold upon the suit jacket and trouser legs. It wore a white tricorn, also trimmed in gold, white stockings and black shoes with gold buckles. The hands were concealed in flesh-colored fabric gloves, and a flesh-colored fabric cowl covered the face and head yet showed the faintest impression of nose-tip, cheekbones and eye-sockets. With a sound of meshing gears and the rattling of a chain the figure began to move, the head turning...slowly...left to right and back again, the right hand rising up to press against the chin as if measuring a thought, and then from the bizarre figure issued a tinny voice with a hint of a rasp and whine, *One of you has been brought here to die.*

Matthew closed that door firmly, but with an unfirm hand.

He stood staring at the fifth door.

Behind that one...what? He feared that one, perhaps more than any other. Behind it was...something he had never known before, something that perhaps he could not survive. Something that perhaps would remove Matthew Corbett from life itself, and distance him from everything and everyone he had ever known and loved.

That door...the fifth one...he could not bear to open, yet it must be opened because he realized it was his destiny.

He reached for it and took the handle. He had no choice but to open it, and see what was ahead for him...if he could indeed take the sight of his future and not lose who and what he was in the present.

He began to open the door.

Wisps of smoke drifted out. He smelled the smoke, very strongly.

"Matthew? Matthew?"

He opened his eyes. He was lying on the ground, with his head on Quinn's lap, and the odor of smoke was not confined to the realm of dreams. Indeed, smoke had drifted into the storm-dark woods and moved sinuously around them like spirits of the dead.

"Matthew?" Quinn said again, shaking his uninjured shoulder.

And he realized then that they were not alone.

He sat up.

Standing not twenty feet away in the thicket were three black men. Two were younger, and supported an older man between them. The older man, who had a pate of close-cropped white hair and a frizz of white beard, looked to be in pain; he was putting no weight on his left leg. The elder was thin, with a seamed face that looked as if it had suffered many hardships, but the two younger men were thicker-bodied and fit-looking. One was bald, with heavy eyebrows and a long chin adorned by a dark patch of beard, while the other had a high forehead, high cheekbones and expressive eyes that also held the darkness of suffering. The elder man wore brown trousers and a gray shirt, his clothing tattered by thorns. The other two were dressed in similar brown trousers, both with patched knees. The bald one was wearing a dark green shirt and the other man a white shirt stained with sweat. All their clothes were much the worse for wear, having been torn at by the claws of the wilderness.

They stood staring at Matthew and Quinn, as if trying to decide what to do. Tendrils of smoke crawled through the woods around them, and not too far behind them the smoke was thick enough to blur out the trees.

Matthew spoke. "Which one of you is Abram?"

They didn't answer, nor did they move.

"Mars," Matthew said to the elder, "I've spoken to your grandmother. Help me stand up, please," he requested of Quinn, and she did. He wavered on his feet but found his balance. "You have to go back to the Green Sea. Abram?"

The man with the expressive, suffering eyes said, "Yes."

"I've come out here to find you. There's a group of men looking for you…all of you. Among them Royce and Gunn. They don't

want you to tell the Kincannons what you know. If they can, I think they'll try to kill you."

"Likely try," said Abram.

"Who're *you*, suh?" Mars asked, pain etched on his face. "Out here with a *girl*?"

"My name is Matthew Corbett. I'm from Charles Town, I was nearby and I heard the bell ringing last night. This is Quinn Tate, from Rotbottom." *My wife*? he almost said.

"Where are the other men?" Tobey asked. "How many?"

"They've gone on ahead. Seven in number, but one of them knows the truth too and he's here as I am...to prevent any more killing."

"The *truth*?" Abram asked, his eyes narrowing. "What truth do you know?"

"I *believe*," Matthew said, "that Griffin Royce was jealous of the attention Sarah was showing you. I believe he thought something else was going on between you in the barn. She was teaching you to *read*, is that correct?"

Abram nodded. "Against the law. Against the law for me to be out of the quarter and in that barn, too. A whippin' offense. Miss Sarah said she'd protect me. Cap'n Royce told me to stay away from her, or he'd fix things. Hurt one of the women, he said, and I'd be to blame for it. I told Miss Sarah...but she say, not gonna let Cap'n Royce tell her what to do. Couldn't tell Massa Kincannon, though. Against the law, all of it."

"Mrs. Kincannon knows all that now," Matthew said. "I believe also that at the Green Sea I can prove Royce killed Sarah and left that knife in her for you to pull out. He knew you'd be walking to the quarter that way. Then he waited and watched. He *wanted* you to run, to look guilty. But what are you doing *here*? Why are you doubling back?"

"Pap broke his ankle, happened last night," Tobey answered. "Figured there'd be men behind us, but didn't know how far they'd follow. We talked 'bout it. Ran into a fire up ahead, saw trees burnin'. Wind's movin' it toward the river. Heard the Soul Cryer last night, too." He had an expression of anguish on his face. "We don't know where we're goin', suh. We thought we could run away...but there ain't no runnin' away. River of Souls leads on and on, but it don't take you nowhere...you just get more lost. Granny tried to help us, said for us to get away and keep goin'…but where do you go, when there ain't nowhere? She was wrong, suh. So we talked 'bout it, and we thought on it. With Pap's hurt…and with what's out there…we're goin' back. Face what has to be faced. That's the all of it."

Matthew reasoned that Stamper would read their trail and see the slaves had turned back, if he hadn't already. He didn't care to wait for Royce and Gunn. Smoke was drifting through the woods and was caught like mist in the tops of the trees, but yet there was no sight nor sound of a moving fire. "We have fresh water," he said, motioning to Quinn's water gourd. "Have some if you like. Then we'll start back."

Quinn took the gourd's strap off her shoulder, uncorked it and offered it to the three men as they came forward. Mars winced with pain as he was supported between his sons, for his injured foot snagged on the brush in spite of their efforts to lift him up. He was indeed leaving a clear trail for Stamper to follow.

"Can't figure *you*, suh," said Mars to Matthew after he'd had his drink. "You say you can prove Abram didn't kill Sarah? How?"

"Leave that to me when we get there."

"Look hardly able to walk y'self, forgive me for sayin'. All that blood, you took a bad injury."

"I'll survive it. Royce and Gunn found your boat. We've got to get back to it. Can you find the way?" Matthew was asking both Abram and Tobey.

"Best way is to get to the river and follow it down," said Abram. "We go southwest, we'll likely get there in maybe an hour or two."

Matthew nodded. It was going to be slow travelling, with Mars's broken ankle. He took a drink of water from the gourd and so did Quinn, who then corked it again and put its strap back around her shoulder. She gave Matthew an encouraging smile, and he had the thought that she was a ragged angel, come to see him through this ordeal. "Ready?" he asked the runaways, and Abram pointed out the direction they should go. Matthew started off, with Quinn right behind him and the two sons helping their father struggle on.

"There's the fire," said Stamper, as smoke swirled around himself and the other six men. A line of trees was ablaze about a half-mile ahead, and the dry wind that had picked up was blowing it in their direction. As they watched, they could see hungry flames jumping from tree to tree. "Lightnin' strike either last night or early this mornin'," he said. "That timber's dry, gonna flare up in a hurry."

The smoke was thickening, burning both the eyes and the lungs. Bovie coughed some of it out and said, "Trail keeps on goin' that way. What'll we do, Stamper?"

"I don't like bein' out here with a fire comin'. That damn thing jumps, it'll get all around you. Could be the skins turned in another direction." He looked past Magnus at Royce. "What do you say, Griff?"

"I say we follow the trail. If it turns, we'll see it."

"Keep goin'," was Foxworth's advice. "Come too far not to get 'em."

"Fire's movin' this way," said Stamper, a muscle working in his jaw. "Could be it's already burned their trail up, we'll never find 'em."

"We won't find 'em by standin' here." Royce looked up at the dark gray sky. "Maybe it'll rain, put the flames out. Come on," he said impatiently, "we've got to move."

"Don't like that fire," Barrows said, angling his good eye at the others. "Wind's pickin' up, too. Not sure we ought to—"

He was interrupted by the sound of a baby crying, off to their right. Instantly all firearms were aimed in the direction of the dense thicket, but nothing alive could be seen in there. The crying noise went on for perhaps five or six seconds, ending with what sounded like a harsh sob of despair.

There was silence, but for the noise of the distant fire eating its way through the wilderness. All the men were frozen in place. Then Magnus heard something coming through the woods...something big and heavy. "Listen!" he said, and heard his own voice tremble: "*Listen!*"

Whatever it was, it was crashing through the underbrush and coming fast. Royce retreated, standing behind and to Gunn's left with his musket raised and ready. Foxworth backed up until his spine met a tree. Barrows' single eye had widened. Stamper and

Bovie both stood their ground, as smoke swept past and the devil's dry wind blew toward the River of Souls.

Magnus' finger was on the trigger of the rusty pistol. He hoped it wouldn't explode in his hand…but whatever was coming, it was going to need more than a pistol ball to stop it.

From the dark, smoke-swept woods burst into the torchlight not just one beast, but three.

Magnus fired. So too did Gunn, Barrows and Stamper, nearly at the same time. Bovie, armed with only the sword, let out a holler and slashed at the first creature that came through…a large buck with a spread of antlers, followed by two does. In the clouds of blue gunsmoke, the buck staggered under the impact of the shots but kept going past the men.

Perhaps two seconds later, Royce's musket went off. Joel Gunn's forehead blew out as the ball that had entered the back of his head made its exit.

"Christ, man!" Stamper shouted. Gunn's knees were buckling, blood streaming down the wreckage of the face. The torch fell from the left hand and the body pitched forward into the brush, shuddered a few times and was still. "Christ!" Stamper shouted again. His face had gone as pallid as gray clay. "Are you *crazy*? You killed him!"

"My gun misfired!" Royce shouted back. "I was aimin' at that thing…pulled the trigger and the pan didn't flash! Then he stepped in the way just as it went off! You all saw it! Didn't you?" He looked around with wild eyes, his chest outthrust as if to dare them to disagree, and Magnus Muldoon realized that it *might* have happened as Royce said, but it was a mighty good way for Royce to take advantage of the moment. With Gunn dead, so had died someone who knew too much.

Stamper started to protest again, but a man who'd already killed another one on this jaunt didn't have much room for indignation. "Damn!" he said, and he took his hat off to wipe the sweat from his forehead with a dirty sleeve. "Royce…I don't know about this… Fitzy dead…that fire comin'…now *this*…I don't know."

Royce was already reloading his still-smoking musket. He had poured an amount of black powder down the muzzle and was now using a ramrod to drive the ball home. "Somebody get Joel's musket," he said, his voice tight. "Bovie, it's yours."

Bovie reached down and retrieved the weapon. Then he had to get Gunn's leather bag of powder and shot from where it had been slung around the man's shoulder. He worked at this for a moment, grimly, as Foxworth shambled forward to get the torch before it could burn up any more brush. He stomped out the fire on the ground, but the fire in the trees was gaining on them. They could begin to feel some heat within the smoke, which was becoming thicker.

From the woods that had expelled the deer came the crying sound, closer now. It again went on for a few seconds and once more ended in the harsh, eerie sob.

Magnus did not believe in curses nor spirits, vengeful or otherwise, but even he felt shaken. He reloaded the pistol, which had performed admirably in spite of its rust, and everyone else with an empty firearm also hurriedly reloaded with powder and lead ball down the muzzle, then a small measure of powder in the firing-pan to prime the weapon.

Stamper had put his hat back on. The raven's feather was crooked. Sweat glistened on his face as he lifted his torch and stared into the wilderness from which the crying had come. His musket was aimed and ready, but his nerve had broken with the second cry. He said, "Royce…I'm clearin' out. It's not worth it…" He was already backing away. "Not worth it, to die out here."

"He's right!" said Barrows, the white eye shining. "I'm clearin' out too…gettin' back to the river."

"Hold on!" Royce protested, but even so his voice had weakened and he too had the tightness of fear on his face.

The smoke was making eyes water and bringing up coughs. "We can't go any further," Stamper said. "I *ain't* goin' any further. Royce, it's got to be given up. The skins are likely dead by now. If not… they will be soon. Anybody wants to go with me, come on. Findin' Corbett and gettin' out of here, 'fore this fire spreads and full dark falls." He turned and started walking to the southwest, toward the river. Barrows followed, then Bovie, Magnus and at last Foxworth.

"*Stamper!*" came the shout.

Magnus turned, as did the others, to see Royce holding the musket aimed at Stamper's belly.

"We can't give it up!" Royce's face had reddened and seemed swollen by blood, and in the drifting smoke he appeared a green-eyed devil from Hell. "We can't let those skins just get *away*! Nossir! They've got to pay for what they've done! Abram the most! Stabbin' her down like she was a damned dog, and her such a fancy lady too good to hardly *speak* to anybody! And flouncin' around there to draw all the attention and all those black eyes lookin' at her, and wantin' her! You could *smell* that they wanted her!" His mouth was twisted, his face contorted into a picture of utter, raging hatred. "Teachin' him to read, they say! To *read*! That wasn't what they was doin' in that barn, night after night! Well, that sweet innocent little girl wasn't so damned sweet and innocent! I watched her, the way she teased! *Readin'*, they say! Those animals want only one thing from a white woman! *One thing!* My Pa found that out, too! And then he paid for it with a cut throat!" He blinked suddenly, realizing something had spilled out from a deep wound. "I mean to say…" He hesitated, not knowing what to say. He tried again, with an effort. "It's that… you've got to be strong with 'em. Keep 'em whipped and scared. If you don't, they'll rise up…burn your house…and everything gone." He looked from one man to another. "Don't you understand that?"

A silence stretched. Then Stamper asked quietly, "You gonna shoot me too, Griff?"

Royce looked down at the musket as if it were an object from another world. He lowered it. "No, Stamper," he said with a hideous grin. "I'm not gonna shoot anybody."

"You can come with us if you like or stay out here. Your choice."

They could hear the trees burning now, a dull roar, and hear the popping of pinecones like little explosions. The dry wind blew and smoke billowed through the woods.

"I'll come with you," said Royce, and he walked past Magnus to the front of the group. Magnus turned to follow them, and saw that Foxworth had gone over to kneel beside Gunn's body. Foxworth was scavaging Gunn's knife in its sheath from the dead man's waist. The others were moving on, and only Magnus saw it happen.

Something on four legs lurched out of the woods. Magnus' eyes burned, he couldn't see it clearly for the smoke, but he had the impression of a large animal that was maybe a panther…its flesh brown but blotched and streaked with black, its black head misshapen and unnatural. Foxworth saw it coming and gave a hoarse cry of terror. He tried to get to his feet or get the torch between them, even as the beast reared up on its hind legs, took two strides forward and fell upon him.

Magnus fired his pistol at the thing, but the distance was more than twenty feet and the ball thunked into a tree. He heard the wet sound of flesh being torn. He saw the beast twist its hideous head and come up with a dripping red mass in its jaws. Its face, somehow deformed and monstrous, turned toward Magnus, who for the first time in his life let loose piss into his trousers.

"Kill it! Kill it!" shouted Stamper, crashing back through the woods and lifting his musket to fire. But the beast leapt forward into the thicket, moving not smoothly like a panther but with a strange jerking motion that was like nothing Magnus had ever seen before. Stamper's musket boomed...too late, the beast had gone into the smoke.

"Foxworth!" Barrows had come back, and Bovie too. They stood over the old man, whose legs still moved in an attempt to escape. Magnus and Stamper joined them, and saw that under the bloodied beard Foxworth's throat had been ripped open. Foxworth's eyes were wide and bloodshot, and he was trying to hold the spurting gore in with both hands. He tried also to speak, but only a harsh rattling came out.

"He's done!" Bovie backed away, scanning the woods on both sides, his face sweating. He had the musket in one hand and his sword in the other, but fear was his greatest enemy. "He's done, that thing's out here with us, he's done!" His voice sounded near breaking into a sob. "Christ Jesus...save us!" He retreated to where Royce was standing, impassive, his face blank of expression.

Foxworth reached up. Magnus leaned over, took one of the bloody hands and clenched it, and he, Barrows and Stamper watched the old man die.

"Did you see it?" Stamper asked Magnus.

"I saw...I don't know what it was. A panther, maybe. Big. But... its head...somethin' was wrong with it. I don't know."

"We've got to move. *Now.*" Stamper had seen limbs in the nearby trees starting to catch fire. The wind was still blowing toward the river, sweeping across the grasslands from the northeast, driving the flames before it. "*Now,*" he repeated, and turned away as Magnus worked his hand free from the dead man's. Magnus retrieved the torch. Then he backed away also, watching the woods to right and left, not daring to stop to reload the pistol, but thinking that night was going to catch them out here and yet the night could hardly be darker than the day. Still he refused to offer his back to the beast. Finally he had no choice, for the earth was rugged and unforgiving, and here in this brutal wilderness even a giant might fall.

Three

Ball or Blade?

Seventeen

As Matthew, Quinn and the three runaways made their slow progress toward the river, Magnus found himself pushing through the woods beside Griffin Royce. He had reloaded the pistol and kept it in his grip, and he thought that if he really was walking with Sarah's killer—and it seemed to him so, according to Matthew, Granny Pegg's story and the cruel ease with which Royce had executed Gunn—then he would stay alert for a musket to be trained on himself, as Royce must realize Magnus shared Matthew's knowledge. Even so, Magnus couldn't help but throw the man a little rope with which he might further fashion his own noose.

"Sarah was my friend," Magnus said, as they moved through the underbrush. Still the smoke pursued them, curling and writhing in the air like the vengeful souls that supposedly haunted this realm. Burning trees crackled at their backs. "I can't believe she was doin' anythin' in that barn but helpin' Abram learn to read," he went on, when Royce failed to respond.

"Little *you* know," Royce said tersely.

"You ever go into the barn and see for yourself?"

"Muldoon, I don't want to talk to you, understand?" The hard green eyes took Magnus in and then dismissed him. "That thing out here…and my friend dead, by my hand. Can't even get his body back for a Christian burial. I don't want to talk, hear me?"

"I hear," Magnus replied, pushing a branch out of his face with an elbow as he moved forward, "but still…doesn't make sense that Abram killed her. Why *would* he? Like Matthew said…it's unproven."

"Gunn saw him standin' over her body with the knife in his hand. Seems like everybody's forgettin' that."

"Not forgettin' it," Magnus pressed on, "it's just that…seein' him standin' over her with a knife is not seein' him *use* the knife. He might've just picked it up when he came out of the—"

"Muldoon," said Royce, and the musket's barrel swung a few more inches toward the black-bearded mountain. Royce's face was reddening and was further blotched by insect bites. "The black skin *ran*. If he wasn't guilty of murder, then why would he run? Why would his blood have stepped in to help him?"

"Too scared to think straight, maybe."

"Scared of *what*, if he hadn't killed Sarah? But tell me this, Muldoon…if he didn't kill her, who did? Corbett have any ideas about that? And what's all this about somethin' he found on her body? What was he doin', pokin' around on that girl's body?"

"Mrs. Kincannon gave him permit," said Magnus calmly. "And yes, he did find somethin' of interest."

"What might that have been?"

"Best he tell you himself—or show you—when we get back."

Stamper, in the lead just ahead, suddenly called out, "Hold up!" and the others paused. "Here's where we left Corbett and the girl," he announced. "Wait a minute…looky here! We've got a new trail! Somebody's draggin' a leg. Damn me if it don't look like… three men walkin' close together. Side-by-side, looks to be. Bovie, you see this?"

"I see it," Bovie said. "Headin' toward the river."

"Three men?" Royce moved forward, past Barrows, to get a look at the wide trail of broken brush. He was no woodsman, but even *he* could follow a trail this obvious. "The skins? Got Corbett and headin' back? Why would that be?"

"Don't know," said Stamper. "Maybe he talked 'em into givin' themselves up."

Magnus took note of Royce's sudden silence. Royce stared at the ground, as if reading his future in the crushed earth.

"We'll find out further on," Stamper said. "Let's keep movin', and everybody keep a sharp eye out. No offense meant, Barrows."

"None taken," said the other man. "I just want out of this damned hell and back to my wife." He looked over his shoulder, through the gray smoke, at the fire that was following them and spreading out to burn a wider path. From the heart of the flames a dry wind blew, sending ashes and embers flying and making the fires jump from tree to tree. They had already seen animals—more deer, rabbits and two good-sized brown panthers—fleeing the oncoming conflagration.

They went on at a faster pace, their advance made easier by the trail that had already been broken before them. After another thirty minutes the ground began to become swampy again, indicating the river was near. Gray pools of water stood here and there under the massive gnarled oaks and weeping willow trees, as smoke from the fire behind them coiled in the branches.

"Bootprints over here!" Stamper said, motioning to the prints in the mud. "Five people. One lamed, for sure. Can't be more than a half-mile ahead."

"I've been holdin' my guts," said Bovie, with a pained expression. "I've gotta take a shit!" He put down his sword and musket, opened his trousers, pushed them down to his ankles and squatted. "Ahhhh!" he said. "Oh my Christ, what a—"

He let loose a scream that might have been heard in Charles Town, and suddenly he was scrambling through the mud with his trousers still down. "Somethin' bit me!" he shouted. "Got me on the balls!"

Magnus saw the ugly brown snake writhing away into the high weeds from where Bovie had rudely disturbed its place of rest. Water moccasin, he thought. Bovie had seen it too, and now he struggled to his feet and pulled his trousers up and looked at Stamper with a fear-blanched face. "Bastard bit me, Stamper! It ain't a poison one though, is it? Say it ain't a poison one!"

"Cottonmouth," said Royce, before Stamper could say otherwise.

"Wasn't no cottonmouth!" Bovie shouted angrily. "It was a black snake, wasn't no cottonmouth!"

There was a moment of silence, and then Stamper said, "We ought to be movin' on."

"It was a black snake!" Bovie insisted. "Got me on the damned balls, but I'll be all right. I'll be all right, won't I, Stamper?"

"Let's keep movin'," Stamper replied, and he went on.

"I'm feelin' all right!" Bovie's eyes were too wide and too glassy. "Stings a little bit, that's all!" He retrieved his weapons and started after Stamper, with Barrows following, then Royce and Magnus. "I'm gonna be fine!" he announced to the others, with a crooked grin. "Laugh about it when we get back!"

Magnus thought that there was nothing funny about being bitten on the balls by a venomous cottonmouth, and even now the poison was moving in Bovie's blood. But he said nothing else, and he kept his head down and watched where he stepped because there might be nests of the things in here somewhere.

"You ever know anybody got bit on the balls by a black snake?" Bovie asked, his question aimed at anyone who might answer. "Damn me, if that won't make a story to earn me a drink or two! Stings a little bit. Nothin' bad."

They continued to follow the bootprints, as the swamp deepened and the pools of gray water spread. The smoke was following them, floating through the brush and hanging from the trees. "Hot in here!" Bovie said. "Damn, I'm sweatin'. My balls are swole up, Stamper! God A'mighty, that black snake got me good!"

"Yep, must've," said Stamper, staring straight ahead.

"I'm all right, though," Bovie said. "You boys gettin' tired? I ain't tired. Nossir. And I ain't afraid of that *thing*, either. Devil panther or whatever it is, I'll stand up to it! You believe in the devil, Stamper?"

"I do, Caleb."

"I believe there's a devil and an angel in every man," Bovie went on, his face, hair and brown beard damp with sweat. "They're fightin' in you all the time, tryin' to win you over. Sometimes I can feel 'em fightin' in me. Pullin' me this way, and pullin' me that. They're whisperin' in your ear, and they're slidin' in and out of your head. You feel that way, Stamper?"

"Yep."

"My balls are kinda hurtin'. Maybe I need to stop for a minute and get a breath."

"Keep goin'," Royce insisted. "We can't stop for a dead man."

"What was that?" Bovie asked. "What'd he say, Stamper?"

"He said, we can't stop right now."

"All right, then." Bovie's voice had weakened. "All right," he said again, as if he wasn't sure he'd spoken it the first time.

They hadn't gone on but a few more minutes when Caleb Bovie said, "I can't hardly breathe, all of a sudden. Damn this smoke... I can't hardly breathe." He dropped his sword to run a trembling hand across his face and he left the sword behind, lying in the mud. "I'm feelin' like I need to rest, Stamper. My legs are 'bout to give out. I don't know...I'm feelin' poorly."

"We're not stoppin'," said Royce.

"Yes," Stamper said, with a hard glare at the other man. "We *are* stoppin'. Caleb, sit yourself down for a few minutes and rest."

"No!" Royce got up in Stamper's face, his green eyes aflame. "The skins are just ahead! You said so yourself! We've got to *stop* 'em!"

"*Stop* 'em?" Stamper's eyebrows went up. "Why, Griff? If they're headin' back to the Green Sea, why would we want to stop 'em?"

"We don't know they're headin' there! Could be they're tryin' to cross the river and cut south! You think they're goin' back to give themselves up? Hell, no!"

Bovie was sitting on the trunk of a fallen tree, his musket leaning beside him. He had begun to shake, as if freezing cold in this swamp's heat. Magnus approached him, walking at the edge of what looked to be an expanse of black, grainy mud. Stamper noted his progress and called out, "Muldoon! Careful! You're walkin' close to a quicksand pit!"

Magnus abruptly stopped where he was. He knelt on the ground a few feet away from Bovie, who had started to rock himself back and forth, his face gray and his eyes fixed on a limitless distance.

"I'm changin' my ways when I get home," said Bovie, speaking to all and none. "Goin' to church every Sabbath. Doin' what I ought to do. I swear it." He realized Magnus was kneeling near him, and he turned bloodshot eyes upon the hermit. "I'm cold," he said, shivering. "Ain't you cold, too?"

"A mite," said Magnus.

"Knew it wasn't just me. My gut's hurtin' bad." Pain was beginning to show in Bovie's face. He clenched his hands over his stomach and squeezed his eyes shut. "Hurtin' bad…oh mercy… mercy on me…"

"We ought to leave him," was Royce's pronouncement. "Wastin' time, waitin' for—"

"Shut your mouth," said Stamper. The way he said it made Royce's mouth close in a tight, thin line. Stamper walked over and stood near the dying man, and Barrows came nearer as well. Royce took a long look at the others, and then he placed his musket against his shoulder and walked over to stand beside Magnus. Royce stared off into the swamp, toward the river and the path of footprints leading to it.

"Stamper," Bovie rasped, his eyes open now, watery and red-rimmed, and he looked pleadingly up at the other man. "Can you help me get home? I can stand up and walk. Swear to God I can."

"You just stay where you are. Just rest a bit."

"I'm hurtin', Stamper. All over. I think I…I need to stand up." Bovie tried, and when he got up halfway he let loose an agonized cry and fell to his knees. He stayed there, his hands still gripped to his belly, his face now taking on a bluish tinge. Foam was gathering in the corners of his mouth. He began to blink rapidly, his breathing loud and harsh. "Oh Christ," he whispered, his voice choked with pain. "Save me…please…save me…"

Magnus started to get up off his knees. When he began to stand up, he was struck from behind by Griffin Royce, who swung the butt of his musket hard against the back of Magnus' skull.

Magnus staggered and dropped both his torch and the pistol. Fireballs exploded in his brain, and he pitched sideways into the quicksand pit.

Stamper looked dumbly at Royce, his mouth hanging open. He therefore saw Royce take a step forward, cock the musket, aim its barrel at his head and pull the trigger. Through the burst of blue smoke the lead ball hit him just under the left eye. Stamper's head rocked back, the hat with its raven's feather went flying, and he fell backward into the mud as if pole-axed.

Royce already had drawn his knife. He walked two paces through the roiling smoke to where Barrows was standing in shocked disbelief, and without hesitation drove the blade downward into the hollow of the man's throat. Barrows had no time to get his musket up for a shot or draw his pistol; he lifted his left arm, the fingers clawing at the bandages on Royce's right forearm. Royce twisted the blade, the thin smile of a true predator warping his mouth. With a blood-choked gasp Barrows tore free and turned to run, but Royce was quickly upon him. His teeth gritted and red whorls in his cheeks, Royce drove the blade into the man's back once…twice…four more times with the force of uncontrolled rage, until Barrows' knees gave way and he fell on his face, the white stone of an eye pressed into the mud.

Royce stepped back to view his work, the breath hot in his lungs and his blood singing in the afterglow of violence. Magnus was a prisoner of the quicksand, Stamper was stretched out and Barrows done for. Bovie had pitched forward on his hands and knees, trembling and retching. "God help me," he gasped, beginning to sob. "Oh Christ Jesus…help me…"

Royce had no more time to waste. He replaced his knife in its sheath and helped himself to Bovie's musket, which he knew to be still loaded after the encounter with the buck. He picked up Magnus' pistol, also still loaded, and slid that into the waist of his breeches. He would reload his own weapon later, he decided, when he got nearer the skins and Corbett. He had plenty of powder and shot in his ammunition bag. Who to shoot first would be the question. He put his own musket under his arm, held the other one in his left hand and then picked up Stamper's torch where it lay guttering in the mud.

Bovie fell on his side and began to curl up, crying and moaning. Royce stood over Bovie for a few seconds more, his eyes narrowed with disgust at this scene of human weakness. In a voice loud enough for Bovie to hear, Royce said, "*Cottonmouth.*" Then he turned away from the stricken man and hurried on after his prey.

Eighteen

MAGNUS awakened in the grip of Death.

He couldn't breathe. His face was pressed upon by a wet, heavy darkness. Panic shook him. In the horror of the instant he realized where he must be, on his right side in the quicksand pit. His head pounded and he could taste blood. Someone had hit him from behind...*Royce.* He had to get his face up into the air. Had to get his legs under himself, and his body straightened out...the quicksand was up his nostrils and in his mouth and sealing shut his eyes, and Magnus knew that if he did not get air within the next few seconds he was finished in this world.

He fought against the mire. It fought back. The paste of black earth had him. He strained his neck and face upward, toward where he thought the surface was. His muscles screamed, and he wanted to scream. Maybe he did, there in the dark pressure of wet, clinging tides.

But in the next instant his nose and mouth broke the surface, which was only a few inches above, and though he remained blind and gripped hard by this demonic mud he was able to spit his mouth clear and draw a howling breath that shuddered through him and gave him a small gift of hope.

He was able then also to expell the quicksand from his nostrils, and breathe air tainted with the sharp and putrid odors of the swamp and the smell of smoke from the fire that burned beyond. The next challenge was getting his entire face and head clear of the muck. It was going to take an effort of muscle and will. Magnus felt both faltering, but by God he had to try before he was pulled down any deeper.

He went about an attempt to get his body straightened out and keep his face at the surface. He worked hard at this objective, but the quicksand worked harder to hold him firm and, indeed, draw him downward. Though he was able to maintain a breathing space, any movement of intended speed or strength was met by a resistance that made him feel he had the weak muscles of a helpless infant. He had the distinct memory of trying to draw a comb through his bear-greased hair, hitting clots and knots and ripping his hair out to spite both Pandora Prisskitt and Matthew Corbett; he felt now like that comb, heavy with bear grease and doomed to fail.

The substance was thick about him, like both a wet sand and a clinging mud. Was there anyone out there to help him? He tried to answer that question by calling for help, but the quicksand threatened to flood his mouth. If anyone had answered, he couldn't tell because his ears were stopped up.

Trapped, Magnus thought. And then the real terror hit him and he began to flail at his fate, to try to fight his way out of this with sheer boulder-shouldered brawn, but the quicksand just seemed to close more tightly around him and once again his face went under. He stopped fighting, for he realized muscle would not overpower this suckpit and hard motion brought forth an equally hard reaction. He suddenly remembered very clearly Matthew's first words to him upon arriving at the house.

Calm yourself, sir.

Magnus ceased all motion. His heart was pounding, telling him it was wrong to give up the fight, yet he intended to fight not with terrified brawn but with a calm brain. Slowly...slowly...he pushed his face upward through the muck...slowly...not incurring the wrath of the suckpit...and his nose and mouth once more broke the surface.

He spat out quicksand and took in air, and determined that slow movements might yet defeat the will of the pit. Thus he began to very slowly push with his legs against the mass of viscous earth, and it took an iron will not to fight hard but it was this or death and he was not ready to give up, and surely not to the evil of a witch-cursed swamp.

He felt the desire of the suckpit pulling at him, even with these slow, sinuous movements. How long it took him to work his head and shoulders out of the mire, Magnus didn't know. Still moving with slowness respectful to the pit, he was able to get his eyes cleared and saw in the afternoon's blue light and drifting smoke the carnage of the scene: Stamper lying on his back with a pool of blood around his head, Barrows crumpled and bloody, and Bovie lying on his side. Royce was gone, and Magnus knew who he was going after.

The man was a mad dog, Magnus thought. An animal who killed on impulse, either in rage or misguided passion. Surely the killing of Gunn had been intentional…and now this.

He had to get out for still he felt the pit pulling at him, accepting his weight and bulk like an offering to the demons below.

If he moved slowly enough, he thought, he might be able to swim out. There were only a few feet to firm ground. So he might use his arms as a swimmer would, to move the muck around and behind him…but even the distance of a few feet would be torturous through this paste. Even so…it had to be tried.

He began his journey from the pit of death toward the shore of life. The motions were slow, the quicksand still heavy and clinging around him and yet it did yield to these more deliberate actions. When at last he reached more solid earth, Magnus dug his fingers into the mud and weeds but found further difficulty in pulling himself out, for the suckpit did not want to let him go. Inch by inch he worked himself from the mire, as if struggling out of a suit of tar. Several times he thought he couldn't get out for even moving by inches his strength was nearly gone, but what fortified him was the knowledge that Royce had killed Sarah in the same kind of blood frenzy the man had just shown, and now Royce was on his way to finish his job of sealing all mouths.

Royce could say the cursed swamp got its victims by alligator, the Dead in Life, quicksand, poisonous snake, accidental gunshot or the Soul Cryer, and it might be many years before anyone would come searching for the bodies. By that time, the swamp and its creatures would have disposed of the flesh, and Royce would be long gone.

"No," Magnus rasped, as he yet struggled to pull himself free. "Not lettin' that happen."

A hand was offered to him.

Magnus looked into the blue-tinged face of Caleb Bovie, who had crawled across the wet earth on his belly like the reptile that had bitten him.

Tears of torment had streamed from Bovie's bloodshot eyes and yellow foam coated his lips, but in spite of his obvious agony he whispered, "*Grab hold*."

Magnus did. Bovie had no strength to speak of, but he tried his best. It was enough. Magnus freed himself from the pit, feeling his boots being sucked off his feet as payment for escape, and he lay weary on the ground next to Bovie like an oversized scarecrow covered head to toe with the black grime of the swamp.

"Muldoon?" Bovie asked, again in a pained whisper. "Will you help me get home?"

"Yes," said Magnus.

Magnus got to his bootless feet with a determination that would have earned an awed respect from even Father Prisskitt. He started to reach down to help Bovie up, when he heard the Soul Cryer's eerie weeping somewhere in the wilderness at his back.

It was close, but it could not be seen. Smoke moved in the trees, and here and there in the higher branches burned sputters of flame like little torches. The dry, hot wind that had been blowing toward the river had calmed to an acrid breeze, but Magnus could see the orange glow of the fire in the sky that meant a large portion of the forest was ablaze. The main part of the fire looked to be maybe a quarter mile away, and was throwing a constellation of embers into the air that drifted down like burning stars.

Again the Soul Cryer wept, closer still.

Magnus walked the few paces to Bovie's discarded sword and picked it up. He retrieved the pistol from Barrows' dead body and cocked it. Soul Cryer smells blood, Magnus thought. It's comin'.

With sword in one hand and pistol in the other, the grimy black mountain of a scarecrow stood over Caleb Bovie and readied himself to fight for both their lives.

⁂

"River's just ahead," said Matthew, who could see it about thirty yards distant through the trees. Quinn was holding his hand, gripped hard, and a few yards behind them came Abram, the crippled Mars and Tobey.

"Need to rest just a minute," Mars said. When Matthew and Quinn paused, Mars' sons eased their father down to the ground with his back against a willow's trunk. "Stepped in a gopher hole," Mars told Matthew. "Heard that ankle snap like a broomstick."

"Does it pain you very much?"

Mars gave Matthew half of a smile; the other half of it was sad. "Not much. You like to see my brand, suh? Now...that *did* pain me much. Pained me more, to watch my wife and sons be branded. God bless my Jenny, I miss her. You own slaves, suh?"

"No, I don't."

"What kind of work you do?"

"I'm..." *A problem-solver*, Matthew was about to say. Instead, he said, "I'm paid to stick my nose into places where it doesn't belong."

Mars laughed, a rich deep sound. "And here you be. Who's payin' you for this?"

"Mrs. Kincannon."

"Why not the mister? He still poorly?"

"I don't know. He was abed when I left the Green Sea."

"Hm," Mars said quietly, and stared past Matthew toward the River of Souls. A whiplash of lightning flared across the charcoal sky, followed by the rumble of thunder. "Boys, we did wrong runnin'. Should've faced up to things, right then and there. Course, you'd be hangin' by now," he said to Abram. "Kincannons weren't gonna take your word for nothin', against Cap'n Royce and Cap'n Gunn."

"I didn't want you two comin' with me," Abram said. "Told you to stay put, I was the one they wanted."

"Weren't gonna let you come out here alone," Tobey answered. "Got to look out for each other, and that's how it is. Anyway...die out here or die at the Green Sea, don't make no difference." He turned his attention to Matthew. "Pardon my askin', suh, but what's this proof you got that says Abram didn't kill Miss—"

Tobey's question was stopped by the *crack* of a musket being fired from the darkness of the thicket behind them, and at once Tobey grabbed at his left side and with a cry of pain fell to his knees. Matthew had seen the flash of the pan, and now the cloud of smoke indicated from where the shot had come.

"Down! Get down!" Matthew urged, and pulled Quinn with him to the ground. Abram crawled over to shield his father, while Tobey gasped and clutched at his bleeding side.

"Who'd I hit?" came Royce's voice, casual and unhurried. "I was aimin' at you, Corbett! That's all right, I'll get you yet! You too, Abram! Gonna get all of you before it's done!"

Matthew realized that might well be the truth, for he had only the short-bladed sword as a weapon. Still...dark was falling...they might yet be able to get to the river. But what had happened to the other men...Magnus, Stamper, Gunn, Bovie and the others?

"Corbett, you were asked a question!" Royce said from his hidden position. "What's your proof?"

Matthew figured the man wanted to get a fix on him when he spoke, but he couldn't resist. He kept low to the ground, right beside Quinn and one arm over her. "The compress Dr. Stevenson gave you for the horse bite," he said. "It broke open when Sarah grasped your arm after you'd stabbed her the first time. You knew it had. I imagine you spent some time cleaning that up after you scared Abram into running. What did you do, work it into the ground? But some of the material inside the compress was under Sarah's fingernails. Mrs. Kincannon knows that, I showed it to her. Are you going to go to the Green Sea and kill *her*, too?"

Royce didn't answer.

"No use in your killing anyone else," Matthew told him. "You're finished, Royce. Where are the others?" A chill passed through him, as he realized what might have happened. "Did you kill *all* of them?"

"Not all, I had some help from the swamp. Abram? You never should've shown any interest in that girl. I watched you. I watched the both of you. Whisperin' together when you didn't think anybody was lookin'. Walkin' together, right in the broad daylight. And in that barn at night...makes me sick to my stomach, thinkin' about it."

"You were wrong, Cap'n Royce," Abram called out. "Miss Sarah was teachin' me to read, and that's the—"

The next musket shot hit the willow tree trunk and threw splinters. Abram ducked his head down against his father's shoulder.

"Don't lie!" Royce seethed. "I know what you were doin' in there! Night after night…I followed her, I saw you go in there too! Only one reason you'd be breakin' the law and meetin' in that barn after dark! Wouldn't even offer me a *smile*, and her givin' herself to that black skin! Well, she paid for it!"

"Royce!" Matthew said, as lightning flashed above and more thunder growled. "Was Sarah carrying a book when you stabbed her? And did she drop that book to the ground? Surely you saw it!"

"That's a damned lie, too! Her teachin' a *skin* to read! Don't matter if she had a book or not, they wasn't *readin'* in that barn!"

Abram had crawled over to tend to his brother, who was in obvious pain but nodded to show he was hanging on.

"You didn't have to kill the girl!" Matthew said. "Why didn't you go to Kincannon? Tell him what you thought was going on?"

"Think he would have believed *me*? About his darlin' daughter? He would've run me off tarred and feathered! I told her I knew what she was doin', and if she was nice to me…show me a little favor…I wouldn't tell. But she looked at me like she always did…like I was lower than dirt…and she'd rather have that damn black skin than me? Treatin' that slave better than a white man?"

"Miss Sarah brought the books and she was teachin' me to read!" Abram shouted back. "That's all!"

A third shot rang out in reply. Matthew heard the ball zip past. It was a higher report than the first two shots. A pistol, Matthew thought. And did Royce have one musket or two? How quick was he at reloading the weapons? Was it worth the risk to charge at him with the sword? But he was hidden there in the thicket, and by the time Matthew crossed the fifteen yards or so between them another musket could be ready. Matthew glanced back at Abram and Tobey. The blood was oozing between Tobey's fingers. It might not have been a killing shot but in time it would be, and time was a precious commodity.

Matthew was still weak from his own loss of blood. He thought he was turning into a bearded ragamuffin himself, a pale piece of parchment as Magnus had said at the Sword of Damocles Ball, which seemed a lifetime away. Lightning zigzagged across the sky and thunder boomed overhead, and Matthew Corbett was caught between what he ought to do and what he feared to do.

"Give it up!" Royce called. "None of you are leavin' this swamp!"

Abram suddenly stood up. He drew a knife from the waist of his breeches. "You won't be leavin' it either, Cap'n Royce," he promised, and with an inhalation of breath he ran past Matthew and Quinn toward the woods where Sarah's killer lay in wait.

Magnus Muldoon knew it was coming. All this blood...the smell of it...the Soul Cryer was coming.

Out of the smoke it skulked, at first a shadow and then a substance, moving with the strange irregular rhythm Magnus had already seen, but this time it crept slowly forward across the mud until it reached Barrows' body. Then its misshapen snout sniffed at the blood, and the slitted yellow eyes stared at Magnus as if trying to determine what this huge muddied beast was...a challenger to its territory, or a fellow monster best left alone.

It was not a ghost nor a witch-created demon but it was surely the biggest panther Magnus had ever seen. Except the dark blotches and streaks across its muscular brown body were burn scars, and its head showed what could happen to an animal caught in a raging forest fire. Both ears had been burned away, its skull hairless and nearly covered with scaly black scars, its muzzle malformed and twisted to expose on the left side the fangs as if in a grotesque grin, one foreleg withered by fire and its tail a blackened stub. It moved in such a manner, Magnus realized, because under the damaged skin some of the muscles had contracted and stiffened, and if this creature had been nearly burned to death seven years ago it must have suffered all the torments of agony. Even now, it must be still in pain...and maybe driven to its own kind of insanity, a thirst for blood and killing not for food but for domination. It could not growl and proclaim itself like an ordinary panther, it could only cry.

Its eyes still fixed upon Magnus, it snapped at the falling embers as if in memory of what had deformed it. Bovie clung onto Magnus' legs, as Magnus awaited the Soul Cryer's decision to attack or not.

With a *whuff* of breath the Soul Cryer suddenly lifted itself up onto its hind legs and balanced there. Bovie gave a strangled noise of terror, but Magnus remained silent and resolute though his heart hammered in his chest. Magnus thought the beast had learned this action possibly to overcome the weakness of the burned foreleg, or maybe as a way to scare off other younger and healthier male panthers. He prepared himself for the Soul Cryer to leap forward from its hind legs, and he aimed the pistol at its heart and the sword's wicked edge at its throat.

Nineteen

As Abram started for Griffin Royce's hiding place with a knife in his hand, Matthew scrambled up from the ground and with two desperate strides crashed into Abram, knocking him aside just as the musket fired. He had not come this far to watch Abram be shot down. The ball passed somewhere behind Matthew's head and into the trees. Abram fell to the ground, and Matthew realized he had no choice but to charge into the smoke-filled thicket with his sword ready to slash flesh from bone because Royce would already be pouring the powder into another weapon.

He leaped into the churning gunsmoke and through vines and thorny weeds that clutched at him like little claws. And there about ten feet to his left and crouched against an oak tree was the figure of Royce, frantically ramrodding a ball and cloth patch down into a second musket's muzzle. Matthew rushed the man, even as Royce turned the musket on him and cocked it with a grimy thumb. As the musket's barrel came at him, Matthew swung out with the sword and deflected it, the musket firing with a noise that shocked

Matthew's eardrums but the shot going wide. Then Royce became a truly wild animal, and with clenched teeth and a growling in his throat he struck at Matthew with the musket's barrel but again Matthew's sword knocked it aside.

Royce launched himself at Matthew, the man's right shoulder hitting him in the chest with bone-jarring force. The musket was dropped and forgotten as Royce fought Matthew for the sword, and Matthew was swung around and slammed so hard against the oak's trunk the breath burst from him and he and nearly lost his grip. Royce punched a fist into the arrow wound on Matthew's shoulder, breaking it open and causing a fresh blossoming of blood. Matthew fought back as hard as he could, catching Royce on the jaw with his left fist and striking him a blow on the throat that caused his opponent to gag and falter for a few seconds, but the man was powerful and adept at close-in fighting. A knee rammed into Matthew's stomach and a fist struck him on the back of the neck, but still Matthew clung to the sword, for to lose that was certain death. Royce gripped Matthew's hair and tried to knee him in the face. Matthew stopped the knee with his free arm and struck into the pit of Royce's stomach. The stocky killer let out a pained gasp of breath, but he would not let go of Matthew's right wrist and began to brutally twist it to weaken the fingers and free the sword. With his other hand he drew his knife from its sheath, but before it could find flesh Matthew saw it coming. He was able to grasp the killer's knife hand and for the moment hold the blade at bay with the strength of desperation.

Matthew gritted his teeth and would not open his fingers. He thought his wrist was about to snap, but let it break; he wasn't giving up to this animal, and letting him kill—

"Stop that, Cap'n Royce," said Abram. "Drop the knife. I don't want to have to cut you."

The pressure on Matthew's wrist went away. He was released. Matthew staggered a few paces, then took in the scene. Abram had come up behind Royce and was gripping the back of the man's shirt. More importantly, Abram's blade was right up under Royce's chin. Royce's knife fell from his hand.

"You all right?" Abram asked Matthew, and Matthew nodded but he was lying; he eased himself down to the ground, and was met there by Quinn. She put her arms around him and held him tightly and might have said to him *Daniel, my sweet Daniel* but Matthew was nearly beyond hearing.

"Got you now," said Abram to Royce, who managed for all his rage and ferocity to remain very still. "Takin' you back to the Green Sea, cap'n. You're my prisoner." And then, because he was yet a slave and Royce a white man, however low, he added by force of habit the respectful, "*Suh.*"

⁂

The Soul Cryer remained upright on its hind legs, as the yellow eyes in its burn-scarred head threw their own fire at Magnus.

"Shoot it!" Bovie croaked. "Christ's sake...*shoot it*!"

But Magnus did not pull the trigger, nor did he slash with the sword.

The Soul Cryer wavered, about to lose its tentative balance. Magnus recognized in the beast the cruelty of this wilderness and perhaps the cruelty of the world itself. He thought it was a tortured thing, a creature forsaken and maybe feared by its own breed. It prowled alone out here, hunted alone and wept alone. He knew solitude, and what it could do to a man. He wondered if years of it could do the same thing to a scarred and tormented panther, and maybe in the slitted eyes there was a death wish, if indeed the creature could think beyond the green walls of its prison.

Embers rained down. The smoke swirled and the fire gave a dull roar as it jumped from tree to tree.

Go home, Magnus thought. *Go*—

The Soul Cryer trembled as its muscles tensed. It took a staggered step forward, its malformed mouth opening at a sideways angle to expose the vicious fangs. Saliva drooled from the jaws and down upon the black-streaked chest.

—*home*, Magnus thought, and he pulled the pistol's trigger.

The ball hit the Soul Cryer as near to the heart as Magnus could aim. The creature gave a grunt of pain and fell backwards but quickly it righted itself again, now on all fours, and crouched staring at Magnus through the banners of gray smoke that moved between them. Magnus knew that one ball was surely not enough to kill it, unless it had indeed damaged the heart. The Soul Cryer was breathing heavily and blood bubbled at the blackened nostrils, but it showed no other sign of weakness or injury.

He had no time to reload. He stood with the sword ready. His hand was trembling.

The Soul Cryer suddenly turned toward Barrows' body, moving with its pained rhythm. With its eyes still on Magnus, the beast angled its head and gripped its jaws around the dead man's skull. It shook the body like a strawman in a display of tremendous power, and the jaws crunched around the skull and the fangs broke bone and the Soul Cryer ate Barrows' brains with the determination of an eager child eating sugar candy.

Magnus noted blood pooling under the panther's chest. The Soul Cryer fed on Barrows' essence, its eyes never leaving Magnus, and in their yellow glare Magnus saw the message *Get away from here. Get away...and never, ever come back.*

When Barrows' broken head was emptied, the Soul Cryer's eyes blinked, releasing Magnus from their spell. The beast backed away, favoring its ruined foreleg. Giving a noise so near to a human sob that Magnus thought he might hear it in his nightmares, the panther turned with its stiffened motion and leaped into the thicket it claimed as home, and then nothing was left of it but a streak of bright red blood upon the swamp's ancient mud.

"Oh Jesus," Bovie gasped. "Jesus help us..."

It occured to Magnus that, though Caleb Bovie had been bitten on the balls by a cottonmouth, the man might be too tough to succumb to snake poison. Either that, or the snake hadn't gotten both fangs to the task, or the venom had not been delivered in an amount to kill, or it was simply not time for Bovie to go. In any case, though Bovie's face was still tinged with blue and his lips caked with dried foam, Magnus thought that if the lout was going to die he would've been dead already.

"Can you stand up and walk?" Magnus asked.

"Give it a try," Bovie answered, still in a weak voice, but it was a moment before he did. The roar of the oncoming fire gave him the will to get to his knees, and then the mud-covered mountain hauled him up the rest of the way. Bovie staggered and almost went down again, but Magnus held him steady.

"My head's spinnin'," Bovie complained. "Legs feel like much a'nothin'."

"I'm not carryin' you out of here, that's for sure."

Bovie took in the bodies on the ground. "Did Royce..." He looked at Magnus with his red-rimmed eyes. "Did Royce kill that girl?"

"Yes," was the answer.

"But *why* would've he have done such a thing?"

"Because," Magnus said, and he'd already spent time thinking on this subject, "some men want what they can't have, some men want to kill *for* what they can't have...and I reckon some men want to kill *what* they can't have. It's that angel and devil fightin', just like you said...and when the devil wins, sometimes an angel dies."

"Reckon so," said Bovie. "Damn...am I gonna *live*?"

"I believe you are."

"Told you it was just a black snake."

"So you did," Magnus said. He glanced back through the smoke at the oncoming flames. It looked to be a solid wall of fire. He wondered if somewhere the Soul Cryer was not watching it as well, and if the creature might lie down exhausted and ready to die, and this time let the flames finish their job of destruction and rebirth. Magnus, however, was not ready to do the same. Royce was still out there, going after Matthew and the runaways. Magnus retrieved Stamper's musket and gave Barrows' musket to Bovie. Both, he saw, were primed and ready to be cocked and fired. He saw also that, regrettably, neither dead man had boots big enough to fit his feet. "Let's get our tails to the river," he said, and he started off with Bovie following, limping and rubbing his snake-bit balls.

They had reached the Solstice River and, following its course, came upon the rowboat the slaves had stolen from the Green Sea. It had been pulled up onto shore through the mud and inexpertly covered with tree branches and foliage. Only a few yards from it was the boat that had brought Royce and Gunn. Overhead the lightning flared and the thunder spoke, and the sky to the northeast glowed red above the burning forest. Matthew could see the flames spearing up into the air and orange sparks flying like swarms of locusts.

He was in a dazed state, clutching at his raw shoulder wound and being supported by Quinn. Mars had been limping along as best he could, using a broken branch as a walking-stick. Tobey was still on his feet, but barely; his eyes were half-closed, he was stumbling from side to side and the blood from his wound had reddened his shirt and the left leg of his breeches. He was in a bad way, Matthew thought; Tobey had to be gotten back to the Green Sea as quickly as possible, or he would die.

Abram had guided Griffin Royce forward by grasping the back of the man's shirt and holding the reloaded pistol to Royce's spine. Matthew had Royce's knife tucked in the waistband of his breeches, and Quinn carried the short-bladed sword.

As weak as he was, Matthew knew he needed to make some decisions regarding the boats. All of them could not travel in only one. "That one," he said to Abram, motioning toward the boat that had brought Royce and Gunn, "should carry you, Mars and Tobey. Give me the pistol."

"I ought to travel with Royce," Abram said. "Get him in faster that way, suh."

"You need to row your brother in," Matthew answered. "Royce can row for Quinn and myself."

"I ain't rowin' for *nobody*," Royce sneered. "What am I goin' back to, a hangin' party?"

"Well, suh," said Abram, who released Royce's shirt and brought up his own knife to place against the front of Royce's throat, "seein' as how Miss Sarah was a kind friend to me, and you took her life, there would be nothin' to stop me from killin' you right here...and when we get back, sayin' you was likely lost on the River of Souls. Who would there be to say any different?" He pressed the pistol's barrel into Royce's backbone. "Ball or blade, suh. You got a choosin'?"

"Corbett won't let you do that! *Would* you?" The hard green eyes glared at Matthew.

"Seems you killed a friend of *mine*, too," said Matthew, returning the glare. "I don't know how you did it and maybe I don't want to know." He reached back and took the pistol from Abram's hand. He placed the barrel between Royce's eyes and cocked the weapon. "You were asked a question. If you won't row, then...ball or blade?"

"You won't kill me! You don't have the *guts* for it!"

Matthew thought about it. Lightning sizzled overhead, followed by a blast of thunder that he could feel vibrate in his bones. "You're correct," he said. He placed the barrel against Royce's right knee. "I won't kill you, but I'll cripple you and leave you out here. How long do you think you would last?"

"Gunn told me you were supposed to be the *law*! You wouldn't do such a thing!"

"Shall we put it to the test?" Matthew asked. And, truthfully, he was asking himself whether to go ahead and blast Royce's knee or give the man another moment to decide, because Tobey was leaning against Abram and beginning to cough up blood.

Matthew's resolve, and the decision that he would do what he threatened, must have shown in his face. Royce looked up at the stormy sky, then at the sword Quinn held and back again to Matthew. It occurred to Matthew that the killer was still seeking a way out of his situation.

"I'll row," said Royce, but something in his tone was yet arrogant and haughty; he was far from giving up.

"I don't like it, suh," Abram said to Matthew, as he supported his brother. "Man's a fox."

"Royce, clear those branches off the boat," Matthew ordered. "Pull it out to the water."

Royce gave a grunt and stood stock-still until Quinn suddenly nipped his right cheek with a quick motion of the blade. He looked at her in shock as blood crept down his face.

"He told you to do somethin'," she said, her eyes dark and dangerous. "Best do it."

Royce put his hand to his cheek and drew it away. He examined the blood on his fingers, and then without another word he turned and began to follow Matthew's instructions, as Matthew stood close enough to wing him with a shot if he tried to run.

The boat was dragged into the river. Abram helped Tobey in, then his father, and he took up the oars.

"We'll be all right," Matthew said. "Get him in as fast as you can."

Abram nodded and began to row downriver. Matthew directed Royce to the second boat with a motion of the pistol, and Royce obeyed. That boat, too, was pulled out of the mud and into the shallows. It took some maneuvering and some caution, but in a few minutes Matthew and Quinn were sitting together at the stern while Royce, facing them, sat on the middle plank seat and, with the oars in their locks, began to row them back toward the Green Sea.

Matthew kept the pistol trained on him. Lightning zigzagged across the dark sky and thunder echoed through the swamp. Quinn pressed close against Matthew, but she was also watching Royce for any trickery. Royce pulled steadily at the oars, his face impassive but his eyes narrowed and searching for a way out.

"Keep to the middle," Matthew told him, as Royce began to let the boat drift toward the right bank. Up ahead, the boat carrying the runaways was rounding a bend and moving out of sight.

"Whatever you say," Royce answered. "Man who's got the gun calls the shots."

Matthew was thinking. What to do about Quinn. Her Daniel would be leaving her, as soon as Royce was returned to the Green Sea and the runaways pardoned. It seemed to Matthew that it would be particularly cruel, for her to lose 'Daniel' again, but what could he possibly do about it? He was looking forward to a cleaning of his shoulder wound, a hot bath at the Carringtons' inn, and as soon as he was able to travel he was taking a packet boat back home. This animal sitting before him, manning the oars, was not worth the rope it would take to hang him. How many had he killed besides Sarah Kincannon and Magnus Muldoon? And Joel Gunn, too? A lead ball to Royce's head might be the more fitting end to him, but Matthew would have to let a court have the final word. He had no doubt what that word would—

Raindrops.

Rain had begun falling. The drops were few, but they were heavy. Lightning streaked, followed by the hollow boom of thunder. Royce kept rowing, unhurriedly. Maybe upon his face there was a thin and cunning smile. Matthew felt a sense of alarm; he knew the pistol's flashpan cover was closed, but when the trigger was pulled the cover opened for the flint to ignite a small amount of powder at the touchhole...and rain was definitely not kind to gunpowder. If the powder at the flashpan became damp, the weapon would be useless except as a club.

Within a matter of seconds, the sky opened up and—Matthew's worst fear—a torrent of rain descended.

The rain fell so heavily, in gray sheets, that he could hardly make out Royce sitting before them; the man was just a shape in the deluge. Rain beat down upon Matthew and Quinn, and the surface of the River of Souls was thrashed as if by the twistings of a thousand alligators.

Royce—or the blurred shape of Royce—ceased rowing.

Water streamed down Matthew's face. "Keep rowing!" he shouted against the voice of the storm. He was aware that this torrent was also beating down upon the pistol and there was nothing he could do to prevent it. "Go on!" he demanded.

Royce didn't answer. Slowly and deliberately, the man stood up. Through the curtain of rain Matthew saw him lift the oar on his right from its lock.

"Stop it!" Matthew shouted, but Royce would not stop. Matthew had no choice. The time had come. He aimed at Royce's chest and pulled the trigger.

The trigger snapped.

The rain-soaked gun remained mute.

"I'll be leavin' now," Royce said. He swung out with the oar and slammed it into the left side of Matthew's head.

Matthew fell to his knees in the boat, bright and searing pain fogging his vision and filling his brain. He dropped the useless pistol, and did not see that Quinn was on her feet and slashing out with the sword. Royce turned the blade aside with the oar and followed that with a fist to Quinn's face that brought the blood from her nostrils and sent her reeling back into the boat, which swayed precariously from side to side on the tortured river.

Under the driving rain, Matthew was aware that he had to fight back. Dazed, his vision cut to a dark haze, he found the knife in his waistband and drew it out, at the same time trying to get to his feet. A second blow of the oar, to almost the same place near the left temple of Matthew's head, knocked the knife from his nerveless fingers and sent him over the side of the boat into the River of Souls.

He went down, his head full of fire. He had the sensation of drifting into a different realm, worlds away from…he could not remember from where, nor could he remember exactly where he was or why, but he realized he could not breathe and he must find air…and yet, this was a peaceful place, this darkness and quiet, and here he might find rest if he so chose.

In the boat, as the deluge continued to slam down, Royce grabbed Quinn by the hair with both hands and dragged her forward in preparation to throw her over the side. She had lost the sword. Her hands scrabbled at the bottom of the boat, seeking the weapon. Royce hauled her up and grinned in her bloodied face.

"Over you go, Rotbottom bitch," he said, spitting water. "But first…I'll take a kiss."

He pressed his mouth against hers with a force that nearly broke her teeth.

Quinn kissed him hard, in return.

Her kiss was delivered by the knife that Matthew had dropped and her fingers had found, and deep into the heart this kiss was driven, and twisted for good measure and good fortune on the journey that Griffin Royce was about to undertake.

He gasped and pulled back, but the knife remained in his heart and Quinn's hand held it firm as the life streamed out of him. His mouth opened and filled with rain. His green eyes blinked, shedding water. All the world, it seemed, had turned to a river without beginning or end. The haunted girl from Rotbottom and the animalish killer from the Green Sea stood together in a rowboat between shores obscured by the downpour, and above them thunder shouted like the voice of God condemning men for sins too foul to forgive.

Royce looked down at the knife, as if to wish it away. He took hold of Quinn's hand but was suddenly too weak to push it aside. Then his rain-beaten face seemed to run and distort like melting tallow, and when Quinn released the knife Royce fell backward into the bow of the boat and lay there, arms and legs splayed and knife still piercing his heart. His sightless green gaze flickered and dimmed, as the River of Souls carried the boat in the direction of the Green Sea on its sinuous path to the Atlantic.

Quinn leaped overboard. Her Daniel had risen back to the surface but his face was still underwater. She swam to him and lifted his face from the river, and there she saw the ugly darkening bruise and swelling at his left temple. For a few seconds he was still and her heart nearly broke because she feared she'd lost him again, and then his body convulsed and water burst from his mouth and nose and he drew in a ragged breath of air strained through the falling rain.

"Stay with me," she pleaded, holding him close lest the river pull him under again. "Daniel...please stay with me."

She thought he might have nodded, but she wasn't sure.

For a moment she watched the boat carrying the body of Griffin Royce drift away until it was obscured by the curtains of rain. He would be no more threat or harm to anyone, she thought, unless he was as strong a spirit as her husband and could also find his way back from the vale of Death. But she didn't believe God, in His final judgment, would allow such a wicked soul to find a way through. Then, holding tightly and lovingly to her Daniel, the girl from Rotbottom struck out for the opposite shore.

TWENTY

MAGNUS Muldoon was again a man on a mission.

Under the bright hot sunlight of morning he rowed up the River of Souls. He had asked for and been allowed this boat by Donovant Kincannon at the Green Sea plantation an hour earlier. The master of the Green Sea was once more on his feet, in spite of Dr. Stevenson's admonitions to remain in bed for a few more days, but Sarah was being buried this afternoon in a plot beside the chapel. Kincannon was determined to bid farewell to his daughter while standing with his arm around his wife. In what was an unheard-of decision, the slaves Abram, Mars, Tobey and Granny Pegg were invited to the service, and Magnus as well. It was doubtful that Tobey would be there, as he was under the doctor's care after the removal of the ball and the tending of two broken ribs. Magnus planned to be at Sarah's funeral, but not in these grimy old clothes he was currently wearing.

Rain had fallen for two days straight, drowning out the fire that had been moving so hungrily through the forest. Magnus and the snake-bit but still surviving Caleb Bovie had found one of the boats left behind by the group of men Seth Lott had shepherded back to Jubilee, and rowing through the deluge they had come upon a strange sight: what at first appeared to be an empty rowboat drifting downriver, but which upon closer inspection revealed the corpse of Griffin Royce splayed at the bow, his eyes open toward the stormy heavens and a knife stuck in his heart.

He was a red-blooded man, that Royce, thought Magnus at the time. A lady-killer, possibly with a trail of dead ladies behind him... or, if not dead, at least changed for the worse. Gunn had known too many secrets about Royce, and might have been persuaded to spill them if Royce hadn't blown his brains out. So there lay Royce, a heartless man felled by a wound to the heart...but who had struck the blow?

Upon reaching the Green Sea, Magnus had been told by Abram that Matthew and Quinn had been in the boat with Royce, but they'd been left behind and out of sight because of the rain and Abram's haste to get help for Tobey. Matthew had had a pistol, Abram had said...but both he and Magnus had realized that the pistol likely was useless in such a downpour.

The question that Magnus intended to have answered this morning, and the reason for his mission, was to find out what had happened to Matthew and Quinn, and for that he was on his way to Rotbottom.

He rowed steadily past dozens of alligators lying motionless in the sun on either side of the river. Several drifted by his boat, and one particularly large beast bumped the bow with its knobby tail as it swam unhurriedly on. Further ahead he passed an area where several men in boats were using spears, nets and ropes to spear and trap their prey, and Magnus wondered if those nets had not recently brought up a few human remains. Not far beyond the realm of reptiles, daylight revealed the harbor of Rotbottom, a wharf around which were standing several weatherbeaten log structures, a few barns and livestock corrals, and back in the woods more log cabins and what appeared to be a larger meeting house at the center of town, if it could be called that.

Magnus approached the wharf and, spying an old man fishing nearby, called for a rope to be thrown to him to moor the rowboat.

Directions were asked to the house of Quinn Tate, and the old man sent him off in search of a cabin "four to the left of the meetin' house, got a flower garden in front, but," the elder added, "that girl's not right in the head, y'know."

Magnus thanked him for this information and continued on his way.

The town of Rotbottom was not the collection of miserable hovels that Magnus had expected. The cabins were small, to be sure, but they were not very different from his own house. In fact, some were better maintained. The dirt streets were clean, willow and oak trees spread their leafy and cooling canopies over the roofs, and except for a fishy smell of decomposition wafting in the air—which Magnus took to be the odor of alligator innards or newly-skinned carcasses issuing from a barnlike structure that appeared to be a warehouse—Rotbottom was a community not unlike many others carved from the wilderness. Some of the houses had vegetable gardens and plots of corn. Apple, pear and peach trees grew in small orchards. There were chicken coops and hogpens, and a few cattle and horses grazing in corrals. Dogs bounded about, following the path of several children playing with rolling-hoops. As a stranger in town, Magnus attracted much attention from the children and from people sitting in the shade of their porches. He was called upon to pause, sit awhile and state his business but he had to go on, and soon found himself approaching the door of Quinn Tate's house, if he'd followed the directions correctly. Someone was inside, because cooking-smoke was rising from the chimney.

He knocked at the door and waited. It was a tidy-looking place with a small porch, but all the windows were shuttered.

Still he waited. He knocked again, a little harder.

Did he hear a movement from within? He wasn't sure. "Quinn Tate!" he called. "It's Magnus Muldoon! You in there?"

And now...yes...he did hear footsteps creak the floorboards. But yet the door did not open, and Magnus had the feeling that if the girl was indeed on the other side, she was standing with her hand on the latch and indecision in her addled mind.

"I need to speak to you," he said, quietly but firmly. "I'm lookin' for Matthew. Do you know where he is?"

A few more seconds passed. And then a latch was turned and the door opened a crack, and there was Quinn's face…strained and frightened-looking, with a bruised nose and dark blue bruises under both swollen eyes.

"Oh," said Magnus, unnerved at the sight. "What happpened to *you*?"

"The man hit me," she answered. "The pistol…it was wet. All that rain, comin' down. He tried to get away." She gazed past Magnus, as if expecting he'd brought someone else with him. "You're alone?"

"I am."

"Thought you were dead. That Royce killed you, with the others."

"He tried," said Magnus. "And he came awful close."

"I thought…somebody might be comin' for me. To take me off, maybe. I stabbed that man in the heart, and I left the knife in him. I had to…after what he did."

"What did he do?"

"He hit Matthew with an oar. In the head, more than once," Quinn said. "Matthew fell into the river. After I stabbed that man, I went into the river to find Matthew…but…" She hesitated, chewing on her lower lip.

"But *what*?" Magnus urged.

"The River of Souls took him," she said, in a hushed voice. "He's gone."

"*Gone?* You mean…he drowned?"

"River took him," Quinn repeated. "He must've been hurt bad. I dove for him, but I couldn't find him. I stayed out there as long as I could, before the 'gators started comin'. After that…I had to get out and leave that place."

"He's not dead!" Magnus's voice cracked. "He *can't* be dead!"

"All I know is…the river took him. Please, sir." She reached out and grasped his arm. "Are you going to send men here to get me? For stabbin' that very bad man in the heart?"

Magnus shook his head. "No. Not my place to do that." He had left Bovie in one boat and rowed back to the Green Sea with Royce's body in the other, just to show the Kincannons what had happened. Bovie hadn't been hesitant to tell the master and mistress of the Green Sea about Royce's murder of Stamper and Barrows, and the killing of Joel Gunn. Magnus figured the story ought to end here, with Abram,

Mars and Tobey pardoned and Sarah's killer gone to his reward. No one at the Green Sea was going to ask who had put the knife into Griffin Royce, but if anyone did...maybe Matthew would want to take the credit for that. But Matthew *dead*, after all they'd been through? Magnus couldn't believe it; or, maybe, he didn't want to.

"How far upriver did Matthew go in?" Magnus asked.

"Just after we got started. I don't know...it wasn't far past where the slaves took their boat out."

It was likely six or seven miles away, Magnus thought. With all those alligators in the water, a body wouldn't last long. He was torn between rowing further upriver in search of the body and giving it up as a lost cause. But still... "You're sure he didn't crawl out? All that rain comin' down...maybe you couldn't see him? And you bein' hurt and all?"

"I looked for him as long as I could," she repeated, with some finality in her tone. "You know...the way I felt about him...I *wanted* to find him, more than anything."

"How did *you* get back?"

"I walked out. Followed the river."

"Matthew might still be alive," Magnus said, mostly to himself. "Maybe pulled himself to shore, but he's too hurt to travel."

"I don't know," she answered, "but I stayed there awhile, and I didn't see him."

"Goin' to Sarah's funeral this afternoon," he told her. "Important that I be there, I think." He frowned and rubbed his forehead with the palm of an oversized hand, trying to figure out what he ought to do. He'd scrubbed himself at his house, but he could still smell the rank mud of the quicksand pit up his nostrils and he thought it would be a very long time before that memory went away.

"Did everything turn out all right?" Quinn asked. "About the slaves?"

Magnus nodded. "Pardoned, one and all. Tobey's not able to be up and about yet, but he'll live. *Damn*," he said softly. "I should've stayed with you and Matthew. Maybe I should never have let him go out there, in the first place. Maybe I should've run him off, when he came to my house. Maybe..." He was overcome by the choices that had been made, and what had resulted. "I don't know," he said, which was as close to the truth as he could get.

"Or maybe," Quinn said, her swollen eyes fixed upon the mountainous man, "things that were supposed to happen...*have* happened. Nothin' can change 'em, just like the flow of the river can't be changed. And nobody ever knows how a journey's going to end, Mr. Muldoon. Happiness or sadness...right or wrong...justice or injustice...even life or death. Nobody knows, but it seems to me everybody has to take their own journey, and square up for it." She paused, searching the troubled, black-bearded face. "Matthew took it on himself to go, as I understand it. I'm sorry for what happened...you *know* I am...heartsick at it...but I think if Matthew was really so much like my Daniel—if he *was* my Daniel, deep in his soul—then he knew he was doin' what he had to do."

Magnus considered that for a moment, as the summer sun shone down through the canopy of trees, birds sang up in the branches, dogs barked across Rotbottom and in the distance children laughed at their game of rolling-hoop. Life, like the River of Souls, moved on.

"Need to be at Sarah's funeral this afternoon," he said. Then he added, with determination in his voice, "Goin' upriver tomorrow mornin', though. If he's there, I'll find him. Seems like...if I can...I ought to bring him back."

"I hope you can," Quinn said.

"Is there anything I can do for *you*? Anything you need?"

"No, but thank you." She gave him a sad smile. "I'm squared up, too."

"Nobody'll be botherin' you," Magnus promised. "The Kincannons have the body of the man who killed their daughter. They have the how and the why of it. That's all they want."

Quinn stared into space for a few seconds, and then she seemed to recover herself. "I'm forgettin' my manners. I've got soup in a kettle and a little tea, if you'd like. Corncake's bakin'."

"Oh...no, I'd best be on my way, with Sarah's funeral comin' so soon."

"Well...good fortune to you, sir," she told him, and then: "Goodbye."

"Goodbye, ma'am," Magnus replied. He waited for her to close the door. He heard the latch fall again, and the creak of the floorboards as she walked away. It was a lonely sound. He thought he might come here again someday soon and bring Quinn a colorful glass bottle or two, something to bring light into the house. At that point he might tell her about the Soul Cryer, and that it was simply a very large, burned and agonized panther...or not, for there was some value in letting a mystery remain a mystery, For now, though, he had to be going, and whether or not his involvement in the solving of Sarah's murder and the safe return of the runaways had any bearing on if he was fated to spend time in Hell, he didn't know. He did know he felt he'd done the right thing...both he and Matthew had...and maybe that ought to be enough, for he was certain he had much more life yet to be lived and a body could step into any number of Hell's suckpits before it was over.

Magnus returned to his boat. He mopped his brow with a cloth he'd brought, asked the old fisherman to release the mooring line, and then Magnus took up the oars and began steadily rowing toward the Green Sea. Before he got too distant from Rotbottom's harbor he looked back, up the River of Souls as far as he could see before the river curved and the trees closed in. He hoped to see... what? Matthew Corbett rowing his own boat back the way he'd come? Matthew Corbett, alive and well and not now drowned and mostly stripped to the bone by alligators? Well, there was a lot to be done soon. He didn't know if the families of the dead wanted the bodies back for Christian burial; if they did, he would volunteer to return into that damned swamp with a group of searchers and bring back whatever was left. It seemed to him that by coming out alive he'd beaten the cursed river and the haunted swamp, and he ought to be mighty pleased with that fact. He ought to...yes, he decided... he ought to.

He had left his ride in the barn at the Green Sea, and mounting his black horse—named, not too imaginatively but rather more wishfully, Hero—he left the plantation. He didn't know how often he would return here; it seemed very quiet and sad without Sarah's presence. The Kincannons had been true to their word and yesterday paid him the twenty pounds that were supposed to be shared by himself and Matthew. He was suddenly in possession of the kind of riches his Pap had searched for all the man's life—and had come to the New World to discover—but had never found. In other times Magnus might have stashed the gold under his thin mattress and defied the world to come take it, but on the day he'd received it, bright and shiny coinage in a brown leather bag, he had decided to return half of it to the Kincannons, for it was not his due. He suggested that Matthew might come back for it, but in his heart he had known something terrible had happened to the younger man. Before Magnus had left the Green Sea yesterday, he'd asked to make a purchase from the Kincannons with one of his coins, but they'd freely given him the three items he'd requested. So it was that now he was on his way home, with intent to make use of these items before returning for Sarah's funeral.

Upon arriving, Magnus drew water from his well into a wooden bowl. He took the bowl into his house, and placed it upon a table alongside one of the three items given to him by the Kincannons, a small mirror on a pedestal. He angled the mirror upward so that he might see his own face.

How did I get to be who I am? he asked himself. And the better question: where does my river lead me, from here?

He recalled what Matthew had said, about his situation: *I say remake yourself, beginning with a bath and clean clothes. Wash and trim your hair and your beard, take your emeralds and bottles to town and see what can be done. You might find your craft much in demand, and yourself as well by several ladies who are worth much more attention than Pandora Prisskitt. But…if you prefer this solitary life way out here, then by all means sink your roots deeper. Sink them until you disappear, if you choose. It's* your *life, isn't it?*

"Yep," Magnus said to the black-bearded face in the mirror. "My life."

Only…it didn't seem like so much of a life anymore. It seemed like a place to hide from life. To curl up and count your woes and plan vengeance upon people who cared not if you lived or died, because you meant nothing to them. It seemed to Magnus that for a long time he'd been waiting to be ready.

And now he was.

Maybe it was the death of the beautiful and kind-spirited Sarah that had unlocked his dungeon. Maybe also the loss of Matthew Corbett had made Magnus decide to throw away the key. For Magnus thought life was too short and fragile to waste as a hermit, shunning all people and thinking all could be painted with the same tar brush. But now he thought that people might be more like the sand and powdered colors that went into his bottles; you never knew what they were going to become, until you woke them up by giving them a breath of opportunity.

Magnus wished for a difference. He wished for his own opportunity to be newly born, as if he were one of his own bottles. And maybe...he could recreate himself, just as Matthew had said, and find his own way in the world that lay beyond his house. He wouldn't start too large or expect too much...but he intended to start.

With a deep breath that indicated his resolve of purpose, he began to use the second implement he'd received from the Kincannons. The sharp scissors hacked away his thick black growth of beard, and maybe a flea or two did jump out. *Goodbye, my brothers*, Magnus thought. He continued to work the scissors until the beard was cut short enough to be handled by the third implement, a straight razor. By that time Magnus' hand was sore; he'd had no idea how long and tangled and dirty he'd allowed his beard to become. He remembered telling Matthew that his Pap and Mam had said it made him handsome. No...it just made him appear more the wild and ragged beast that at heart he was not. And as Magnus soaped his face and began to scrape the razor over the contours of jaw, cheeks and chin—carefully, carefully, for this had long been forgotten territory to him—he saw the emergence of a new man, much younger-looking, and really—if he wished to be a little jaunty about it—somewhat kind of handsome.

He would wash his hair and wear his best and cleanest clothes to give his respects to Sarah. He would give his respects to Matthew Corbett by searching for him tomorrow, but he doubted the body would ever be found. It was a strange thing: he might have imagined that beyond the crack of the door Quinn Tate was hiding Matthew in that house, if the young madwoman had not invited him in for tea, soup and corncakes. But if Matthew had really been in the house, then why hadn't he proclaimed himself?

Going out on the river tomorrow, Magnus told the younger and handsome man in the mirror. Going out and look for Matthew, one last time.

And then what? What about the day after tomorrow?

That would be the day Magnus Muldoon would take his green stones and some of his bottles to Charles Town, and he would present himself where he needed to be presented along the shops of Front Street, and maybe he would never be a true gentleman like the problem-solver from New York because he would always have too many rough edges that resisted smoothing, but still…

…it seemed to Magnus that any man who had come back alive from the River of Souls had somewhere else to go. Somewhere important, a destination not yet in sight, hidden around many further bends and twists. Like Quinn had said…everybody has to take their own journey, and square up for it.

He was ready for the first step out into the world. And day after tomorrow, he reckoned his journey would begin.

Twenty-One

When Quinn Tate closed the door and latched it, she went to the hearth and ladled out a bowlful of corn soup. To this she added a small corncake. Then she opened the door to the second room, where the bed was, entered it and sat down on the bed beside her man.

"Daniel?" she said quietly. "I've brought you some food."

He didn't stir. He'd been sleeping a lot. He was badly injured, of course. A bandage was wrapped around his head, his swollen face a dark blue mottled bruise, his black stubble growing into a beard. That was as it should be, for Daniel had always worn a beard.

"Can't you eat anything?" she asked him.

He'd been awake a short time earlier, if only for a few minutes, but now it seemed he had slipped back again into the heavy depths. He was breathing all right, though. She had removed his sodden clothes before helping him into bed, and yesterday morning had cleaned the arrow wound on his shoulder with wellwater and applied a dressing made from crushed onions and ginger to draw out infection. She would be very attentive to that wound for the next few days, as some yellow pus had collected there.

As for the condition of his head and the regaining of his senses, she didn't know. He had been mostly dazed and silent on their journey through the driving rain, and several times his legs had given way and they'd had to rest in the shelter of the trees.

But her Daniel was going to be all right, Quinn thought. Yes. He hadn't come all this way to leave her again.

She set the bowl on a table beside the bed and stroked his unruly hair, which stuck up from the bandages like a black rooster's tail. For awhile she sang a song to him in a quiet, clear voice, the verse being:

"*Black Is the Color of my True Love's Hair,*
His face so soft and wondrous fair,
The purest eyes and the strongest hands,
I love the ground on which he stands."

Daniel would soon be standing. Quinn was sure of it. He would be up and about and back to himself. It would take time, and healing, but he had returned to her from the gates of Heaven and she would guide him with a gentle hand back to her heart on Earth.

For the next few days she was patient. She went about her work of accepting clothes from her neighbors to darn and sew, for that was her way of bartering for food. No one need know about Daniel's rebirth yet, she decided. No one had seen them return in the downpour of a dark night, and no one yet needed to know, for she feared someone might come and take him away from her again. She had feared so with the man named Magnus Muldoon. She had thought he sensed that Daniel was in the house, in that bed in the other room, and so she had decided to offer him entry and food thinking that if she did not do so, he might know for sure. But the man had politely declined and gone on his way, and that was the last she'd seen of him.

At night she lay close against her Daniel and listened to him breathing. Sometimes he awakened with a jolt and tried to sit up, but always he gasped with pain and put a hand to his bandaged head where the oar had struck, and then he slipped away once more. Quinn believed he was not ready yet to rejoin the world, but it would be soon. Until then, she changed his bandages, tended to him, drove the infection out of the arrow wound and sang to his sleeping form at night, by the light of a single white taper.

Then came the morning, four days after their return from the River of Souls, when she brought a cup of apple cider into the room and found her Daniel sitting up on the pillow with his eyes open. They were hazy and unfocused, his face still mottled with bruises and burdened with pain.

But he had spoken to her, in a raspy voice, and the words were: "Who are you?"

Quinn had thought this might be. That her Daniel, newly born in the body of another man, might not know her at first. It was like the fresh awakening of a new soul. And, after all, it was her task to guide him back to her heart.

"I am your wife, Quinn." she told him. "And you are my husband, Daniel."

"Daniel?" he asked. When he frowned, something hurt his head and he touched the place where the oar had struck. "Daniel *who*?"

"Tate."

"Daniel Tate," he repeated, and stared at her with his hazy gray eyes that held hints of twilight blue. He looked around the room as if searching for something familiar. "Why don't I remember anything?" he asked.

She was ready for this question, and if it had to be a falsehood at first then so be it. "We were both harmed in an accident. On the river." Not quite a falsehood, but not exactly the truth.

"What river? And what was the accident?"

"The River of Souls," she said. "It runs not far from here. Your head's been hurt. We were in a boat that turned over, and you struck your head on a rock. It's goin' to take you time to remember me. To remember *us*," she corrected.

He lifted up his hands and examined them, like a child might. "I don't work with my hands," he said. "What do I do?"

"You teach the children readin' and writin'. Oh, Daniel!" she said, and putting the cup of cider aside she got into bed with him and pressed herself close and felt both his heart beating and her own, and suddenly there were tears in her eyes. She wasn't sure they were tears of joy or tears of sadness, because though Daniel had returned to her as he'd promised she had so much to tell him and teach him and make him understand, and was it wrong that the man named Matthew Corbett had had to die so that her Daniel might live again?

She must have sobbed, because he put an arm around her and held her tighter, and he said, "Don't cry. Please. I want to remember, but...I can't, just yet. Everything is dark. Will you help me?"

"Yes," she answered. "Oh yes, I will." And she kissed him on the cheek and then on the lips, and he returned her kiss but it was like the shadow of the kisses she had known from Daniel before, and she knew he was still far away and wandering on his journey from death back to life.

But there was time. There would be much time for the burning of white tapers in the night, and much time for two souls to cleave together once more.

Daniel Tate awakened in a cold sweat from the occasional nightmare. In them, a masked figure wearing a white suit with gold trim and a white tricorn also trimmed with gold reached out for him with a hand concealed in a flesh-colored fabric glove. In his nightmare Daniel shrank away but his movement was slowed as if mired in mud, and the masked figure of a man turned into an octopus whose tentacles also reached for him in horrific but determined slow-motion.

Quinn listened to these nightmares, but could never help him understand why he was having them. She just held him close and whispered "I love you, Daniel," into his ear until he fell again to sleep.

Came the day he stood up from the bed and walked shakily across the room. Came the day he dressed in clothes he did not remember ever wearing, the clean white shirt just a little too big for him, and came the day Quinn opened the front door and he stepped out onto the porch and drew in the faintly-decomposed scent of Rotbottom. By this time he knew all about the alligators and that he was in the Carolina colony, that he was a teacher and would get back to teaching when he had fully recovered. His appetite had returned, the bandages were removed from his head and the bruises were nearly gone yet he felt deeply bruised within his brain, and things were floating in there like thorns that caught and snagged and left the brief quick flash of images he could not decipher.

It occurred to him one afternoon that he faced problems he could not solve. This greatly disturbed him but he took the cup of tea that his wife offered and thought how lucky and blessed he was to have such a woman loving him and to love, and he thought no more of such disturbing things.

At length he was able to walk around the town, with Quinn always at his side. The citizens of Rotbottom knew that people came and went, there were always empty cabins that individuals and whole families moved into and out of, and everyone generally minded their own business. Thus it was noted that Quinn Tate was living with a new young man, and after one neighboring woman asked Quinn his name and was told it was "Daniel, my husband," people gave her a wide berth. They also looked at Daniel strangely, but since this whole world seemed strange to him he dismissed their interest.

One afternoon nearing two weeks since Daniel had sat up in Quinn's bed, they were walking back from the wharf with a bucket of freshly-caught catfish when Daniel noted a cabin far down in the hollow, about forty yards beyond their own. It was untended, covered with vines and nearly obscured by the wilderness. The front porch sagged, the roof appeared near collapse, and the whole place had an air of supreme neglect. But obviously someone did occupy the place, because there were two horses in a corral and a wagon nearby.

"Quinn," said Daniel, "who lives there?"

Her face tightened. "We don't want to bother him. He's a very mean man…like that Royce was." She had spoken without thinking, and immediately wished she could take the name back.

"Royce? Who is that?"

"A man we knew, a time ago. But the man who lives down there," she said quickly, changing the subject, "is to be left alone. Been here…oh…maybe six months. Heard he comes out after dark to go fishin'. He took up with the widow Annabelle Simms, and it was frightful how he beat her when he got drunk. After he broke her nose and her arm, she came to her senses and left."

"Hm," said Daniel, pausing to stare down at the unkempt hovel. "He sounds dangerous. What's his name?"

"Annabelle said he used to be royalty, from some other country. Could hardly speak English, she had to teach him. Called himself Count…" Quinn hesitated, trying to come up with the name. "Dagen. Somethin' like that. He's got a crooked left wrist, looks like a break that didn't set right."

Daniel nodded, but said nothing.

"I say he's to be left alone," Quinn continued, "'cause a month or so past I saw him down in the woods swingin' a sword around.

Looks like he knows how to use one...so he's not somebody I care to invite to supper." She gave her man a smile and a playful nudge in the ribs. "Just enough catfish for *us,* anyway."

Daniel agreed, and he carried the bucket of fish on into their home.

What night was it that he had the dream? Maybe not the same night he'd heard about the widow-beating count, but one soon after. The name *Dagen* kept bothering him. Something about it...it wasn't right. In his dream he had been seated at a banquet table, with all manner of food on silver platters spread before him, and scrawled on the wall was the shadow of a swordsman at work, carving the air into tatters with a vicious and well-trained arm, and the air of danger had swirled thick and treacherous through the room.

Dagen.

Count Dagen.

He used to be royalty, from some other country.

In the middle of the night Daniel had sat up, not so quickly as to disturb his wife, and listened to a dog barking in the distance. Otherwise the world was silent, but questions pressed upon Daniel's mind.

What was a count from some other country doing in Rotbottom? A swordsman? A man with a crooked left wrist? And the name—Dagen—wasn't right. No...that wasn't the man's name. Close, but...no.

"Go to sleep," said Quinn, reaching up to rub his bare shoulder. "Darlin'...go back to sleep."

He tried, but he could not. He lay there for a long time, beside his sleeping wife, thinking that there was a problem he desperately needed to solve but not quite sure what it was.

Twenty-Two

IT worked on him.

He kept it from Quinn because he didn't wish for her to be as disturbed as himself, but she knew something was wrong. He could see it in her eyes. It was a kind of shiny fear, and where it came from he didn't know but it was there all the same.

One night, as summer moved on, the black-bearded and wiry Daniel Tate got up from their bed slowly and carefully so as not to wake his wife. He knew the small room by now and he was able to dress in the dark. In the front room he lit a candle and put it inside a lantern, and then—still moving quietly—he left the house and walked toward the harbor.

The little town slept beneath a blaze of stars. Frogs croaked in the swamp grass and far off a nightbird sang, happy in its solitude.

Also in solitude sat a man on the end of the wharf, a lantern and a wooden bucket beside him. He was intent on watching the bobber of his fishing line, but as soon as Daniel's boots made noise on the planks the man's head jerked around and he stared coldly at the newcomer through the darkness between them.

"I vant no company!" said the man, in a heavy foreign accent.

Prussian, Daniel thought…but he had no idea why he thought that. He continued onward, his boots thumping the boards. "I have need to speak to you," he said. "If…indeed…you are the Count?"

The man suddenly trembled. He grasped his lantern and stood up, fishing line and pole forgotten. By the yellow light Daniel saw the man was wearing a brown-checked shirt and dirty tan-colored breeches with patches on the knees. The left arm was grotesquely crooked at the wrist, indicating a severe break that had been poorly mended, if tended to at all.

"*Who are you?*" asked the man, whose pale blond hair was matted and shaggy and hung limply about his shoulders. There was a note of frantic urgency in the voice, and Daniel saw the fingers of the man's left hand grip with some difficulty around the wooden handle of a knife in a leather sheath at his waist.

"I am Daniel Tate," was the reply. "You are Count…is the name *Dagen*?"

"Get avay from me!"

"I want no trouble," said Daniel. He lifted his own lantern higher to reveal his face. "Only a moment of your time."

The man drew his knife, which appeared a painful process to the warped wrist. He took a few steps forward, holding his lantern toward Daniel, and then stopped again. "*You*," he said; a single word, delivered with both stunned disbelief and like a curse. "Of all to find me…*you*."

Daniel shook his head, uncomprehending. "Do you *know* me?"

"I came here…to hide," said the Count, his English strained and hard-earned. "From him. From whoever he vould send after me. I failed. He does not tolerate such." The Count gave a bitter, anguished grin. "Of this place I heard in Charles Town…this vas the end of the earth. And now…*you*." He came a few steps closer, the knife ready for a stabbing blow.

Daniel did not retreat. He was thinking that if this madman came much nearer he would smash him in the face with one swing of the lantern. "I've never seen you before. Who do you think *I* am?"

"You don't know your own name?"

"I told you my name. It's Daniel Tate."

"Oh, no. Oh, no," said the Count, still grinning. "You're Matthew Corbett. You haff the scar on your forehead. I don't forget that." He held up the crooked wrist. "This too I don't forget."

"I have no idea what you're talking about. My wife is Quinn Tate. I have lived here for..." Here Daniel had a stumble, for this part was blank. He tried again. "Lived here for..."

"How long?" the Count taunted, coming a step closer.

Daniel had a headache. He touched his left temple, which seemed to be the center of his pain. "I've suffered an accident," he explained, his voice suddenly weak and raspy. "I hurt my head, and some things...I don't remember." What name had this man called him? "Who is Matthew Corbett?" Daniel asked.

The Count stood very still. Then, slowly, he lowered his knife.

And he began to laugh.

It was the laughter of the king of fools, a giddy outpouring of stupid mirth. He laughed and laughed and laughed some more, until his pallid, wolfish face had bloomed red and the tears shone in his green eyes. He laughed until he was too weak to stand and had to lower himself to the planks, and there at last he was silent but breathing heavily and staring at nothing, his lower lip curled with aristocratic disgust.

"May I know the joke?" Daniel asked when the laughter was done.

It was a moment before the other man replied. He seemed to be thinking very hard about something. Then he said, "Ve haff met before. Do you not remember me?"

"I do not, sir."

"The name Count Anton Mannerheim Dahlgren means to you, nothing?"

"Dahlgren," Daniel repeated. Not *Dagen.* He had the memory of that dream again, and the shadow of a swordsman upon the wall of a banquet room. Perhaps at the center of the dream was the feeling of fear. The man sitting before him was very dangerous. But how and when they had met...*if* they had met...he had no idea. "You're a swordsman," Daniel ventured.

"Ah, that! Yah...or...I *vas.* The sword demands balance. Timing. As vell as strenght. You see my crooked arm? Isn't it lovely?"

Daniel knew not what to say, so he said nothing.

"My balance is no more. I am too veak on this side. Oh yah, I can still use the sword...but I am no longer her master. And for me…ah, such a shame." Dahlgren gave Daniel a pained smile. "I vas taught…if you are not the best, you are nothing. All my years of training…of hardship…lost and gone. How do you think my arm vas broken? Do you haff any…guesses?"

"None," said Daniel. "I *am* sorry for your condition, however."

Count Anton Mannerheim Dahlgren came up off the planks with silent fury. Before Daniel could retreat, Dahlgren's face was pressed nearly into his own and the knife's sharp point was placed at Daniel's throat. The man's smile was a ghastly rictus.

They stood like that for a few seconds, motionless on the edge of violence.

Sweat had risen on Dahlgren's face. His smile began to fade. The knife left Daniel's throat.

"Forgiff me, sir," he said, stepping back and giving a slight bow. "It is not anger at you…but much anger at myself." He put the knife away. "I vish that ve should be friends. Yah?"

Daniel rubbed the place where the blade's tip had not broken skin but certainly had left an impression. "I don't know why you believe me to be someone else, sir," he said, "but I will repeat that my wife is Quinn Tate, my name is Daniel, and—"

"And you are wrong!" came the reply. "You believe these things because the voman has *told* you? Her husband Daniel *died* last summer. Everyone knows her head is *verruckt*! She is insane. This is not your home, and you are not Daniel Tate."

"You make no sense."

Dahlgren's grin darkened, his eyes glittering above the lantern. "Then…please allow me to *prove* what I say is correct."

"Prove it? How?"

"There is a man," said Dahlgren, leaning closer as if not wanting anyone else to hear yet they were entirely alone upon the wharf, "who vishes to find you. I know this is true. This man is…a professor. A man of great learning, and great power. He knows all about you, and he vill embrace you with gladness once I bring you to him."

"The man's name?"

"He is called Professor Fell."

Did that name cause a shifting of shadows within Daniel's brain? He knew the name, yet he did not know how he knew. "Why does he seek me?"

"To reward you, for services you haff performed. But he does not seek Daniel Tate. He seeks Matthew Corbett…your true name, and true self."

Daniel felt pressure building once more in his head. "You said…you came here to hide. From *him*?"

"I vas involved in a…shall ve say…failed business venture, and he is a var' hard taskmaster. But I vill tell you…all vill be forgiven, vhen I bring you to him. He vill greatly reward both of us."

"I think you're mad," said Daniel, with some heat in his voice. "I know who I am."

"Do you? Then…valk the town…alone, and ask anyone to tell you about that voman. My voman Annabelle told me, before she left. Ask about Daniel Tate, and how he died. Now…how can there be *two* Daniel Tates?"

"*Mad*," the tormented young man repeated, and began to back away. "I *am* Daniel!"

"You are *not*. The professor knows you. Allow me to prove so, by taking you to him."

"And where would you take me, to meet this professor?"

"*England*, young sir," said Count Dahlgren. "Ve vould board ship in Charles Town, and set sail for England. I haff two horses and a vagon to sell. That vould be enough for our passage."

"I'm going nowhere with you," Daniel replied, continuing to back away. "Certainly not across the Atlantic! My wife is here, and so is my life."

"Your vife is *not* here," Dahlgren countered. He motioned toward the east with his crooked arm. "And your life is out *there*."

Daniel had had enough. He turned and began to walk back the way he'd come.

"Think on these things!" said Dahlgren. "And…Matthew…no vord of this to the madvoman who shares your bed, yah?"

A confused young man returned to the Tate house, and slipping quietly inside he extinguished the lantern's flame but found he could not put out the small fire that had begun to burn in his brain. He undressed and settled himself against Quinn's body, and she moved to rest her head against his shoulder. He lay listening to her breathing. He tried to remember his childhood, or how he'd met Quinn, or their wedding day, or anything about the empty cradle—made from a hollowed-out log—that stood on the other side of the room.

He could remember nothing. *Do we have children?* he'd asked her, thinking how sad it was that he did not know even this, and she'd replied, *No, but we will in time.*

That name Dahlgren had called him. Matthew Corbett? And the other name…Professor Fell. Why did that name both repell and attract him? Why did it give him quick images of fiery explosions, rolling ocean waves and cannons being fired from a ship in the violet twilight? And stranger still…why did he think of what appeared to be a bloody fingerprint pressed upon a white card?

These images could not be kept. They could not be held long enough to be more closely examined. But he knew they were important, and he knew they said something about himself that he had to rediscover.

"I love you, Daniel," Quinn whispered to him, from the depths of sleep.

"I love you, Berry," he whispered back, but he did not hear himself answer and Quinn had already faded away.

He did not return to the wharf on the following night. Neither did he on the next night, for Quinn was aware of him getting out of bed and she grasped his hands and bade him return, for she'd suffered a bad dream that he was lost in the smoke of a burning wilderness and she could no longer even see his shadow.

But on the following night, after they had made love in their gentle, sweet way and Quinn had fallen asleep, Daniel kissed Quinn's cheek and smoothed her hair, and he wished he might stay exactly where he was until morning's light but the fire of curiosity was burning in him, it was a blaze beyond endurance, and it would not let him rest. He dressed, lit a candle for his lantern, left the house and returned to the harbor, where Count Anton Mannerheim Dahlgren was both fishing and waiting.

"Ah, there you are!" said Dahlgren, from his sitting position at the wharf's end. "I vas sooner expecting you."

The young man walked out to him. "A warm night," he said.

"Yah, var' varm. I myself like cold days and colder nights. I like the snowfall. The sound of it hissing through the pines. Someday I vill get back to my Prussia. Perhaps you vill help me?"

"By going with you to England?"

"Yah, that."

"I tell you, I am Daniel Tate. I am—" He stopped, because he had no memories of being Daniel Tate and these mental flashes he was having spoke of a different life altogether.

"You are not anymore so sure," the Prussian said. "Othervise... you vould not be here." He saw the bobber go under and felt the line jerk. "Ah! Caught something!" He pulled up a small silver fish, enough for a pan, took it flapping off the hook and dropped it into the wooden bucket with several of its kin. Then he rebaited the hook using a live cricket and put the line again into the water. His boots, Daniel noted, were nearly in the river.

"You're not afraid of alligators?" Daniel asked.

"Alligators," answered the Prussian with a slight snarl, "are afraid of *me*."

"Yet you fear this Professor Fell? Why is that?"

"As I say, I was involved—much against my vill—in a failed business. But that is in the *past*, my friend. In the present, he is seeking *you*. All vill be *right*, when you present yourself to him. You see?" Dahlgren smiled up at Matthew Corbett, exposing a mouthful of gray teeth.

"No, I do not see."

"You do know you are not Daniel Tate. You do not belong here, and neither do I. You *know* that. But...your problem is...you do not remember who you are, and you are trying to decide if you can trust me. Yah?"

"I'm not sure I can trust someone who recently put a knife to my throat."

"Forgiff me, I am sometimes hot-headed. Also..." Dahlgren smiled again. "Bad mannered." He returned his concentration to his fishing, as if he were again alone upon the wharf.

Daniel waited for the man to speak once more, but nothing was offered. He realized the next move was his. "If I believed you...then tell me, how do you know me? And from where?"

"Ve crossed—" The Count was silent for a moment, as if deliberating his choice of words "—paths once. More than that, I cannot say."

"What did I do for this professor that warrants a reward?"

"You were born," said Dahlgren.

"I say again, you must be mad."

"And *I* say again…board ship and go to England with me. I vill pay all. Do you haff a travel bag and clothing?"

"I'm not going to England with you," Daniel said. "Leave my wife? *No.*"

"Then let it tear you apart, young sir."

Daniel frowned. "Let *what* tear me apart?"

"Not ever knowing who you really are." The Count shrugged. "Small pieces, you may remember. Things may come back to you. But *years*, it may take…and I say it vill tear you apart."

Daniel said nothing. He stared off into the dark, which seemed to go on forever.

"It is tearing at you even now," said Dahlgren. "Ah! I think… yah, I've caught another!"

"Goodnight, sir," Daniel told him, and began walking away.

"In the morning," the Count said as he took another silver fish off his hook, "I vill bring you some of my catch. Ve should be good friends, yah?"

Daniel didn't answer. The planks creaked under him, the frogs croaked, and the swamp seethed with life. Why then, had the cobblestoned streets of a large town flashed through his mind for just an instant…an image of coaches and carriages and the signs of shops he was unable to read? The image was gone just as quickly.

London? Had that been London? His *real* home, possibly?

Or…rather…the real home of Matthew Corbett?

If that was true…then was Quinn out of her mind, as the Count had said? And if he was *not* the first Daniel Tate…what had happened to the first one?

Let it tear you apart, young sir.

He feared he had already begun to be torn apart, that he was possessed of two minds, two hearts and perhaps two souls. One might wish to remain here, as husband to a loving and beautiful wife and a teacher of reading and writing when he got back to that, the other…

Your life is out there, Count Dahlgren had said.

He walked on, following the lantern's spear of light, his head down and his shoulders burdened as if with a crushing weight.

Twenty-Three

THE sun was barely up. It was going to be a hot day, the hummers and buzzers already singing out in the woods.

Quinn was cooking breakfast of eggs and corncakes at the hearth and singing quietly as she worked. She was wearing an apron over an ankle-length pale blue shift, and he wore the slightly-oversized yellow nightshirt that hung to his knees, taken from the trunk of men's clothing that he did not remember ever wearing before.

He sat at the pinewood table, drinking from a cup of tea, and watched his wife with appreciation. She was so beautiful and so lively. There was to be a dance this coming Friday night, in the meetinghouse, and she was very excited to go. Daniel had agreed, though he'd said he might need help to get through some of the more complicated steps, for he could not recall if he was a very able dancer or not and he wished to bring no shame on the Tate name.

Yet as he sipped at his tea he also watched her with questions in his mind that he could not answer. Only she might answer, and though the need to know pressed at him he felt that asking these questions might cast a shadow upon their happy home, and in the deepest part of his soul he was weary of shadows. He felt he already carried a darkness within himself, something he could not shake, and yet…the need to know—the desire to *discover*—was so strong in him it was nearly a sickness.

"Are you happy?" he asked her.

She stopped in reaching for the skillet in which the corncakes were browning over the low flames. "Yes, of course I am!" she said, with a smile. "Why do you ask such a question?"

"Because *I* am happy," he replied, "and I want to be sure that you are, as well."

"You can be assured, then."

He nodded. "I look forward to starting my teaching again. I feel worthless sometimes, watching the other men go out to hunt, but—"

"*Hush*," Quinn said, and crossed the room to put a finger against his lips. "We have gone over this road before. Everyone has his or her place. Besides, the hunts are dangerous. I don't want you out there."

He put the cup aside and looked at his hands again. They were unmarked and unscarred, very different from the gnarled hands of the men who went out and trapped the alligators. Had he ever done physical labor in his life? he wondered. How had he even gotten to this place? Where and when had he been born? A question came out of him before he could stop it. "Have you ever heard the name… Matthew Corbett?"

Quinn continued to work at the hearth, but perhaps her face did tighten. She didn't look at him. "No," she said lightly. "Who is it?"

"I'm not sure," he answered.

"Where did you hear that name?"

"From…" He decided not to bring the Prussian into this. "From my head. I'm wondering…if it's someone I know."

"It could be, but I don't know the name."

"Well," he said, and took another sip of tea, "there's much I need to remember. Maybe, in time, it will all come back."

"Some of it may not, ever." She turned from the hearth to face him, and gave him a determined stare. "Daniel, you just have to trust me. You *do*, don't you?"

"Am I really Daniel Tate?" he asked, and he saw her wince just a fraction. "Or was there a Daniel Tate before me?"

She shook her head. "I don't know what you mean."

"I mean…everything before I woke up is so dark. I only get pieces of pictures, and they fly away so quickly. This name… Corbett…haunts me. I saw in my head the image of a large town, with coaches and carriages upon the streets. It startled me, because I think I know that place. I think…somehow…it's important."

"It's Charles Town," she said, and now in her voice there was a faint quaver. "Some memory you have of Charles Town."

"Maybe it is," he replied. "I should like to go there, to see if I recognize anything."

"We shall, then." She straightened up from her work, rubbed her hands on her apron, and came over to perch herself upon his lap. "I love you, Daniel," she said, with her lips close to his. "I want you to know that I'm goin' to help you come back, as you should be. As you *used* to be. Everythin' will be fine, as long as we're together. As long as we have our love between us. Like we were, before."

"Before?" he asked.

"Before the accident," she said. "Before you left me for a little while."

There came a knock at the door. They never had visitors, so Quinn said, "*Who?*" as she stood up. She unlatched the door and peeked out, and through the crack Daniel caught sight of Count Dahlgren.

"What is it?" Quinn asked sharply. "What are you wantin'?"

"I've brought fish." Dahlgren lifted the bucket he held. "This heat…they von't last var' long. I saw your smoke. I thought you vould like to clean and cook these."

"No, I wouldn't. Thank you, but—"

"Daniel knows," Dahlgren said, and he pushed his way in. He was still wearing his dirty tan-colored breeches with the patched knees, but he wore a gray shirt that was already damp with sweat. The shaggy blond hair was lank and oily. His smile never wavered. "About the fish, I am meaning," he added. "Good morning, Daniel."

"Good morning."

"You see, I've brought vhat I promised." He came over to the table to show Daniel the four small silver fish. "Enough for a meal, I think."

"Yes, thank you."

"Do you *know* each other?" Quinn asked, still standing with the door open.

"Ve haff spoken." Dahlgren set the bucket atop the table. "If you vould like me to clean these for you?" He touched the sheathed knife at his waist.

"We'll do that," said Quinn. "When have you spoken?"

"Oh, at night, vhen I am fishing." Dahlgren ignored the open door and the invitation to leave. He sat down across from Daniel in the other chair. "Your husband likes to valk at night. So he valks out to me, and we talk."

"We were about to have our breakfast," Quinn said.

"Yah, I see." Dahlgren gave her a gray-toothed grin. "You should close that door. Flies vill get in."

"Daniel, please tell this man to leave our house," Quinn said. "I don't care for him."

Dahlgren looked across the table into the eyes of Matthew Corbett. "And how is your *head* this day, Daniel?"

"Please *leave*," said Quinn, her teeth clenched.

"Perhaps you *had* best leave," Daniel said quietly. "Now is not the time."

"Now *is* the time," came the count's reply, delivered as sharply as if by a rapier.

They sat in silence for a few seconds, and then Daniel said, "Quinn, close the door. Go ahead. It's all right."

"I don't want to," she said, with something of a frightened child in her voice.

"It's all right," he repeated, and slowly the door was closed.

"Yah, var' good. Man of the house. Var' good." Dahlgren kept his eyes fixed on those of Matthew Corbett. "Ve should talk about some things, the three of us."

"Talk about what? What things?" Quinn asked, as she cautiously neared the table.

"Your husband here," Dahlgren said. "Your *man*. You know, Annabelle was a fine voman. I never should haff let her get avay. She had var' good things to say about Daniel. He vas a *gentleman*, yah?"

"*Is* a gentleman," said Quinn, coming to stand beside her man and put her hand on his shoulder.

"It seems to me...a gentleman does not belong here, in this place." Dahlgren took a moment to look around the room, which was surely better-scrubbed and tended to than his own. "Not just *this* place, but this town. This *nothing*. I say this has been a good place to hide and lick one's vounds—if one had to—but the time has come."

"What time?" Quinn asked, narrowing her eyes.

"The time for Matthew Corbett to go vith me to London. This is the name of the man who is sitting across from me. Not Daniel Tate." Dahlgren's green gaze slid toward Quinn. "Your Daniel is dead, and he is not coming back."

Quinn stood very still. But then the young man who could not remember his name or his past felt her shiver, as if the cold of the grave had passed through her. Tears bloomed in her eyes. "You don't...*know*," she rasped. "You don't know what you're sayin'." Her hand tightened on Matthew Corbett's shoulder, as if trying to grasp more firmly the spirit of Daniel Tate. "Tell him, Daniel. Tell him who you are."

He covered her hand with his own, and squeezed it, and he had to say the truth: "I'm sorry, Quinn. I'm not sure who I am." And now was the time, indeed, for his decision. "But...I know I love you, as a husband would love his wife, and I am staying here with you, until I can—"

He was not able to finish his sentence, because suddenly Count Dahlgren was on his feet and the knife was out. It flashed as it went across Quinn's throat and as she fell backward, her eyes wide with shock and surprise, the blood sprayed in a ghastly red arc from the mortal wound.

"No," said Count Dahlgren, very calmly. Blood reddened the blade's edge. "That is not the plan."

If the spirit of Daniel Tate did indeed possess the body of another man, then it directed both a cry of anguish to burst from the throat and the right hand to pick up the bucket of silver fish and swing it hard against Dahlgren's head. The count was able to get his shoulder up to deflect the blow, but even so it brought forth a grunt of pain and knocked the man to his knees. The silver fish scattered across the planks around him, and one was caught in the oily thicket of his hair.

A kick to the ribs made Dahlgren curl up and shout a curse in the Prussian tongue, and then the young man without a memory rushed to kneel beside Quinn and press both hands against the gushing wound. She looked up at him with terror, seeking the help he could not give for he knew she was doomed. "Help me!" he shouted to Dahlgren, but the count waved his request away and sat on his knees rubbing his sore ribs.

"I love you!" he told the dying girl. "I love you! Don't leave me! Don't leave! I love you!"

She grasped his hands, as if to cling that way onto life. But there was too much blood, the wound was too savage, and she was fading. Her dark blue eyes were darkening more, her face becoming chalky. Her mouth moved, leaking blood, but it seemed she was trying to speak. He put his head down, right against her mouth, even as he tried to seal the slash with his fingers but it could not be sealed.

She spoke three words, but whether he heard them correctly or not he didn't know, and later he would think that at the end some clarity had entered her mind, if indeed she was living a life of desperate fantasy.

She said, or he thought she said, "*My Daniel waits.*"

And then he could do nothing more but watch her as she left.

At last Matthew Corbett took his bloodied hands away from the wound, crawled away and sat with his knees pulled up to his chin. He began to rock himself back and forth, his eyes wide and Quinn's blood streaked across his face.

"Get up," said Dahlgren, who had gotten to his feet. He realized he had a fish caught in his hair, and he frowned with dismay as he worked it out. He wiped the blade clean on the fish, tossed it aside and sheathed the knife. "Clean yourself and get dressed. Get clothes and something to carry them in. Ve are going to Charles Town."

"Murderer," whispered Matthew, as he stared at nothing and rocked back and forth. "Murderer. Murderer."

"I haff opened the path for you," Dahlgren answered. "For myself, as vell. Ve go to Charles Town today, sell my horses and vagon at the livery stable, and ve set sail for England on the next ship out. Go ahead, get up."

"Murderer. Murderer. Murderer."

"Yah, I hear that." Dahlgren knelt down, his face a few inches from Matthew's. He saw the shock deep in the young man's eyes; Master Corbett was a bloody mess, and would have to be washed before he could leave this cabin. "But *who* is the murderer? Shall I leave you like this? Shall you go out calling for help, telling all vhat you haff seen? In that case, I shall leave the knife here...for this girl's neighbors know she vas insane...and she found an insane young man—from somewhere—to pose as her Daniel." He reached out and tapped Matthew's forehead. "*Think*," he said. "Vhy should I haff reason to kill her? But...a lovers' spat between two people who are *verruckt* in the head? Ah, me! Vhat a tragedy! So...get up, Matthew, and let us go forward together, for you surely cannot stay here now. You see?"

In his tormented mind he did see. He wished only to stay here, frozen in this posture and in this moment, but he knew he could not.

Matthew's eyes moved. They stared into Dahlgren's with cold ferocity.

"Someday I'll kill you," he whispered, as tears streaked down his cheeks.

"As you please." Dahlgren patted the young man's head and grinned with his gray teeth. "But it vill not be today, for ve haff things to do. Get up, now. I'll help you. Yah?"

TWENTY-FOUR

THE two-masted brigantine was called *Wanderer.* From its shabby, near-derelict appearance it looked to have wandered on one too many voyages, yet here it was in the harbor of Charles Town on an early morning in the second week of August, taking on trunks, crates and barrels and a few passengers who wished for the comfort and cobblestones of the Old World beneath their feet.

A modest crowd had gathered on the dock to see the ship off. It was the next vessel bound for England, and ships coming in and out invariably drew sightseers. Count Anton Mannerheim Dahlgren and his young charge moved through the throng toward the gangplank, carrying canvas bags that held their clothes. They had lived together for three days in a small boarding-house on the outskirts of Charles Town, waiting for this vessel to be prepared for the crossing. They had hardly spoken to each other, even as they took their meals in the kitchen, and because there was only a narrow single bed the younger man slept on a mat on the floor. They spoke to no one else, either, and the landlady decided there must be something wrong with the younger man, for the way he sat and stared into empty space for such long periods of time.

A bell had begun ringing on the dock, signalling the imminent departure of the noble but weatherbeaten and ill-used *Wanderer*, that all who should be aboard were aboard and all who were visiting should be off.

The black-bearded and gaunt Matthew Corbett would never be recognized by any of the proper gents and fine ladies who had attended the Sword of Damocles Ball little more than a month ago. His clothes were clean and simple and he was well-washed, but he was a different man. Surely in this crowd there *were* some of those who had attended that night, and seen the young problem-solver from New York best the brutish Magnus Muldoon in a duel involving a comb, but that young man had returned to New York, as far as they knew. But still....weren't there whisperings that the young man had left his clothes and belongings at the Carringtons' inn, and that—the shame of it—he had neglected to pay the total of his bill?

It was so hot these days in Charles Town. Who knew what became of some people? Many came and many went, and if this young man was missing someone would come from New York to look for him, eventually. Or perhaps not, but life and the parties went on.

The talk of this summer, however, was centered on an unlikely source. The beast himself, the hermit from the woods, the black-bearded monster. Only...Magnus Muldoon was no longer such a beast, and certainly he appeared to be no monster after shaving off that horrid beard. Oh yes! said the women at their gatherings. The man is *young*!

And he has set up shop right there on Front Street, to sell the most beautiful bottles. He makes these himself, if you can warrant it! Of course the shop is rather *small*, but one should stroll in there to take a peek...and not just at the bottles, but at Mr. Muldoon himself. For in a clean suit, a white shirt and with his hair combed—properly so—and his square jaw showing...well, he nearly appears a gentleman.

And—lean in closely, for here is the real story! Have you heard... that Pandora Prisskitt *herself* has walked into that shop? Yes, her curiosity got the best of her! She had to go in, but accompanied by Fanny Walton so as not to seem too brash. And here...*here*...

is the thing. Fanny Walton told Cynthia Meddows, who told Amy Blair...that Pandora Prisskitt batted her eyes at this new version of Magnus Muldoon, for you have heard that he has come into some money, have you not? And...you will see this for yourself, ladies, if you happen to stroll in there...he could be said to be *handsome.* Now of course he has not the family, nor the estate, that matters...but... isn't it just too *delicious*?

Oh...his reaction to Pandora?

He smiled at her, sold her a bottle at the regular price, and said *Good day to you, ma'am.*

The stories, the stories...how they swirled around the parties, lawns and porches of Charles Town. But what was lesser known was that Magnus Muldoon had returned the horse Dolly to her stable, and had twice rowed seven miles up the Solstice River to seek a body that could not be found.

Matthew Corbett, a man without a past, followed Count Dahlgren through the crowd. He was still having flashes of memory—a blurred face here, the snippet of a name there, such things as the quick images of a hawk descending with its talons ready to rip and tear, a man crashing through a mansion's window and what appeared to be a castle of white stones crumbling into ruin over a cliff—but nothing would remain. He could not hold onto anything. He had no choice but to follow this killer onto *Wanderer*, and hope that in three months' time and in the city of London he might discover who he truly was, and why this Professor Fell wished so fervently to reward him.

As they moved through the crowd, Matthew happened to look upon a man and woman standing nearby. They were both dressed extravagantly and seemed to be among the elite, though they were an odd pair. The woman was high-wigged and corpulent and dressed up like a pink piece of cake, or rather a hasty pudding. The man was long and lean and much older than the female, and he wore a black suit with gray stripes and a black tricorn atop a powdered wig. Matthew's gaze went to the man's face and stayed there. He abruptly stopped and felt a chill on this blazingly-hot morning. The man's head turned and the dark, hooded eyes in a long-jawed face that seemed a virtual patchwork quilt of deep lines and wrinkles fixed upon Matthew with what might have been holy—or *unholy*—power.

"Move along," said Dahlgren.

"Wait," Matthew said, trying to put this man's face in its proper picture, but he couldn't frame it. "I think...I *know* that man."

"Come on!" Dahlgren's voice was harsher. "Keep moving!"

Suddenly the man seemed to recognize Matthew as well, and took a jolt. Dahlgren reached out to grasp Matthew's shirt, but Matthew pulled free and approached the man even as the other fellow worked his way through the crowd to Matthew.

"God above!" said the man, in a voice that might soar up to deafen thunder but in this case was quiet, restrained and earth-bound. "It's *you*! Much the worse for wear, I see! I hardly recognized you!" He glanced back at his dollop of pudding. "Listen, Matthew," he said, leaning in close. "I have no idea why you are here, but I have a good situation. I am no longer Exodus Jerusalem, I am called Earl Thomas Kattenburg, from the country of...well, that matters not, as long as *she* doesn't study her geography and she is liberal with her purse. I know we had our differences, but...please...refrain from any attempt at vengeance, would you? Here." He slid two gold coins from a pocket and into Matthew's hand. "And again, my sympathies at the untimely passing of Magistrate Woodward."

"*Who?*" Matthew asked.

The man's frown might have knocked ravens from the air. "*Who?*" he repeated. "You know fully well who!" He peered more deeply into Matthew's eyes and saw they were glazed over like ice on a millpond. "What's wrong with you?"

"I know you," said Matthew. "But...from where? I can't remember. My head...is so full of fog."

"Ve are to be aboard our ship. Come along!" Count Dahlgren was suddenly at Matthew's side, grasping an elbow to guide him. "Good day, sir," he said to Earl Thomas Kattenburg, known in another life and guise as the hellfire preacher Exodus Jerusalem, who had been so bent on throwing Rachel Howarth to either the witch-burning flames or his own lecherous desires.

"Here! Just a moment! What's wrong with Mr. Corbett?" the earl inquired, grasping hold of Matthew's other elbow.

"He...has suffered an accident," Dahlgren replied tersely. "Ve are going to London, to get him cured. Again...good day, sir." With a forced, gray-toothed smile the count pulled Matthew away, and the wrinkled earl took the opportunity to remove the two coins from the young man's hand and replace them where they ought to be, in his own pocket.

"Pity," he said as they moved off, but his flesh-hooded eyes were cold. "Farewell, Matthew!" he called. "Surely we shall meet again, on this winding and unpredictable river we call life!" Then he realized he was becoming too much Exodus Jerusalem again, and anyway the stricken lad did not respond, and neither did Matthew Corbett look to left nor right as he went up the gangplank, but only ahead as if gauging his life one careful step at a time.

Soon the lines were cast off, *Wanderer* was rowed out by its pair of pilotboats, its sails bloomed wide and the ship shuddered like an old woman just waking up from a bad dream. It caught the wind and began to sail away, into the tides of the Atlantic, on one more journey of its often-erratic and sometimes calamitous existence. After awhile the crowd moved on, as crowds do when there is nothing left of any interest to see.

But one man stopped and looked back toward the dwindling sight of *Wanderer*, and as he stood next to his corpulent pink lady of the open purse he frowned and rubbed his chin, and wondered whether someone ought to know that Matthew Corbett was ill, had seemingly lost his memory, and was being taken to London by—it also seemed—a small measure of force. Or was it a larger measure than it appeared?

But who would he tell? He was many things, but no Good Samaritan. It would be too much of an effort, as well. He recalled something his father, a true hellfire preacher, had told him as a little boy.

Every soul must bear their own burden, fight their own fight, and break free from their own prison.

He stared at the departing ship, with a valiant young man aboard who was obviously faced with all three of those tribulations.

"I wish you well," he said, and he surprised himself because he meant it.

Then he turned away, took hold of the offered hand that gave even a wretch such as he a place in this troubled and turbulent world, and he returned to the comfort of his life.